JAX
COCKY CAGE FIGHTERS
BOOK ONE

LANE HART

COPYRIGHT

This book is a work of fiction. The characters, incidents, and dialogue were created from the author's imagination and are not to be construed as real. Any resemblance to actual people or events is coincidental.

The author acknowledges the copyrighted and trademarked status of various products within this work of fiction.

© 2015 Editor's Choice Publishing

All Rights Reserved. This book or any portion thereof may not be reproduced or used in any manner whatsoever without the express written permission of the publisher except for the use of brief quotations in a book review.

Edited by Wendy Ely

WARNING: THIS BOOK IS INTENDED FOR MATURE AUDIENCES 18+ ONLY AND CONTAINS EXPLICIT SEX SCENES AND ADULT LANGUAGE!

CHAPTER ONE

Page Davenport

I tap my perfectly manicured nails rhythmically over the laptop keys while watching the clock. I'm bored out of my mind waiting for this "urgent and extremely important" meeting to commence. The one my father's secretary said would begin promptly at three p.m. sharp.

And he's late.

But really, what else is new?

Ever since I started full-time at the firm, I've felt like dad's errand girl. While some of his requests have actually involved trips to the United States Attorney's Office, my responsibilities in the building only included delivering or picking up documents. I've also been assigned the extremely important task of hole-punching a thousand pages of discovery before organizing them into binders. And last, but certainly not least, to remind me I'm the lowest on the totem pole he's actually sent me out to pick up his freaking lunch! I keep wanting to remind him that there is, in fact, a law degree hanging in my office, just like the one in his. I may have only recently graduated and passed several state bars, but being treated like a freaking intern is getting tiresome.

"Page," my father says when he breezes quickly into the room. "Sorry I'm late, got held up on a conference call. We may have just settled our trade secret violation case with SynTech for a million."

"Good for you," I say with as much enthusiasm as I can muster. It's not much since I know our clients are making a killing stealing their old company's ideas.

My dad, Miles Davenport, has always specialized in corporate law. My older brother, Logan Davenport, is an expert at patent law. My uncle, John Davenport, has been doing wills and estates for twenty-five years. All three areas of law put me to sleep faster than an elephant-sized tranquilizer dart. I'm still trying to figure out my specialty; what cases I'll actually enjoy doing for the long-term.

The senior Davenport settles into the rolling chair at the head of the conference room table, slapping down a brown accordion file in front of him with a thud. Could it be that he's actually going to give me a real case to handle on my own? Usually the closest I get to a case is when I'm assigned research projects for him or my brother.

"Our three o'clock is late, not that I'm surprised. His father just posted his bond this morning, so they probably got held up at the jail," he tells me while checking his phone.

Oh no, no, no. I'll practice any area of law, but I won't do...

"It's a new criminal case," my father says, grinning greedily from ear to ear.

Criminal?

Represent *miscreants*? He can't be serious. There are two attorneys in our firm who do all of the criminal work. Ryan handles the state court cases, and Mark takes all the federal cases. So why the heck is my dad, a corporate attorney, talking to a potential criminal client?

"I'm sure you've heard of him, Jackson Malone, the famous MMA fighter?" he asks. I probably dislocated my jaw based on the speed at which it hit the wooden table. "His head coach, Don Briggs, and I grew up together. Don called me this morning and asked if we'd take his case."

"You mean Jackson *'The Mauler'* Malone, the man who *raped* and *strangled* a woman?" I ask in horror. It's been all over the news ever since the story first broke three days ago.

"Innocent until proven guilty, remember?" my father says, finally glancing up at me to raise a condescending gray eyebrow that matches his perfectly combed hair.

"Yeah, that's the motto of all criminals," I snort. "So what am I doing here?"

"You're going to represent him," he says, sliding the file across the table to me.

"Like hell I am!" I exclaim, jumping to my feet and raising my voice at my father for probably only the third time in all my twenty-four years. "I don't have any criminal law experience other than a summer internship with the DA's office, and even if I did have experience, I wouldn't represent *him*!"

"You are," he says with the narrowed cobalt blue eyes I inherited, and the cold tone of finality I've always dreaded. It means he isn't going to budge, and there's no convincing him to change his stubborn mind. "This is going to be a huge case. Not only is he going to pay us a small fortune, but the national publicity we'll get will be incredible! It's also exactly what you need, to put yourself in the spotlight to boost Elliot's campaign."

Oh please! Like I give a rat's bare bottom about Elliot's campaign. I don't even bother responding to that nonsense.

"There are nine other attorneys in this firm, why can't one of them do it? You know, maybe one that has *actual* criminal courtroom experience," I argue.

"You and Logan are the only ones who've passed the bar in New Jersey, which has jurisdiction in this case. And you're the only female in the office. It'll look better to the media and the jurors to see a woman sitting beside Mr. Malone at the defense table. Don't worry, Ryan will carry the brunt of the load."

Oh no. Now I'm starting to understand. My father isn't giving me this case because he thinks I deserve it. No, he wants me to be the sacrificial lamb. The woman the media and feminist groups will all tear into for representing a chauvinistic pig. He really doesn't give one shit...ake mushroom about my reputation. After this case, I'll be nationally known as the idiot woman who represented the rapist jerk. Speaking of...

My dad's secretary cracks the conference room door, and announces in her nauseatingly sweet voice, "Mr. Davenport, the Malones are here."

I have a slight dislike of Margo. Okay, maybe a tad more than slight. She's so freaking pleasant, it's obviously fake. As soon as her back turns her smile falls and is replaced with a gaping maw of gossip, spewing filth to anyone who will listen.

"Show them in," my father instructs her while straightening his blood red tie, the color appropriately representing his strict conservatism. Then he turns to me, and says, "Be nice, and don't you dare fuck this up," sternly through his clenched teeth.

I make an attempt to ignore the knife sticking out of my chest from the second half of my father's directive, and instead, try to come to terms with the idea that he wants me to be nice. Be *nice* to a ruthless, cocky meathead who thinks that since he's all rich and famous because of a brutal, barbaric sport that he has the right to do whatever the heck he wants with women and get away with it.

Maybe my uncle will hire me if I get up and walk out the door. Sure it'd be tedious work filling in blanks on templates for old people, but at least I wouldn't be stuck working with an actual hardcore, violent criminal.

An older man, looking roughly in his fifties with shaggy black hair and a beard sprinkled with a dusting of white, steps into the conference room first. The heavy bags under his hazel eyes and his deep frown lines make him look tired and highly annoyed. I paste on my fake smile and reach across the conference table to shake his hand.

"Mr. Malone, I'd like you to meet my daughter, Page Davenport. Page, this is Martin Malone and his son. I'm sure you'll recognize Jackson Malone from his outstanding MMA career," my dad says when he makes the introductions.

JAX

"Nice to meet you," I lie as I hold out my hand to the older man. Shaking it, he gives me a polite nod of his head while assessing me. He's not looking at me in a creepy, sexual way, but his eyes are narrowed, and his crinkled brows meet, making it obvious that he's asking himself, *'Is she really old enough and experienced enough to represent my son?'* Of course not, and everyone in the building knows that.

My curious eyes finally dance around the older man to the one standing behind him. The spacious conference room that can easily accommodate ten ego-inflated attorneys suddenly feels too small. Intimidating doesn't even begin to describe the vibe this man is putting off. He practically comes with his own flashing neon sign over his coal colored pompadour cut that says in big, bright letters, *"Danger! Stay back at least 100 feet!"*

It isn't necessarily the guy's size that makes him scary, even though he's built like a tank at more than six feet tall, with a broad, muscular build. But when you add in his black bottomless pit eyes and tight, unshaven jaw...he looks like Mount Vesuvius about to erupt. Violence and tension radiate off of him in waves that are almost visible. In nothing special faded jeans and a plain white tee contrasting nicely with his golden tan skin, he's absolutely, without a doubt, the most... scrumptious looking man I've ever laid eyes on. His mug shot photo plastered all over the television and Internet doesn't do him justice.

How the heck is it physically possible for someone who lets other people punch him in the face for a living still look like...like...a gorgeous *Abercrombie & Fitch* model?

And how can someone so bad-ass and angry still come across as...well, I'd never actually say this to his face, but pretty?

The man is nothing like the type of guy I'm usually attracted to. He's missing the requisite white collar and tie. I have a feeling that the brute before me never wears either. Instead of clean cut, he's ruggedly and dangerously handsome, singularly able to make women stop, drop their panties, and roll over...and cause men to run away like cowards with their penises tucked between their legs. Speaking of penises, I bet his is...

5

"Page?" my father's commanding voice interrupts my perusal, that has gone on far too long and much further south than is professional.

He is a monster, not a sexy man you should want a life size poster of for your bedroom! My inner sanity finally surfaces and reminds me of the rape and strangling he's charged with. Yes, that's exactly what I need! A reminder of why he's here and the horrible things he did.

"Nice to meet you," I lie again, intentionally not offering him my hand to shake. It would've been a serious stretch to reach him across the table anyway.

The dangerous man's dark, seemingly soulless elevator eyes assess every single inch of my body. And, unlike his father, his gaze is definitely sensual, lingering on the buttons and fabric of my dress shirt that is stretched tautly over my breasts. He runs his tongue over his full bottom lip like I'm a brand new flavor of *Ben & Jerry's*. One that he can't wait to dip his...spoon into the cream, gorge himself on until he scrapes the very bottom of the carton, and then lick the sticky container completely clean with his tongue.

Even if I had looked at him the same way, his sensual stare helps calm my overheating hormones, seeing him for the pig that he is. I retake my seat, using the table in front of me as a shield from his intensity.

There isn't even a hint of a polite smile on his perfectly sculpted face, and he doesn't speak a word to my father or me. When he realizes that everyone else is already sitting down, he finally lowers himself into the chair beside his father.

"We're really sorry you have to deal with this media circus, Jackson. We appreciate Don's referral, and you can be assured that our firm will do whatever it takes to clear your name," my dad begins his ass kissing spill right away.

"Do you think I'm guilty?" Jackson's voice is a deep and gravely rumble, causing the goose bumps on my arms to stand up and take notice.

"It doesn't matter whether or not you did it," my dad responds coolly, clasping his hands in front of him on the table. "We're going to make sure your case is ready for trial, and do whatever it takes to defend you. Page is licensed in New Jersey as well as Maryland, and Pennsylvania. She'll be first chair since we believe having her leading the defense team will go far in how the public and media views this case."

"Do you think I did this shit?" Jackson asks again intently, directing his question at me.

My heart stops, and my mouth and mind are suddenly paralyzed. I'm unable to form a single thought. How the heck do I answer that? If I'm honest I'll piss him off, and he might not hire us, which will make my dad furious. If I lie, well, he'll probably see through my bullshit and call me on it.

He continues staring black daggers at me, waiting for my response, along with the other two men in the room.

"I haven't heard your side of the story, seen any of the reports, or evidence yet." I force my mouth to respond with a politically correct response.

"Are you going to ask me?"

"Well, of course we'll need to get your statement," I respond, annoyed when my shaky voice makes me sound like an uncertain little girl.

"Mr. Malone, why don't you and I head to my office to discuss the general procedures and timeline we're looking at while Page and Jackson get to work. The attorney-client privilege is severed whenever there's someone other than the client and attorney present during confidential communications," my dad explains, narrowing his gaze at me in warning when he stands up as if to leave.

My heart is suddenly racing in my chest with the onset of my panic. He's leaving me in here? *Alone with an angry rapist?* I'm so surprised that he's abandoning me in this situation that I'm too paralyzed to react. Without a backward glance, the two men leave the room before I can think of an excuse to ask them to stay. The door clicking shut makes me jump, instantly putting me on edge. The room falls silent, and I can't yet find any words for several awkward seconds.

"So," I finally say, and have to pause to clear the fear from my throat. "Let's start at the beginning." I poise my shaking fingers over the laptop home row keys in front of me, the cursor sitting on a blank Word document on the screen, ready to take notes.

"The beginning of what?" the delinquent asks, leaning back casually in his chair like he's posing for a photo shoot.

My father just threw the file in front of me when I was ambushed, so I haven't had a chance to see what information it contains. I grab the folder and quickly thumb through the pages, but the only thing inside is a few emails about setting up this appointment and a stack of the articles printed from various media outlets.

"Well, what are you officially charged with?" I ask.

The man suddenly rises to his feet, towering over the table, and I can't help my startled twitch. After he removes some papers from his back pocket, he practically throws them at me, making them slide across the table before he sits back down. "See for yourself."

I try to take slow, deep breaths to calm down my galloping heart when I pick up the tri-folded documents to begin scanning them. The conditions of his release are listed on the first sheet, showing he posted a fifty thousand dollar secured bond. He isn't allowed to contact the victim, of course, and he can't travel out of his state of residence without the permission of pretrial services. Flipping over, the next page is a warrant for First Degree Rape. The New Jersey General Statute is cited word for word, along with the name of the victim, Christina Loftis. The second warrant is for Assault by Strangulation, alleging that the defendant wrapped both hands around the victim's neck during intercourse, squeezing until the victim couldn't breathe. Wow, that is some sick stuff even for me, and I've unfortunately been exposed to some freaky fetishes.

"How the fuck are you going to represent me if you think I'm guilty?" The criminal practically snarls at me, startling me with his tone and profanity.

"I didn't say I think you're guilty." I'd only thought it.

"You didn't have to, it was all over your snobby face from the moment I walked into this room." He hangs his head with a sigh after calling me out, rubbing his temple like he has a headache. I know the feeling.

"Look, I don't give a shit what you think. Are you going to actually help me or not? Because if you're not, I'll find someone who will."

I want to beg him to take his case somewhere else, but if I let him walk, I'll never hear the end of it. According to my father, this is a huge case that our firm needs. Maybe, just maybe, if I show my dad that I *can* handle something so screwed up as this particular case, he'll actually let me start practicing law on my own, and give me a little credit for accomplishing something for once.

"I want to help you," I tell him.

His dark eyes narrow and cut to mine, likely trying to read my sincerity. "You want the free publicity? Trying to make a name for yourself? That's all fine with me as long as you don't fuck me over."

"I won't...fuck you over," I respond, forcing the f-bomb past my lips, which earns me a small smirk. The slight lifting of the corners of his lips even manages to make him appear a little less frightening for a brief second.

"Good to know," he mutters softly.

I may not be able to sleep at night knowing I'm trying to help a beautiful monster get off scot-free after doing something so abhorrent, but ethically...well, I'll do what I've been hired to do. Defend him to the best of my abilities.

"Okay, so let's get to work. Who's Christina Loftis?" I ask.

He shakes his head and scoffs. "A cage cunt I wish I'd never met. Or fucked."

Oh God, that chicken salad I had for lunch is threatening to spew all over the conference room table.

"*Consensually*," the criminal adds, probably after seeing my stricken expression. "I didn't even remember who the bitch was until I went back through my phone on the way here. I think she first threw herself at me after a fight I won back in April in Atlantic City." The man's ego knows no bounds. "I'm pretty sure we went back to my hotel room, and well, you know..." he trails off.

"Actually, *I don't* know, so you need to be honest and tell me everything. Something you may feel is a minor detail may actually be relevant to your case. What happened in the hotel room in April?" I forced myself to ask as I type up a few notes.

He stays silent for a minute, and when I lift my eyes back to his, he gives me a cocky, lecherous grin before he continues. "The slut was on her knees trying to suck my cock before the hotel door shut."

Holy cheese on rice! I gulp, swallowing that crass little tidbit down, and hope my eyes aren't bulging like a cartoon character.

"If she's the one I think she is," he continues. "I'm pretty sure I pulled her mouth off of my cock, hiked her skirt up, and fucked her against the wall. *Without* her protest."

My cheeks suddenly feel sunburnt. Hearing about this man's sexual exploits is so freaking uncomfortable. I'm not sure if I'm going to be able to do this after all.

"Afterward, we both undressed and got into bed. I think I fucked her from behind if that detail's important, and then we fell asleep. The next morning I had an early plane to catch, so she gave me her number," he says, then pauses, reaching up to scratch his head like he's thinking. I don't drool over the sight of his massive, flexed bicep like it's a three layer chocolate cake. I was just um, really thirsty, that's all.

"Actually," he continues. "I'm pretty sure *she* put her name and number in my phone herself and told me to call her. She must have gotten my number out of there, too."

"Okay, so did you...talk to her again after that?" I ask, while my fingers click rapidly over my keyboard to keep up with his story.

"Not until recently. I remember her name showing up in my call log a few times over the last few weeks. I ignored all of her text messages and voicemails just like I do to all the other sluts. The next time I was in Atlantic City was for my brother's fight last weekend. I still have the voicemail she left me saying she knew I was in town since she'd seen me in the crowd on TV, and she wanted a repeat. After the fights were over I was...bored, and decided to call her back. She asked to come up to my hotel room. We met up about thirty minutes later," he says.

"Which hotel were you staying at?" I ask him.

"The Trump Taj Mahal both times, which is where both the fights were hosted, too."

"Got it. Keep going with as many details as you can remember," I encourage.

"I knew she was drunk when she walked in. Her speech was slurred, and she was staggering. I remember smelling the alcohol on her breath. She bitched about me not calling her before she tried to push me backward toward the bed. After I had sat down, she climbed on me and unzipped my pants to start trying to fuck me. I had to stop her to grab a condom because she was in such a hurry to get it in without one. When we were finished, she asked if I wanted her to stay. I told her she got what she came for and that I was going to sleep, so I didn't give a fuck either way. She called me an asshole and left. The next thing I know, two Montgomery County cops show up to my apartment and arrest me last Friday. They took me to the local shithole jail, and since it was the weekend, I was held there for three goddamn days on a writ before the Atlantic City PD finally showed up to take me into their custody. Late last night I went in front of the magistrate and was eventually given a bond. My dad said he got there early this morning to post it, and the bastards took until noon to release me."

"Okay," I say, thinking through the next step of gathering evidence based on what he's told me. "I'm going to need you to get me the hotel receipts, plane tickets, and your cell phone records. Also, I'll need copies of all the voicemails you have and screenshots of text messages from her. Oh, and we should probably hurry up and get a subpoena ready for the hotel to see if they have any surveillance video from that night before it gets recorded over. So that we can narrow it down for them, what time was it when she arrived at your hotel room and when she left?" I ask as I type up a to-do list. I'm greeted with silence for so long I finally look back up at his startlingly beautiful face, meeting his dark stare. "What?" I ask insecurely.

"Um, yeah, sure. I can probably get you all that," he finally responds. "And she got there about midnight and left probably before one."

"Great. So what about witnesses? Anyone see you with her that night?"

"Jude heard me on the phone with her on the way back to our rooms. His room was next door to mine, so if she *had* protested he would've heard through the thin-ass walls."

"Jude?" I ask. "What's his last name?"

"Malone. He's my little brother," he says, sounding softer and much less hostile than most of the previous conversation.

"Is he at least eighteen years old?"

"Yeah, even though he still acts like a juvenile, he just turned twenty." The criminal snorts, and I swear it looked like he almost smiled.

"Do you think he'd be willing to sign an affidavit swearing he didn't hear anything...unusual?" I ask.

"I'm sure he would," Jackson says immediately like his brother would lie and say it, even if it wasn't true. Relatives are crappy witnesses because they always side with their family members, but it's better than having no witnesses.

"Are you friends with this woman on Facebook, Twitter, or any other social media site?"

"Hell no."

"Well, if you can give me some details about her, it'd be worth doing a search to see if we can find her profile and print any public pictures or posts. Do you have any social media accounts?" I ask.

"Yeah, there are some fan pages, but the coaching staff maintains them for me."

"Is there anything negative, harmful, or damaging to the case on any of them? Because if there is you should shut them down."

"Um, I don't know. I'll have them double check."

"Okay, but do it as soon as possible, and I want printed copies of all of them to see for myself. The prosecutor's investigator is probably printing off every word on there as we speak."

"Fine."

"Any questions?" I ask even though I'm not qualified to answer any with my very limited criminal defense experience.

"No. I just...you've got to make this shit go away. I can't fight until the case is over, and I need to fight."

"We'll do our best," I tell him, standing up and walking to the door to show him out.

"Good," he says as he follows me to the door.

Even at my gigantic, unfeminine height of five-eight, not including my three-inch heels, standing beside Jackson Malone makes me feel petite. He's hovering so close, looking downright dangerous with muscles twice the size of most normal men. Although, his midnight eyes aren't quite as menacing when he makes his parting comment. "You might actually be worth the fortune I'm paying you."

CHAPTER TWO

Jackson "Jax" Malone

What a fucking week. It's not that I never expected my ass to get thrown in jail. After my trouble-making and brawling youth, I'm sure everyone who knows me is surprised that it took me to the ripe old age of twenty-seven before I was put behind bars. It's a shame, however, that my first arrest is for complete bullshit.

I head for the lobby of the big, fancy law office to wait for my dad to finish up in his meeting. Sitting down, I pull out my phone to type a list of all the shit the uptight, elitist bitch lawyer asked me to bring her. Her disgust and instant judgment had pissed me off, but I have to admit, she does seem to be really damn smart. And she's hot as fuck.

With her long, lean legs and light blonde hair pulled back in a neat little bun, she looks like a *Playboy* pinup or a *Victoria's Secret* model dressed up to do a naughty attorney photo-shoot. In my fantasy of her as a centerfold, she'd be unbuttoning the professional suit jacket to reveal thin pieces of black lace that barely cover her perfect tits.

Okay, so maybe I'm a *little* horny after going four days without getting laid. That had to be a record for me. While I was locked up, it was hard to think about fucking when I feared for my life every goddamn second.

I'd thought the local jail was bad until they threw me in general population in Atlantic City. Both smelled like dirty, sweaty men, shit, and piss, but in AC the floors of the crowded cell actually contained dirt, piss, and shit. There were only two bunks for four dudes, so the unlucky two of us won the lottery to receive roll out mats. I leaned against the wall last night rather than risk floating away in the river of filth. Also, I didn't want to close my eyes and get attacked or shanked. The crackhead trapped in the cell with us couldn't stop scratching himself or fidgeting. He said all kinds of delusional shit, like the cops hid cameras in his apartment, and he knew for a fact that one of us had snitched on him. After that, he alternated staring at me and our other two cellmates with his unblinking crazy-eyes and a goofy-ass smile that had me convinced that he'd kill us in our sleep just for shits and giggles.

Thank God I was only in AC for one night. I never want to see the inside of that type of cage again in any district. I'll probably have nightmares from the trauma of the last four days.

I'm a badass motherfucker, spending the last seventeen years training to fight. It's not that I'm worried about taking on any of the punks in there, or even three or four of them at a time. But the feeling of suffocating because it was so goddamn hot, with the air rank and stale in such a small box? That's some scary shit.

I swear there was a lack of oxygen, and more carbon dioxide than can possibly be healthy in that bitch. I'll probably have to sleep with all my doors and windows open with the air conditioning on full blast for the next few weeks.

So despite how much this whole situation sucks, I'll do whatever it takes to avoid going back to that hell hole. I'll even follow the orders of the blonde, bitchy lawyer.

Finally, after what seems like forever, my dad and the father of the prude ice princess come out of one of the offices.

I hate seeing my dad so upset, and I'm still not sure if he and Jude believe I'm innocent or not. They both know my battle with rage better than most. The anger I've been struggling with since I was ten years old, beating and bloodying anyone and everyone who said a wrong word to me. That's the reason I got into legitimate fighting in the first place. The classes were a bribe to motivate me to stop getting suspended from school. So it's probably not a stretch for them to think I'd do this type of thing.

As a newly single father raising us on one income, my dad scraped up money we didn't have in order to give me some type of outlet to constantly grapple with my demons. And Jude, well, he's taken the most punishment over the years. The fucked up part is he always kept coming back for more, no matter how many times I knocked him down or out.

I'd like to think that in some way I've been helping Jude get his fighting career to where mine is today or more like where it was a week ago. But for the first few years when he started training with me, that thought never crossed my mind while I was repeatedly beating the shit out of my younger brother. I'm not sure which is worse; being angry at him or feeling guilty for taking my jealousy out on him.

I can't say I'm real happy about the loss of income while this shit drags out, or the dent I just made in my bank account either. A huge chunk of my hard earned money flushed down the toilet all because some cage cunt decided it'd be fun to ruin my life.

Before my dad posted my bond and my feet even hit the ground, Mack Miller, the President of the IFC, the International Fighting Championship, had left me a voicemail saying that my contract with him at the largest and best MMA promotion company has been put on hold until the disposition of the case. When I talked to Coach Briggs on the way here, he told me that just like the IFC, all of my sponsors have dropped me until this nightmare ends.

I'm not worried about making ends meet, just pissed I'm throwing money away. As the reigning middleweight champion of the world for the past five years, between promotion purses and advertisers, my bank account sits comfortably with seven figures, even after this unexpected hit. I'm worried that I might not ever be able to get in the cage again, and I have to admit that the idea of ending up behind bars for the long haul is scary as fuck.

"Jackson, did Page get your statement?" the arrogant, white-haired attorney asks. I'm pretty sure the old man's scared of me. I'm an expert at reading people's fear in and out of the cage. He avoided eye contact with me and ran out of the conference room like his ass was on fire. His daughter's got more balls than him. Even though she was practically shaking with nervousness being alone with me, she held her ground and didn't run scared.

I stand up when they approach and nod in response before taking a few steps toward the old man to test my theory. "Yeah, pretty much."

Retreating a step, Davenport says, "Don't worry about her inexperience or timidity. Ryan Warburton may technically be the second chair in the courtroom, but he'll be running the show behind the scenes. He's got over a hundred trials under his belt. Page will just add a nice, feminine touch for media purposes."

Wow, so this pussy doesn't think his own daughter is capable of handling my case. He sounds like he just wants her to basically be arm candy for photo-ops. What a sexist prick. I might fuck more women than I can count, but I do know that just because someone has nice tits and a fine ass doesn't mean they can't do any job just as well as any man, maybe even better.

"Page already has some great ideas on how to go forward and gave me a list of receipts and things to get her. She seems to really know her shit," I tell him. Why I feel defensive on her behalf, I have no fucking idea. Especially when my first thought seeing her was that she's just a snotty, spoiled, dumb blonde getting by on her daddy's coattails. I can occasionally admit when I'm wrong.

"Right. Well, I'm sure you need to get some rest after the hellish weekend you've had. Here's my card and Ryan's. Call either of us if you need anything." Davenport hands over two business cards, not bothering to offer me his daughter's, and then after a polite handshake, he's gone.

"So how do you feel about them?" my dad asks when we sit down in his Explorer in the parking garage.

"Davenport is an arrogant asshole who's terrified of me, and his daughter thinks I'm a piece of shit rapist. But she seems like she's going to actually put in the effort."

"Don't worry about her. Miles assured me that Warburton is a top-notch defense attorney. As soon as he gets out of his murder trial in a few weeks, he'll take over your case."

So Davenport had also convinced my dad that his daughter isn't capable of handling me. No wonder the girl comes across as such a frigid bitch if she has to deal with her own father's shit every day.

~

Page

I'm surprised the day after our first meeting when Jamie buzzes me around eleven a.m. to say Jackson Malone's up front and wants to see me. I tidy up my office so I can bring him in here and leave the door open instead of having to close us in a conference room together, then go to the lobby to get him.

"Mr. Malone?" I ask when I get to the waiting area. He rises from the chair with a bizarre masculine fluidity I've never witnessed before. Today he's dressed even more casually, in a pair of black nylon workout pants and a white tee stretched tight over his broad chest that says *Havoc* in large bold letters, with *Fight Club* underneath. The "V" of the word Havoc is actually a detailed bird or griffin of some sort, and it looks like his wings are spread out and flexing like a man would flex his biceps. How cute.

I don't miss Malone's dark eyes drifting down my gray pants suit before they eventually come up and meet mine.

"I've got all that shit you wanted," he says, holding out a stack of papers and a thumb drive that I accept.

"Um, that was quick. Thanks."

I slip the thumb drive into my pocket so I can flip through the pages to see what all he's rounded up. There are plane tickets, fight promotional flyers, hotel receipts, his own social media posts, and phone records with yellow highlights on a certain number, which I assume belongs to the accuser.

"Just for future reference, don't mark on any original documents," I warn him.

"Excuse the fuck out of me. I spent two goddamn hours going through this stack of shit, picking out her number from hundreds of other calls, trying to save you some time."

I jerk back from his hostility and fire back with my own, even though we're standing in the front lobby with onlookers. "Don't worry. I'm not hourly since you paid a flat fee, so even if it takes me hours, it won't cost you another penny."

"I don't give a shit about the fucking money," he snarls, his black eyes fiery like liquid lava. "Despite what you instantly judged and assumed from looking at me, I actually have plenty."

Based on the way our conversation is growing rather inflamed, I decide we both need a cooling down period, but I still can't help taking another shot at him.

"Why don't I give you a few minutes to extract those wadded up panties that seem to be causing you some discomfort, and when you're ready to talk to me without the attitude Jamie will show you to my office," I tell him, pointing to the cowering receptionist behind her window before turning on my heel and storming back to my office. I pretend to ignore the muttered "itch" with a capital "B" that follows me down the hall.

That man is so freaking infuriating! Instead of going back in my office I march right on past it and don't stop until I get to the break room. I toss the papers down on the lunch table and then grab a bottle of water from the refrigerator, quickly twisting off the cap.

My brother, of course, chooses that moment to stroll in. "What's all the shouting about?" he asks before I can swallow my first sip. "You need some help?"

JAX

I roll my eyes and let out an annoyed huff, taking my time sipping my water, so he's forced to wait in silence for my response.

"I've got everything under control, *Logie*." I tack on the hated childhood nickname I gifted him and smile to myself when he winces.

"Didn't sound like it," he says, leaning back against the countertop in front of me while crossing his arms over the front of his crisp white dress shirt. "Are you going to cry? Do you want me to take over the case for you?"

My jaw drops and my back straightens, bristling at his insinuation. "I am perfectly capable of handling that cocky jerk all on my own, thank you very much!" I can't help the screech caused when my teeth grind against each other. "Why do you even care? You don't practice criminal law, either. You're just a weeny patent lawyer."

He raises a light blond eyebrow at my assertion before flashing both rows of his perfect white teeth. "I'm the best damn patent lawyer in the country, beanpole. And there's an office pool running on you."

"Are you kidding?" I ask, placing my hands on my hips. "For what exactly?"

"A variety of things." He laughs before he begins ticking them off on his fingers. "One, for how long it'll be before he makes you cry. Another is for how long before you fuck up. When you'll actually give up and quit. Oh, and one for how long before he fires the firm because you piss him off. So yeah, I think that's all of them."

I try really hard not to let the hurt show on my face, knowing he'll use it against me. The whole office doesn't think I can handle the angry criminal, or probably any other case, for that matter.

"So what are the bets?" I ask. I'm going to make sure I surpass them all.

"For crying, anywhere from today until Friday at the latest. Fucking up in the next forty-eight hours. On quitting, the bets range from today until next Monday. And on him firing us, well, we all give it less than a week."

Now I'm no longer hurt, I'm angry. I work with an office full of jerks. No wonder female attorneys haven't lasted longer than a year, two at the max, in this place. The men are dicks, and the assistants are all gossiping hens...well, except for Jamie. I'm by God going to prove them all wrong, and I don't care what it takes. This jerk of a client is no different than the men I work with. I'll just have to finally show them that I'm actually tougher and smarter than I look.

My whole life it's always been, "*Oh, Page made the honor roll? Well, Logan got a perfect score on his SAT.*" And "*Page got into Georgetown? Well, Logan was offered a full scholarship when he got accepted.*" I'm so freaking tired of it!

Turning my back on my brother without another word, I pick up the stack of documents and glance through them while heading back to my office. That's when I notice the screen shot of Christina Loftis's Facebook page.

He'd actually found it.

I have to admit that he's done a good job gathering everything he could in less than a day's time.

I pause in the middle of the hallway to close my eyes and replay our most recent conversation. Malone had flipped out on me after my criticism for marking on potential exhibits. There was no way he'd know that, having never done this sort of thing before now. He was probably pissed that after all the time and hard work he'd put in that the first thing I did was snap at him. Of course he got all defensive. That's what he does for a living. Okay, so now that I understand that I'll try not to be so quick to attack him again.

My eyes are still on the paperwork in my hand when I get back to my office. I'm lowering my bottom down into my computer chair before I realize I'm not alone.

"Ah!" I squeal, fumbling to hold on to the stack of documents.

"About time," Malone grumbles from the chair he's currently slouching in across from my desk.

"Geez Louise, you scared me," I say, holding the papers to my galloping heart.

"Everything okay in here?" Mark, our federal criminal attorney, asks from my open doorway. He purses his lips like he's trying not to grin but epically fails when a snicker escapes.

"Perfectly fine. Now run along, imp," I mutter, getting back up from my chair to go slam the door in the annoying dwarf's face. I swear the man's only a few inches taller than Peter Dinklage and tells more dirty offensive jokes than Daniel Tosh.

"Listen," I say to Malone when I take my seat again. "There's an office pool going that I don't intend for anyone to win."

"A pool?" he asks, slanting his thick black eyebrows together. Somehow they're actually sexy as all get out, and nothing like Bert's on *Sesame Street*.

"Yeah, my lovely coworkers are betting on me. You, too, actually."

Malone leans back in his chair, both hands behind his head with his elbows out. Can the man do anything without making it look sexy? "Really? What's the bet?" He asks.

"How soon before you make me cry, how soon before I screw up, how soon I'll quit your case, and how soon you fire me."

"Well damn," he mutters. "You a crier or something?"

"No, I'm not a crier! I've never shed a tear in this office, and can't recall the last time I shed one at all."

Although, it was most likely when I was around ten or eleven years old. I'd found a litter of newborn kittens near the dumpster behind our Methodist Church. After my parents and I had dropped them off at a local vet because they wouldn't let me keep them, I told them I wanted to save puppies and kittens when I grew up. In response, my mom said, "No, Page. You're too smart and pretty to shovel shit for strays. You're going to marry a rich man." And my dad followed up her statement with, "Or you can go to law school just like your brother." That had been it, my only two options, end of discussion. It was the first time I realized my life would never actually be my own if I didn't want to disappoint them. Any variation from their decree, and to them I'd be a failure. That pressure's only gotten worse as I've gotten older.

"But all your coworkers think *I'm* going to make you cry?" Malone asks.

"Yep."

"That's pretty fucked up."

"Tell me about it," I agree with a burst of laughter. "So, here's what we're going to do. I'm not going to cry, and I'm going to try to be nicer to you. You're going to stop yelling at me, and we're going to work together on your case so that everyone else in this building can go screw themselves. Deal?" I ask.

He looks at me a second before he finally nods. "Deal."

"So," I say with a deep calming breath. "You found her on Facebook?"

"Yeah, I tracked her down from her liking my fan page. She apparently doesn't know how to make her shit private since I could see all her posts and pictures. There were several photos of me on there, before last weekend. I printed them out, along with her comments."

"This is good stuff," I tell him honestly. I start spreading everything out into piles based on separate categories. One for receipts, one for phone records, and one for Facebook.

I read each page before putting it in the appropriate stack, closely reviewing the victim's Facebook profile and posts for anything that might be helpful. I do a double take when I get to a picture of Jackson. My cheeks warm, looking at such a revealing photo while actually sitting in front of the man.

The black and white photo is...breathtaking. Every single line of his smooth, sculpted chest, arms, stomach and... legs are clearly shown. Feet shoulder width apart, only his two hands cupping himself block his privates from the camera. His head is hung, chin to his chest like there's an enormous invisible weight on his lethal shoulders.

Under the photo is a comment by Christina Loftis, "Even yummier in person and tastes divine."

Wow.

So maybe his ego isn't as inflated as I first thought, or at least not without merit. Hell, if this is what he looks like naked then I'm surprised a stampede of women isn't currently running through our building to get to him.

"Find something you like?" the arrogant jerk asks.

I shuffle on through to the next few pages. "I'm just...reviewing them, you know...to see if ah, there's anything helpful," I stutter.

"If you need me to undress for you to confirm that those are, in fact, pictures of me, well, I'm happy to oblige," he says. I can practically hear his smirk.

"That won't be necessary," I assure him even though my body completely disagrees.

"I don't have to take advantage of anyone to get some ass. If I posted, 'I'm horny' and listed this address on *Twitter* to my more than two million followers, plenty of women would show up, ready to fuck me anyway and as many times as I want. Faster service than a *Domino's Pizza* delivery. So why would I do something as stupid as rape a woman?"

Holy guacamole. After seeing that picture, I knew he wasn't bluffing. He's probably the one responsible for the sudden influx of female fans to MMA over the last few years. That doesn't mean he didn't overpower this woman against her will this time or choke her during.

"That brings up something important we need to discuss. While this case is pending, you shouldn't be seen with any women in public, and you certainly shouldn't...engage in intercourse with anyone," I tell him.

He scoffs. "You can't be serious." When I don't respond, he eventually asks, "How long are we talking?"

Looking up, I quickly run the timeline in my head. "Depending on when we get all the discovery from the district attorney, how soon he goes to the grand jury, and when the judge decides to put the case on the trial calendar, a few months at least."

"Months!" he exclaims, his dark eyebrows reaching for the ceiling.

"Yes, months. Do you really want copycats coming forward with more accusations? Preparing for a trial takes time. We'll get ready as soon as we can, but we have to get your direct testimony and cross-examination ready and practiced. You'll need to decide on a few character witnesses. I may need to hire a medical expert to review the victim's records and injuries, and have you mentally evaluated. I'll want to interview the officers involved. There's a ton to do."

"How do you expect me to go *for months* without getting laid? My dick has high expectations and demands. He's a hardheaded, overeager bastard that gets angry when he's denied servicing for longer than a day."

I try not to smile at his way too detailed description.

"I'm sure you and your...dick will survive the famine. Also, do I really have to tell you not to use any drugs or get drunk in public?"

"For Christ's sake, woman, I'm a professional athlete! I don't ever touch any of that shit," he replies.

"Well, good for you," I say, surprised by his statement. "But don't start now because of the stress of all that's going on."

"If I can't fuck and I can't fight, then I guess I'll be doing a shitload of training."

"That should be fine," I agree. "As long as you're available when I call and need information from you, or for you to come in to do some trial prep work. This case has to be the most important thing in your life for the next few months."

"I get that. If we lose, I'm out of the cage for good."

"Not only that, but these are very serious offenses. If you get convicted, you could get an active sentence of up to three hundred months..."

"Three hundred months! What the fuck!?!" he yells, practically coming out of his seat.

"That's just for the rape charge. Add another maximum of twenty months if you're convicted on the assault by strangulation charge."

"*Goddamn!* What the hell is three hundred and twenty months?" he asks, his forehead so furrowed trying to do the math that he looks like he's in pain.

"A little less than twenty-seven years."

Malone's face goes slack, his tan skin turns pale white, and then he really is out of his chair, scrambling for the small black trash can beside my desk.

In that moment I feel an unexpected twinge of sympathy for him. He's known for being a tough, badass fighter, and at the moment he's on his knees losing all the contents of his stomach. He almost looks...vulnerable.

I grab a few tissues from the dispenser on my desk and hand them to him when it sounds like he's finished. He eventually accepts my offering, looking up at me with dark, watery eyes, seeming more like a scared boy than a violent criminal.

"You can't let them convict me," he pleads. "I swear I didn't do it."

I have to look away from his sad, pitiful, puppy dog eyes before they suck me in. I'm still a sucker for strays. "Those are just the maximum sentences. You know the worst case scenario sentences. With a clean record and a decent judge, you might only get the minimum of a hundred and fifty-four months. A little less than thirteen years," I say, doing the math for him.

"Thirteen...*fuck*! I wouldn't get out until I'm forty fucking years old," he mutters, hanging his head while wiping off his mouth.

Eventually, he rises gracefully to his feet and sits back down in his chair with hunched shoulders. I go around my desk and pick up the smelly trash can, taking it out in the hallway for my fellow coworkers to enjoy. Ha! Take that you bastards.

"It's important for you to understand what you're facing upon conviction," I tell Jackson as I return to my seat. "Because if the prosecutor offers a plea deal to a lesser offense like assault on a female with just a few years active, it's worth considering."

"I'm not pleading guilty," he says gruffly.

"Even though serving three or four years is a heck of a lot better than twenty-seven or thirteen years?" I ask in disbelief.

"I'm not. Pleading. Guilty. I didn't rape that bitch, and I'll take the risk of doing the extra time before I fucking say I did it."

He may think that now, but when the evidence starts coming in, he'll probably change his mind.

"All right, so let's get ready for trial."

"My head coach wants to know if we're going to do a press conference anytime soon, you know...to calm things down with the media?"

"Your coach wants to know?" I ask curiously.

"Don Briggs. He's like my coach, manager, and agent all rolled into one."

"Oh. Well, there are rules of professionalism that limit what attorneys can say about pending trials. We have to be careful, or the prosecutor will argue that we're trying to influence the jury pool. Why don't I work on drafting something up, and then email it to you for approval? Just one that's short and sweet like, "Mr. Malone adamantly denies all of the charges against him and intends to plead not guilty and go to trial to prove his innocence. He appreciates the support of his fans during this difficult and stressful time."

"That works." Malone nods. "I probably shouldn't say that I've never choked the bitch, but I'd really like to do it now that she's made up these bullshit charges."

"Yes, let's not mention choking any...bitches, especially not the victim. You'll need to watch your temper because any sort of outburst will just add fuel to the prosecutor's fire."

"Right."

"We may need to take a trip to Atlantic City soon to get the video surveillance, and you can show me the hotel room, so we can take some pictures to possibly use as exhibits. We can talk to the hotel staff to see if they remember seeing her, and I'll set up an appointment with the District Attorney to get acquainted."

"Yeah, whenever. Just let me know. It's not like I've got anything else to do," he says with a shrug of his broad shoulders.

"All right, how about tomorrow? I can get the subpoena for the video ready, and my Notice of Appearance and Motion for Discovery typed up to file it with the clerk while we're there."

Yesterday I was terrified of the man, but after watching him toss his cookies in fear, he doesn't seem quite as scary. I think hearing the possible consequences of a conviction will likely have him on his best behavior from now on.

"Sure. On one condition, though - I get to drive," he says with a smirk.

"Fine. That way I can get some work done. I'll put a call into pretrial services to get authorization for you to travel..."

A knock on my office door interrupts me mid-sentence.

"Come in," I grit out, wondering which jackass is checking up on me now.

"Page?" Jamie asks from the doorway.

"Hey, what's up?" I ask our receptionist, glad it's not another snickering attorney.

"Sorry to interrupt, but Elliott wanted me to catch you before you left," she starts, then drops her eyes to the post-it in her hand.

"Let me guess, he has to cancel lunch?" I ask, leaning back in my chair and crossing my arms over my chest in annoyance at the man, not the messenger.

"Yes. He apologized and said he would make it up to you tonight," she says reading from the post-it note in her hand.

I groan, already hearing how he'll "make it up" to me by talking nonstop about whatever budget plan or new piece of legislation they'd worked on today. How important his job is, how wonderful he is, blah, blah, blah.

"Thanks, Jamie," I tell her as she backs out of the office and suddenly covers her nose and mouth. That reminds me. "Oh, and, Jamie? Can you have someone from housekeeping come grab my trash for me?" I ask, and she nods quickly before pulling the door shut.

"Sorry about your trash can," Malone murmurs. I swear he almost sounded embarrassed with his eyes cast down to the floor.

"Don't worry about it." I shrug it off.

"Friend stand you up?" he asks.

"Fiancé, and yes. Not the first time and won't be the last." Self-centered prick. Why make plans if three out of four times they get canceled? Why not just say, *"Hey, I'll call you if I get free?"*

"You're not wearing a ring," he says, interrupting my internal ranting.

"Um, excuse me?" I ask.

"A ring," he repeats, holding up his hand and pointing to where the circular piece of jewelry would go.

"Oh, well, we just sort of, you know...agreed to get married. It wasn't like he went down on one knee or made a big scene."

"Sounds like a really romantic guy." He snorts with a shake of his head and his trademark smirk.

"And you think you're what, a regular Casanova?" I scoff. The guy who chokes and rapes women wants to be critical of *my* love life?

He shrugs in response. "Maybe not, but if a beautiful woman actually agreed to marry my dumb-ass, I wouldn't skimp on a ring. I'd want everyone to know she's taken and that she's mine."

Was that a compliment or just a general statement? Either way, it doesn't matter.

"Our relationship is not a bunch of hearts and flower nonsense." Because that would require an actual effort on Elliott's behalf. "It's basically a...realistic partnership."

"What, like a business deal?" he asks.

"Actually, yes."

He shakes his head. "That's weird."

"Weird? What's weird about marrying someone you're compatible with?"

He shrugs again. "Whatever. Marriage is a waste anyway," he says, standing up to go. "What time do you want to leave tomorrow?"

"Um, how about ten?" I suggest.

"See you then," he replies over his shoulder. I watch as the man strolls out the door of my office with so much sexy swagger it should be illegal.

CHAPTER THREE

Jax

I pull up in front of the high-dollar law firm in Silver Spring two minutes late. The tall, bitchy blonde is already waiting for me at the curb, looking put out with her briefcase over her shoulder and arms crossed over her chest.

It's going to be a long fucking day.

I turn the booming bass of my stereo down and climb out. The ice princess opens the passenger door before I have a chance, so I just hold it open for her while she sits down with her nose wrinkled in disgust.

After I settle back into the driver seat, I glance over at her while I put my seatbelt back on.

"What?" I ask in annoyance when her face remains scrunched up like she smells shit. My car is my baby, and I keep it spotless. The only thing I smell inside of it is the scent of new leather and *Armor All* from the dashboard.

"This is your car? What the heck is this thing?"

"Are you fucking kidding me?" I ask in disbelief. "It's a brand new Dodge Viper. The most awesome car ever."

"It's cramped and...impractical," she remarks, while twisting around to reach for the seatbelt.

"It's fun to drive. Do you even know what the term *fun* means?"

"Yes."

"Right," I snicker. "You should be happy I didn't insist we take my bike."

The thought of her arms wrapped around my waist, breasts pressed against my back while weaving through traffic on my Beemer, shouldn't be as arousing as it is. I can already tell my unfortunate vow of celibacy is gonna last about as long as the flavor in a stick of gum. I turn the radio back up as a distraction from my wayward thoughts, even louder than before just to tick Miss Priss off.

She shifts her long, lean body, one I'm almost certain would be damn fine if it wasn't always covered up with expensive pantsuits like the black one she's got on today until she's as far away from me as possible in the confined space. Her revulsion shouldn't bother me, but it does. I'm pretty sure she still thinks I'm guilty, and I don't like how she assumes I'm a bad guy. Sure, the IFC league casts me as a crazy motherfucker that bloodies people and knocks their brains loose. That's all true, but they're just trying to hype up the volatile maniac image to sell tickets and merchandise.

I go along with it, playing up the role of the jackass fighter everyone loves to hate but still watch, because I'm able to backup my talk in the cage where it counts. Most women seem to go for the bad boy, even if some, like this ice princess, are afraid of me. Now with these charges, everyone probably thinks I'm a loose cannon.

I don't care what the fans think about me, but my attorney that I'm paying to defend me so I won't spend the rest of my life in prison? Well, I need her to see that I'm innocent and worth her precious time to try and save me.

I turn down the volume on the radio as I take the exit for the highway. "So, Ms. Davenport, how long have you been practicing?" I ask as nicely as possible.

"I know what I'm doing," she responds snidely.

"I didn't *ask* if you know what you're doing, I *asked* how long you've been practicing."

"Almost a year," she says, lowering her voice like she's embarrassed and hates losing face.

"Where'd you go to law school?"

"Georgetown, just like everyone else in my family."

"Nice. Go Bulldogs. That's a pretty tough school, right?" I ask.

"Yeah, it's ranked thirteenth in the country."

"Wow, that's impressive. You must've worked your ass off."

She sighs. "Not really. My dad just made a few calls."

"What?" I ask in disbelief, glancing over at her highness.

"Kidding. That's what everyone probably thinks, though."

"I've never really cared much about what everyone thinks," I tell her. Well, except for one sassy, uppity lawyer bitch.

"Must be nice."

"I take it criminal law is not your favorite area to practice?" I ask.

"No, it's not. I don't know what area I want to practice in, though, so right now I take whatever cases my dad gives me."

"What about your fiancé? Is he an attorney, too?" I don't know much about him, but he has to be an asshole for standing her up on a regular basis. Oh, and what kind of dick doesn't even buy a fucking engagement ring?

She gives a soft sarcastic laugh. "Technically, although he's currently serving as a state senator and not really practicing."

"Ah. So he's a politician. Those are even worse than attorneys, right?" I tease.

"Oh yeah," she agrees. "Elliot has his eye on the U.S. Congress and then running for the Presidency after he's been in office a few years."

"As in the President of the United States?" I ask in awe.

"Um-huh, but that's way down the road."

"So you could be like the First Lady someday?"

"Yeah. I'm a lucky girl," she says quietly while looking out the window, not sounding like she feels the least bit lucky.

"So how long have you been mauling people?" she asks after a few minutes of silence, catching me off guard.

"A long time," I reply, unable to prevent the bloody memories of my youth from surfacing. "Since I was ten."

"You mauled people when you were only ten years old?" she asks, her voice going all high and squeaky like she's appalled.

"That's when I first started getting into fights, yeah. I used any reason to beat up a kid. If someone said a wrong word to me or messed with one of the other kids, I went ape-shit on their asses. After my third suspension from school, my dad told me that if I could go a month without getting into another fight, he'd let me enroll in the new kickboxing school."

"So you started kickboxing?"

"Yeah. I stopped fighting at school, took the kickboxing class once a week, and then eventually bumped it up to three times a week. In middle school, I added football and wrestling to burn off the anger. After I won the state championship in the one-seventy weight class in my freshman and sophomore year of high school, Jon Baker, a local MMA coach, approached me. He asked if I wanted to train with him to fight some tough ass men instead of weak little boys. I gave up school sports in my junior year and started training at his gym. When I was twenty-one, I signed up with former championship heavyweight boxer Don Briggs, my current coach, when he opened *Havoc Fight Club* in Silver Springs. A year later I won my first world championship belt."

"And the rest is history," Page remarks.

"Yeah. I've never lost a fight."

"Never say never," she mutters.

"As long as I stay in shape no one will ever beat me. I train with some first class heavyweights, and if they can't do it, no middleweight will, either."

"Not lacking any confidence are you?"

"It's the truth, not me just running my mouth."

"Uh-huh," she says, sounding less than impressed. Why that bothers me, I have no idea.

When she pulls her laptop from her bag and goes to work, I figure my attempt to make small talk is over. I turn the radio back up to an acceptable level and keep my thoughts to myself the rest of the trip.

As soon as we arrive in Atlantic City, I take Page to the courthouse and wait for her in the car while she goes inside to file shit and talk to the prosecutor. I don't care anything for stepping foot into that terrifying place until I have to. When she returns, she's smiling triumphantly with a manila folder in her hand.

"Good news," she says, fastening her seatbelt. "I talked to the District Attorney Franklin, who seems like a decent guy. He went ahead and gave me a copy of the discovery."

"What's discovery?" I ask.

"The evidence. Mostly police reports, the victim's statement... that sort of thing."

"About that. You keep saying, 'the victim', but she's not a fucking victim," I point out in aggravation. Every time I hear that word I want to hit someone.

Page's expression blanks and she finally nods. "Sorry, does 'alleged victim' sound better?"

"Can't we just call her 'the bitch'? Or cunt? Whore. Slut. Any of those would work," I tell her. Her soft laughter hits me in the chest harder than a battering ram. I rub my palm over the strange, unfamiliar ache.

"Fine, we'll call her 'the bitch,'" she agrees, even though I can tell she has to force the profanity from her prim and proper lips.

"Good. So what did the bitch say?" I ask as I pull out of the courthouse parking lot and head to the hotel a few blocks over.

"I've only skimmed through it," she says, pulling out the three-inch stack of documents. "You drive, and I'll read, then we can go through everything together when we get to the room." The room, where the *alleged* rape and strangulation occurred.

I hear Page shuffling through the papers while I drive. "Oh no," she says solemnly when we come to a stop under the hotel's canopy.

"What?" I ask.

She shows me a close-up photo of a woman's neck. Not just any neck, but one with black bruises resembling fingertips on the side.

Fuck!

"I didn't do that shit!" I tell her.

"Are you sure? Could you...could you have been a little rough with her...during—"

"Fuck no! I might like it rough, but I'd remember putting my hands around a woman's neck. I wasn't even rough with her at all that night. My hands never once touched her neck when she was on top, fucking me. All I touched were her hips. And maybe her tit...breasts."

"This is not good," Page mutters, continuing to thumb through more photos that I can't make out.

I jump out of the car, give the valet my keys, and take the offered ticket. I open Page's door since she's still immersed in her reading.

"Come on," I tell her. "Let's go somewhere, so I can read that shit, too."

She finally climbs out with her bag and handful of documents. After we stop by the front desk and give the security manager a subpoena for the surveillance video, he goes to check on making a copy for us while the front desk clerk gives us a key to the same room I'd stayed in less than two weeks ago.

The oceanfront king suite on the eleventh floor looks just like I remember. I stand in the kitchen out of the way while Page takes a few pictures with her phone.

When she sits down on the red leather couch across from the bed, I sit beside her, so we can both see what all they've given her at the courthouse. I don't understand some of the shit I scan as she passes the sheets to me, but then we get to the reports.

"She said you tore her blouse and shoved her onto the bed before forcing her to perform oral sex..."

I bark out a laugh. "How do you *force* a woman to suck a dick? Because I can tell you right now, my dick's not going anywhere near the teeth of an unwilling participant."

Page's cheeks redden, apparently offended by my crassness. Too bad, she needs to get used to dealing with this sort of shit before trial.

"That is sort of a preposterous accusation," she admits.

"You think? And I didn't tear her shirt. She was wearing a button down and yanked it open herself."

"She doesn't say anything about you removing her skirt or panties."

"Because she wasn't wearing any. Panties that is."

"Oh-kay. Let's see. Then she ends by saying you grabbed her by her throat to hold her down before penetrating her vaginally, so rough that it caused tearing..."

"If she tore something that's her own damn fault for riding my dick five seconds after walking through the door."

"Uh-oh. You said you used a condom right?" she asks.

"I did use a condom. I *always* use condoms."

"Well, this lab report from the rape kit shows that semen matching the DNA sample you gave them was found inside her vagina. The exam nurse gave her *Plan B*, to prevent the chance of pregnancy."

"No! No fucking way!" I say, jumping to my feet. "That is bullshit! I used a condom. I came in the goddamn condom!"

"Maybe...maybe it leaked," Page offers softly.

"Trojans don't leak!"

"Calm down and stop yelling at the messenger," she says, offering me the stack of documents. "Here, you take them."

I yank the reports from her hand, probably harder than necessary, and sit on the bed so I can spread them out to look through them again. I re-read the lying sack of shit statement one more time, wondering how I can prove I didn't do any of the things she accuses.

"What about if I do one of those lie detecting things?" I ask Page, who's standing in front of the sliding glass doors, looking out at the ocean. She's a breathtakingly beautiful woman when she's not wrinkling her nose like an elitist bitch.

"A polygraph?" she turns around and asks.

"Yes! One of those things."

She shakes her head. "They're not admissible in court."

"Then how the hell do I prove I *didn't* do something?"

She blows out a breath and gnaws on her bottom lip in thought. "I might be able to get you an appointment with a retired FBI polygrapher, but it's going to cost about a grand."

"But I thought you just said they aren't admissible or whatever."

"Not as evidence in a trial, but if you pass...I could use it as leverage with the prosecutor."

"I will pass."

"Well, we can just shred the report if you don't."

"I will pass it," I repeat, and she looks back out toward the ocean. "What? You don't think I will? You thought I was guilty this whole damn time, so will this finally prove to you that I'm innocent?"

She finally faces me again. "It doesn't matter what I think. It matters what twelve jurors believe, and I'm telling you, one look at those pictures, and you're going to get convicted."

"Your job is to make sure I don't!"

"I'm just an attorney, not a freaking miracle worker," she says, crossing her arms over her chest.

"You're really starting to piss me off," I warn her.

"Then maybe you should hire someone else to represent you," she replies, her jaw tight, face blood red, looking as angry as I am at the moment. "Because if you get convicted, I don't want you blaming me for the fact that you were too stupid to take a plea!"

"You are such a stuck-up bitch, you know that?"

She scoffs at the insult. "Well, you're an arrogant, rude, overcompensating..." she sputters.

"Yeah, so what? That doesn't mean I'm guilty!"

"You know what, I'll just take the train home, so you can go on back without me," she says.

"Hell no, you won't! I'm not leaving you in this city by yourself. You're going back with me, even if I have to throw you over my shoulder and carry you to my car."

She huffs out a breath, and her blue eyes narrow when she puts her clenched fists prissily on her hips. Damn if that doesn't make her even sexier. It's also pretty funny to see her wound up like a feisty, aggravated kitten. The ones you can't help but keep teasing, trying to get them all riled up until they arch their backs and hop around on all four feet like they're little badasses.

"What's the smirk for?" she asks in a huff.

"You're kind of cute when you're trying to look pissed off."

"You're not taking this seriously."

"I'm as serious as a motherfucking heart attack. This is my life at stake here!"

"Then listen to me when I tell you that those pictures are going to get you convicted, whether you're guilty or innocent. That's why a plea might really be the best thing-"

That does it. I throw the papers down and stand up to get in her face. "I'm not pleading guilty! Maybe *you* should try listening to *me* for once!"

"I'll be committing malpractice if I let you go to trial and get twenty or more years active when you could've taken a plea and gotten out in just a handful!" she yells.

"Seriously, woman, I don't want to have this discussion with you again. No fucking plea is going to happen! So don't you lose another single wink of sleep worrying your pretty little head about malpractice nonsense."

She blows out another breath, and I'm so close I can smell the peppermint scent. "Fine. Then you won't mind signing something stating that I advised you to take a plea, and you refused?"

"I'll sign any fucking thing you want as long as you quit talking about that shit."

"Fine."

"Good. Glad we could clear that up," I say, taking a step back to put some space between us.

"I'm going back down to the security desk to see if the video is ready and if so, try to get them to print a few pictures of her. I think I can pick her out from her Facebook photos. Then I'll find out who in the hotel was working that night based on the other people visible on the camera.

I'll show those people her picture and see if anyone remembers seeing her."

"Great. I'll be at the pool when you're ready to go," I tell her.

Of course she scoffs, crossing her arms over her chest. "This is not a vacation, Mr. I'm-Serious-as-a-Heart-Attack."

"I'm serious, but there's nothing else for me to do while you do that shit, is there? And since I had to pay for this room for us to come look at, that makes me a guest here, and I'm going to the fucking pool."

"But you don't have a swimsuit."

"I'm not going skinny dipping for Christ's sakes. They have like three huge ass clothing stores downstairs."

"Fine," she says in a huff, gathering all the paperwork and shoving it into her briefcase.

"And you better not fucking leave without me," I warn her. Then I have no choice but to watch her ass as she storms out the door. That incredible ass has me thinking all sorts of things I shouldn't.

CHAPTER FOUR

Page

What *a jerk*. I'm working my ass off while my client lounges by the pool. After sweet talking the security officers I was able to get a copy of video surveillance from that night on all the relevant cameras, and even a few printed photos. I also found a valet who remembered Christina Loftis asking him to call her a cab. He said her appearance had been disheveled, but she'd seemed calm, and even smiled and thanked him before climbing into a taxi.

Finished for the day and ready to head home, I throw my briefcase over my shoulder and go in search of Mr. Personality. We definitely need to work on his attitude before cross-examination.

I consider taking the train home like I had threatened earlier, but I wanted to share my success with someone. I'm even starting to believe Jackson may have a better chance of getting a *not guilty* than I originally thought. Small, but better than zero chance at least.

I follow the signs to the hotel pool, weaving my way through the slot machines and restaurants, along with the choking cigarette smoke.

Finally, I walk out the double glass sliding doors to head outside. Since it's a warm late May day, the rows and rows of lounge chairs around the pool are all occupied. It'll take me forever to find the arrogant man in this crowd.

Not having my sunglasses, I raise my hand to shade my eyes as I glance around. After several minutes I spot him. Hard to miss the one man in a sea of scantily clad sluts, I mean women. Moving closer, I notice they've formed a circle around him, and several are even sitting on the same lounge chair with him, practically draped over him. Does he not remember our conversation about staying away from females? *Idiot.*

When I reach the outer perimeter, Jackson looks up and notices me, giving a head nod in my direction. "Ready?" he yells.

"Yes."

A chorus of disappointment sounds around us, making me groan.

"We love you, Jax!" A woman exclaims. Her fangirl support is followed up by the sounds of many others.

"There's no way you did that shit!"

"Call me if you need *anything*!"

I roll my eyes at the comments until Jackson finally breaches their skanky barrier and appears in front of me.

Holy ravioli!

Wearing nothing but black sunglasses and low, very low, black boardshorts, the man's golden muscles glisten from water or tanning oil, making him look like a walking wet dream. His biceps are like small boulders, his waist narrow, stomach and pecs chiseled from stone and begging to be licked. I snap my mouth closed when I realize it's fallen open. I need to look deep inside my professionalism and find some dignity here before I embarrass myself even further.

Of course, Jackson is smiling at me when I look back up at his face. No wait...the man is actually *smiling*, not smirking for the very first time. The effect of that expression on his gorgeous face, along with his near nakedness is too much for me to handle.

"I'll, ah, just wait for you in the lobby," I say, spinning on my heel to quickly get away from him. Only instead of actually retreating, one of my black Stilettos loses traction on the slick patio when it lands in a puddle of pool water. My arms start wind-milling as I struggle to find my balance, but it's futile. The weight of my heavy shoulder bag throws me off kilter, and I'm going down.

Or I *was* going down, until a steel band knocks the air out of me when it hits my stomach, squishing me against a brick wall. No, wait, that's just Jackson's big, hard body behind me and his arm wrapped around my waist, standing me back up.

"Careful," his deep voice whispers beside my ear. His lips are so close I can feel his warm breath. That, along with his yummy tropical smell and the hardness of his body pressed intimately against mine, causes a shiver to run down my spine. "Can't have you busting that pretty little head of yours. It would be a real pain in the ass to have to find another attorney."

"Thanks," I mutter, trying to slow my racing heart. The racing caused by imagining what it'd feel like to have those lips brush against my skin. Idiotic thoughts, but I don't seem to have any control over them or the goosebumps they cause.

"You good?" Jackson asks.

I nod, steadying myself, and he releases his hold on me. Slowly, putting one foot carefully in front of the other, I walk back into the hotel, not stopping until I reach the front lobby. I fall backward onto one of the plush couches and groan in embarrassment. The egotistical jerk will never let me live it down, neither the part about how I looked at him nor how I almost pulled a *Humpty Dumpty*. My cheeks burn hotter thinking about the replay.

I get my laptop out and check my emails as a distraction while I wait for him. Finally, Jackson strolls out from the casino and heads straight to the valet. Thankfully he's back in his jeans and a gray tee, all that gorgeousness covered back up.

After handing over the ticket for his car, he returns to the lobby, pulls off his sunglasses, and starts looking around. When his dark eyes finally land on me, I expect his cocky smirk to be back in place. I can handle his cocky smirk better than the intense, hungry gaze fixated on me now, taking my breath away. Bastard. I lower my eyes and busy myself with packing up my bag.

"Did you get the video?" Jackson asks a minute later, right from above me.

"Yeah. This is her, right?" I ask, pulling out a photo to show him.

"That's the bitch."

"Notice anything significant?" I ask, standing up and having to get on my tiptoes to look at the zoomed in picture in his hands

"Ah, what do you mean?"

"I don't see any redness or bruises on her neck."

"Holy shit! You're a fucking genius, Page!" he exclaims.

"Nah, this was an obvious piece of evidence anyone would've known to get," I respond, taking the picture carefully from his hands and putting it away in my bag.

"Give yourself a little credit. The video could've been gone or taped over if we'd waited much longer."

I can't help but smile at his very correct assessment. "Yeah, and it would've been two days from now. They only save them for fourteen days."

"*Holy fuck!* I knew you were worth the fortune I paid!" he laughs as he lifts me off my feet in a bone crushing, spine popping bear hug.

"Put me down!" I squirm to get out of his hold. He smells too damn edible, like coconuts and sweat mixed with a woodsy, masculine cologne. I'm terrified I might accidentally lick him. Right up the inside of his neck and along the dark scruffy jawline. "Seriously, Jackson, people are looking at us." *And I might bite you if you don't let me go.*

"You called me Jackson," he says, finally loosening his hold and letting me slide down the front of his big, warm, sun-kissed body.

"Oh, um, s-sorry," I stutter, staring at his broad chest, swallowing back the uncalled for and extremely unprofessional flare of desire.

"No, I mean, you don't have to be all formal and shit with me. Just Jax is fine, too."

"We should probably start heading back," I say, stepping out of his thick arms. I really need to stop ending up in them.

"Car's out front. I'm just waiting on you, princess," he says, and when I look up at his face, he's smirking at me yet again.

Glad to be back on solid ground, I walk past him, heading out the sliding glass doors to his ridiculous black and green car.

"Why do you hate my car so much?" Jackson asks over the hood when he walks around to the driver side.

"I don't hate it," I say, taking a seat and putting on my seat belt while he does the same. "It just looks sort of ridiculous and reminds me of the Batmobile."

"Let me guess. You drive a Mercedes?" he asks, expertly shifting the gears to pull away from the curb.

"Maybe."

"Ha! I knew it. That's what all the spoiled little rich girls drive." The stereotype stings, but I can't really complain since it's true.

"You're one to talk. Aren't you the highest paid MMA fighter of all time?" I counter.

Jackson chuckles, and it's obvious he's in a much better mood than earlier. "Have you been Googling me?" he asks, glancing over and raising one dark, sexy eyebrow in question. Just like that, he makes something so common sound sexual. Boy, would I like to...Google him. I bet it'd be the best Google of my life, and afterward, Googling would never be the same.

Stop that! I yell at my hormones in disgust.

"No. It's just a rumor I've heard." I have actually searched him, but his salary didn't show up in Google images.

"Are you trying to get a bigger fee out of me? If so, I'll gladly pay it after you just saved my ass with that video."

"I don't want a bigger fee, rich boy. It's not like I'd see a dime of it anyway."

"Why not?" he asks.

"I work for my father. He pays me the same salary every month, regardless of what I do."

"That sucks."

"I'm a brand new attorney, so I have to slowly make my way up the ladder."

The two of us fall silent as we drive down the highway, and the sun begins to set. It's been a long day, but at least it's been productive. I don't even mind most of Jackson's punk rock and hip hop song choices as we roll along. The peacefulness of the drive is broken when my phone rings. Sheesh. *Elliott.*

"Hey," I answer.

"Where the hell are you?" he yells, and I instinctively pull the phone away from my ear.

"On my way back from Atlantic City."

"Yeah, I know where you've been. With Jackson *fucking* Malone."

"Elliott, you know I can't talk about my clients."

"You don't have to. The picture of the two of you is all over the Internet," he snaps.

"What picture?" I ask.

"The one showing you crossing the attorney-client line."

"What?" I exclaim. "I haven't-"

"How long have you been fucking him, Page?" Elliott yells the unexpected question.

Is Elliott actually jealous over some picture? It shouldn't make me happy that he's upset thinking I've been with another man, but it does. He never shows any sort of emotion when it comes to me, so it's a nice change of pace.

"What are you talking about? You know I wouldn't cheat on you, and I'd *never* sleep with a client," I respond, even though I still have no idea what the heck he's so pissed about. I could lose my law license for having any sort of sexual relationship with a client. Not that I've ever thought about doing...that with a client, and especially not with the man next to me. Okay, maybe such an inappropriate idea has filtered through my mind once or twice since I met Jax. Sometimes that often in an hour.

"Do you know how embarrassing it is for me to have my *fiancée* seen with another man? Especially *that* maniac! The media is going to make me look like a cuckold loser!"

Oh, so he's only worried about his precious reputation. I should've known better than to think he'd actually express some sort of feeling with regards to me. "I haven't done *anything* like that with him, and you can't technically be a cuckold since we're not married," I point out, just to piss him off.

"You better watch it, Page," Elliott warns. "As soon as you walk through this door I'm going to wear your smartass out to remind you who you belong to. When I get done, you won't be able to sit tomorrow, and my palm will burn for days."

"I think I'm just going to go home tonight."

The idea of him getting off on his fetish while my poor bottom suffers the consequences doesn't sound all that appealing at the moment...not that it ever has.

"Fine, I'll meet you there," he barks, then hangs up.

Son of a mother...trucker!

Jackson clears his throat from the driver seat. I cringe, wondering how much of that conversation he heard since he's less than a foot away in the cramped car.

"He's a *really* loud man," he remarks, telling me he'd likely heard it all.

"Yeah, he is."

"Do you want to go home?" Jackson asks without taking his eyes off the road.

"Not anymore." I laugh as much as I can given the situation. I'd just been yelled at and accused of sleeping with the man sitting next to me, who probably heard my wonderful fiancé treating me like a piece of crap.

"Then let's go to my dad's house."

"What?" I ask.

"You need Jude's statement, right?"

"Well, yeah, but we don't have to do it tonight."

"Why not?"

I can't actually think of any more reasons not to, and I did want to go ahead and get his affidavit. Being able to avoid Elliot is an added bonus.

"Do they have a printer?" I ask Jackson.

"Yeah."

"Then okay. If you're sure he'll be home."

Jackson snickers. "Jude's *always* home unless he's at the gym, which is within walking distance from the house."

"Oh, so unlike you, he doesn't spend all his time with hordes of women at his beck and call?" I joke.

"He probably could, but he doesn't date, like *ever*."

"Why not?"

"He says women are a distraction from his training." He chuckles, pulling his phone from his pocket. "I swear I think he's a fucking twenty-year-old virgin."

"The anti-Jackson?" I tease.

"Yeah, I guess. The two of us are pretty much opposites."

"But he fights, too?"

"Uh-huh. Jude's had a string of bad luck lately, losing his last three to submissions. He thinks he's not good enough to beat these guys, but he is. In the cage, he's the fastest SOB I know. But ever since he dislocated his shoulder a while back, as soon as he thinks he's trapped in a hold he taps out."

Jackson's affection and pride for his younger brother is obvious, and it's...sweet. This is definitely a strange side of him to see, so contrary to his image.

Quickly pushing a few buttons, he puts his phone to his ear.

"Hey, man. You at the house?" Jackson asks who I assume is Jude. "Good, I'm going to swing by with my attorney, so she can get your statement." He pauses for a few seconds while he listens. I can't hear the other end since his brother isn't yelling like Elliott had. "Did you hear the bitch protesting that night?" Jackson asks, then laughs a few seconds later. "That sounds about right. We'll see you in a few," he says, and then hangs up.

"Does he remember hearing her?" I ask.

"Oh yeah, but I'll let him tell you himself." Jackson chuckles again, putting on his signal for the exit to Silver Spring.

CHAPTER FIVE

Jax

I'm still barely containing my rage after hearing that asshole Page is seeing on the other side of the phone. Yelling at her, talking down to her, and accusing her of bullshit. Then when he mentioned wearing her ass out like it was a punishment and not just a little kinky foreplay, well I didn't want to let her go home. She doesn't deserve that shit.

My opinion has nothing at all to do with the fact that she's sexy as fuck, and I want to see her naked. Nope, I just feel the need to look out for her for some damn reason. Maybe because it seems like she's constantly dealing with pricks. Her dad doesn't give her any credit, and her coworkers are all betting against her. Then her fiancé is a huge fucking tool, too? How can someone so smart and beautiful end up surrounded by so many assholes? Myself included.

I'm actually kind of nervous about bringing Page to my dad's place. I've never brought any women over since there's no point in having Dad and Jude get to know one-night stands. Hell, I don't even get to know them. My dad has already met Page and didn't seem all that impressed. Since she's a knockout, I'm pretty sure I know what crude opinion Jude will have about her before I unlock the front door of the two-story brick house I grew up in and step inside.

The woman may not have much experience in court, but she has been getting shit done, which makes me respect her a little more. For some reason, the more I respect her, the more I want to fuck her.

I'll never forget the way those blue eyes widened, and her mouth fell open while checking me out at the pool. Her usual unfazed, ice princess facade crumbled for just a few seconds. She wanted me, despite the fact that she thinks I'm a guilty jackass. That's why she had tried to bolt and nearly knocked herself out on the cement. She was embarrassed that I'd witnessed her lustful perusal. She was probably pissed at herself for even considering fucking a lowlife like me. The woman's supposed to be marrying a future Presidential candidate for Christ's sakes. Although, she'd have to be an idiot to go through with that shit based on what I just heard him say to her.

"Dad? Jude?" I call out, stepping aside in the foyer to let Page through.

A second later, my brother is sliding down the staircase banister on his ass, wearing nothing but navy blue sweatpants. With an airborne, flying leap dismount, he lands with a loud thud when both of his bare feet hit the foyer floor inches in front of us. I swear he acts like he's still twelve instead of twenty.

"Hey, bro. Your attorney is fucking hot," Jude says with a lecherous grin. His eyes, the same dark chocolate as our mother's and mine, look appreciatively up and down Page, making her cheeks redden.

While he's distracted with ogling her I pounce, effortless putting him in a headlock until he's bent over, his upper body parallel to the hardwood floor.

"Jax, you fucker!" he yells as he flails about trying to get free, elbowing me in the chest and pulling on my arm that's over his throat.

I bring my knee up on his head but not hard enough to break anything, then sweep his legs with my foot, taking him down to the ground.

"Jax, don't choke your brother out in front of company," my dad says when he joins us in the foyer.

Point made, I let Jude go and get back to my feet while he collapses flat on his stomach.

"He needed to learn some manners," I reply, straightening my now crooked t-shirt.

"Cheap shot," Jude grumbles.

"Hi, Page. What are you two up to?" Dad asks the woman whose back is pressed against the door, looking at us like we're all nuts.

"We just spent the day in AC. Luckily Page was able to get the video today, or we would've been shit out of luck," I tell him.

"I also spoke to a valet that remembered seeing...the bitch when she was leaving that night," Page speaks up for the first time since we've walked through the door.

"You did?" I ask in surprise.

"Yes. His name is Steve Sanders," she replies proudly. "I've got his contact information, and I'm going to draft up an affidavit that he's agreed to sign. He said she was fine and perfectly happy when she asked him to get her a cab. Her appearance was somewhat disheveled, but that's to be expected. He didn't see any redness or bruising on her neck, either."

Dad's eyebrows shoot to the ceiling, and he gives a small smile like he's impressed with the attractive young attorney. Lord knows I am.

"We're hoping to get Jude's statement since he was in the hotel room next door," she tells them.

My little brother slowly gets to his feet, sending a pissy look my way, probably for besting him in front of Page.

She turns to him and explains, "If you'll tell me anything you heard, I'll type it up and then get you to print and sign it."

At that, Jude smiles wickedly at her. "Well, at first it sounded like she was bitching, something about Jax never calling her. Then after that, it was '*Fuck yesss! Oh! Oh! Oh Godddd!*'" He uses a falsetto to make his imitation sound more authentic.

"Geez," our dad mutters, shaking his head before thankfully retreating.

Page is still blushing, but she quickly finds her composure. "So you didn't hear her say 'no' or 'stop'?"

"Nope, definitely not," Jude responds, flashing her his dimples. "The only thing I heard after the bitching were cries of pleasure."

"And how would you know what a woman sounds like when she's getting off?" I joke with him.

"Shut the fuck up!" my little brother snaps at me. "If you weren't such a whore then maybe you wouldn't be in this mess, charged with rape and shit!"

"That's an excellent point, and he's agreed to stay away from women until the trial is over," Page tells my brother.

"Ha! Jax staying away from women? I give it less than a week!" Jude laughs. I have to admit that his guess is rather generous.

"Hey, I can easily stay away from women," I respond. "The problem is getting *women* to stay away from *me*."

"Has he always been so...cocky?" Page scoffs loudly and asks Jude.

"You have no idea, sweetheart. Have you seen his apartment yet? There's wall to wall mirrors in that bitch so that at any given moment he can see his oversexed cock multiplied by infinity."

Page throws her head back and laughs. "You're adorable and freakin' hilarious. I bet you have to beat the girls back with a stick."

Was the ice princess actually flirting with my little brother? I was stunned and...jealous, which was nothing new.

"Trifling trashy cage cunts are always trying to hit this," Jude says, running his palms down his naked upper body, making Page giggle like a little girl again. "But unlike my bro, I'm looking for quality, you know, a beautiful, classy woman like you, and not secondhand sluts bought in bulk. Jax has been fucking every skank that flashes a little tit or ass his way since before he could drive."

"Oh, please cut the bullshit before I knock your ass out," I groan, not happy with Jude telling Page about all of my sexual exploits, even though she basically knows as much. "Page, you can set up anywhere,

JAX

then let me know when you're ready, and we can get the shit printed," I tell her. "Are you hungry?"

Her eyes finally leave Jude's to meet mine. "Sure, I could eat something. I had a busy day while you lounged at the pool."

"What a lazy ass," Jude mutters as he tries to punch me in the gut. "You going soft during your hiatus from the cage?"

"I can still take you," I say, dodging his fist, and nailing him in the side with mine.

"Ugh. Damn it," he grunts, clenching his ribs. "Yeah, you outweigh me by twenty pounds, and are three inches taller, asshole."

"Excuses," I counter, heading for the kitchen before I make my brother bleed.

...

Page

It's fun watching Jackson and Jude joke and tease each other. My brother and I have never been close since he's six years older than me. When we were growing up, Logan had been just as condescending to me as my father.

After Jackson had told me that he and his brother were opposites, I hadn't expected them to look so much alike. They could pass as twins! I guess he was referring to their personalities since Jude has the exact same dark hair, although almost completely shaved, and eerily similar midnight eyes. Jude seems happy and outgoing, unlike his introverted, brooding brother. He's incredibly charming, probably able to make women swoon just by flashing his adorable dimpled smile. And I couldn't help but notice in his state of undress that, even though he's a little slimmer and a smidge shorter, Jude has the same rippling muscles as Jackson. The only attributes Jude lacked were his older sibling's cockiness and scorching hot natural swagger.

"You finished flirting with my brother?" Jackson asks when he strolls back into the living room.

"I wasn't flirting with your brother," I scoff, looking up from my laptop. "We've been working on formulating the most accurate wording for his affidavit." I can't help but smile as I remember some of Jude's more hilarious versions.

"Uh-huh. Ready to eat? Stuck-up rich girls like fajitas, right?" he asks snidely, crossing his massive arms over his puffed up chest.

"I'm not stuck-up."

"Yes, you are. You're an elitist bitch, and you think you're better than everyone else," he snaps, making me gasp at the insult.

"No, I don't. And you're the one being a judgmental jerk."

He barks out a laugh. "A judgmental jerk? Is that the best you can do? What else you got for me, ice princess?"

"You know, I'm really getting tired of your snarky comments about me being a spoiled rich girl," I tell him. Setting my computer down I get to my feet, slapping my fists on my hips to show him I'm seriously tired of his attitude.

Jackson smiles in response like I'm missing out on some inside joke. "But if I didn't make 'snarky comments' then I wouldn't get to see you like this, trying to look angry."

That momentarily catches me off guard. "You...intentionally provoke me?" I ask in confusion.

"Hell yes. And unlike the asshole on the phone, I wouldn't spank the shit out of you to punish your smart mouth. I'd fuck you so good you'd forget your name, along with whatever it was you were pissed about. You wouldn't be able to sit down the next day, but only because you'd beg me to keep pounding my cock into you until you pass the fuck out."

I'm paralyzed by his crude words, mostly offended, but a small part of me is so instantly aroused I think I might combust where I stand. It's the annoying anatomy between my thighs, pulsing and suddenly so wet the moisture coats the inside of my panties.

"You can't...that's not..." I stutter.

"Quick, what were you pissed about less than thirty seconds ago?" Jackson asks.

"Ah, what?" I'm drawing a blank about everything in my life prior to the speech he just gave. I know my name is Page...something-another. That's it, that's all I've got.

"I guess I don't need to fuck you to make you forget since just talking dirty does the trick." Jackson doubles over with a full belly laugh. "You should see your face, princess. *Priceless!*"

He's making fun of me, taunting me. He didn't actually mean any of the things he said, he was just trying to get a rise out of me. "You're an a-hole."

"Well, this *ass*hole does have food ready if you're hungry," he says before heading back down the hallway still chuckling.

Since it's either stand in their living room and sulk or finally have something to eat after a full day of going without, I follow him. The house smells delicious, like green peppers and sautéed onions. Just inhaling the aroma has my empty stomach growling.

Quickly finding the kitchen, Jackson thrusts an empty plate in my direction before he sits down, joining his dad and brother at the dining table with his plate of food. It's then that I finally notice what's missing. Where is their mother? Jackson has never once mentioned her.

I decide it's none of my business, and after making two fajitas, I take the empty seat beside Jude, mostly just to annoy Jackson since he thinks I was *flirting* with his brother.

I fold up my tortilla tightly, noticing Jude and Jackson forgo the shells and are only eating meat and vegetables, and lean down to take a bite. Holy moly, these things are delicious! When I open my eyes from savoring the flavor all three men are looking at me.

"Do I have something on my face?" I ask, grabbing my napkin and patting the corners of my lips.

"You eat funny," Jackson says before digging his fork back into his food.

"What?"

"You're all delicate and shit, like a girl," Jude explains.

"Um, okay?"

"We're not used to having any ladies join us for dinner," their dad explains from the head of the table. "One of my sons is a whore, and the other is celibate. Between the two I may never have daughter-in-laws or non-bastard grandchildren."

I can't hold in my snort of amusement. It's hilarious that he's so blunt!

"That's definitely unladylike," Jude says in response, which causes warmth to spread across my cheeks. "Now you fit in a little better with us."

"Gee, thanks," I mutter. "And thanks for letting me join you for dinner. These are great," I tell them, digging into my fajita.

"So how are you going to respond to that picture of you two?" their father asks.

"What is this picture I keep hearing about?" I ask.

His dad pulls his phone from his pocket and hits a few buttons before sliding it across the table to me. Jackson intercepts it before I can see it.

"Ah, fuck," he groans when he looks down. Now I *really* want to see it.

"Let me see!"

"Um, you really don't want to see this right now, Page. Maybe later."

"Give me the phone, Jackson!"

"No."

I wipe my hands on my napkin then pull out my own phone from my pants pocket. In the search engine, I type Jackson's first and last name then wait for the images to load.

"Son of a...biscuit eater!" I exclaim and cover my mouth when the first photo pops up. It's a side view of Jackson and me at the pool earlier. I'm clenching his arm that's around my waist as he presses my body against his huge, mostly naked one. His head is bent down awfully close to my ear, which makes it look like he's kissing me. The title of the article from a sleazy gossip magazine says, "Felony charges forgotten while MMA fighter Jackson Malone fraternizes with his legal staff."

"Whheeeww," Jude whistles when he leans over to look at the phone in my hand.

"She was about to fall," Jackson explains.

"Sure, the old, 'I broke her fall excuse.'" Jude chuckles.

"This is so not good. I can't believe my dad hasn't called to yell at me yet. Dang it, he'll probably take me off the case!"

"No. I don't want you off the case," Jackson says right away, sparking a warmth inside me despite the current circumstances.

"If there is even an *appearance* of a conflict, I'll have to get out, or I risk losing my law license."

No wonder Elliott was pissed. This is bad, and it does look like something's going on between Jackson and me even though it's completely innocent. Okay, mostly innocent.

"Maybe that's just a still shot from a video, like what we did with the hotel surveillance video. If we can find someone out of all those people around the pool that captured the whole thing then it won't be an issue, right?" Jackson asks.

He has a good point. "No, probably not."

Jackson sits his dad's phone down and pulls out his, while I put in a few keywords for videos. I finally come across one on a video sharing site with Jackson's name and today's date. I hit play, hoping this is it. And thank you cheese and rice, it's us from before I turned around through my embarrassing slip and windmill, and finally his save and then release.

"Got it!" I tell him, handing over my phone.

Jude and his dad both jump up from their seats to go and take a look at it over Jackson's shoulder.

"Huh, that really is what happened," Jude admits disappointedly, then returns to his plate of food.

"That's a relief," his dad says before heading back to his seat to finish eating.

My phone starts ringing in Jackson's hand. He frowns and stretches across the table to hand it back to me. "It's your dad."

"Hey, Dad," I answer.

"Goddamn it, Page! What the hell were you thinking! I didn't give you permission to go to Atlantic City, and I sure as hell never expected you to screw around with our client!" He yells at me like I'm an unruly teenager.

"It's just a misunderstanding. There's a video-" I start to say, but he interrupts.

"Not only are you fucking things up with Elliot, but you're already fucking this case up after we just got hired!" he yells, making my eyes water at his harsh chastising. He's always expressed his disappointment in me, but never at this level. I stand up to leave the room and breakdown in private, but before I can escape, Jackson reaches across the table and jerks my phone from my hand.

"Mr. Davenport? This is Jackson Malone," he says. His eyes are focused on the hardwood floor as he paces with his usual fluid grace alongside the dining room table. He reminds me of the angry caged tiger at the zoo, plotting who he's going to maul first once he escapes. Oh, and he *will* escape.

"If you look on the internet there's also a full video showing I caught Page before she cracked her skull on the cement. And if we'd waited just two more damn days to subpoena the hotel video surveillance footage, it would've been gone. Permanently. Fucking. Erased. And then we wouldn't have the blown up photos of the bitch leaving without any marks on her neck, contrary to the pictures the prosecutor gave Page in the discovery today. Oh yeah, and Page wouldn't have found an employee that actually talked to the bitch when she was leaving the hotel that night. If it weren't for *her* getting shit done, I'd be fucked, waiting around for someone else at your firm to finally get off their ass. From now on this is *her case* or we're done," he says in a growling tone, making it clear that he's pissed and deadly serious before he hangs up on my father.

I remain standing at the table absolutely dumbfounded. I've *never* heard anyone talk to my father that way. I've also never actually had someone defend me before, either. And in that moment I'm completely helpless when a little tiny sliver of my heart becomes his.

CHAPTER SIX

Jax

That motherfucking son of a bitch! It takes all my willpower not to pulverize her phone to prevent her from having to put up with his shit again. Instead, I set it gently back down on the edge of the dining table.

When I look over at Page, her wide eyes are on mine. I wait for her to bitch at me about how she can take up for herself. Of course, I know that, but for some reason when I saw the tears welling in her eyes, and sadness replace her usual stubborn strength and confidence I just snapped. She's been working her ass off to defend me, even though she thinks I'm guilty, so standing up to her father's completely wrong accusations and totally out of line criticisms were the least I could do.

"So what's for dessert?" Page asks in an exhale, ending the silence, and sitting back down all prim and proper and shit at the table.

"Dessert?" I repeat, amazed when she doesn't bitch at me.

"Yeah, you know like ice cream or chocolate. Maybe cookies? Dessert is the best part of every meal."

"Fighters don't get to have unhealthy shit like dessert," I reply at the same time Jude says, "We've got some Oreos."

My dad gets up and leaves the table, giving me a disappointed look when he passes. He probably thinks I was out of line with Page's dad. *Screw that.*

"Oh yeah!" Page replies excitedly. "Oreos would be awesome. If it's not too much trouble, could I also have like a small glass of milk, too? Or do fighters not drink milk, either?" she asks with a smirk in my direction.

"Yes, we have milk, and for you, sweetheart, I'd bring the whole fucking cow," Jude responds, making Page laugh and me groan before he's up and ducking into the kitchen.

Before I can sit back down, her goddamn phone starts ringing again and vibrating on the dinner table. Only instead of her dad, this time, it says, *"Elliot"* on the screen. Awesome. I'm raring to go 2-0 tonight with another telephone showdown. Since I'm closer, I grab it before she can.

"Page's phone," I answer.

"What the...who is this?" the angry man asks. "Where's Page?"

"I'm sorry, but since Page and her fine ass are unavailable tonight, it looks like you'll just have to spank yourself."

"Jackson!" Page hisses, lurching across the table but still unable to reach me. "Give me the phone!"

"Who the hell is this?" the asshole asks. "Do you have any idea who the fuck you're talking to?"

"Let me tell you who *you're* talking to. You're talking to a crazy motherfucker who will beat the shit out of you if you lay another finger on her ass without her express written permission to do so. And I don't give a fuck what soft, pussy job or title you have, buddy. You could use a big healthy dose of *watch your goddamn mouth* when you talk to her before I knock a few teeth out of it." I end the call, chest still heaving with adrenaline. Fucking bastard. I finally hand over the phone to Page's outstretched hand, knowing she's going to bitch me out for sure this time.

"That...was the funniest shi...znit I've ever heard," Page says, looking up at me with a smile.

"Shiznit?" I ask with my own grin, breathing deep to calm myself down. "What are you, ten?"

"Excuse me if every other word out of my mouth is not filth like yours."

And it is a damn fine mouth, I can't help but notice. Plump pink bottom lip, fuller than the top which forms a perfect fucking bow. I'd love to force those lips apart with a gasp of pleasure. Or watch them part even wider when they wrap around my hard cock. The cock currently pressing against the fly of my jeans so hard it'll likely have a permanent zipper imprint down it.

Jude returns with the pack of cookies and a glass of milk, giving Page a low bow when he says, "Here you go, m'lady."

"Thanks, Jude. You are definitely the more pleasant brother," she says when she accepts the offering and returns to her seat.

"Yeah, Jax is a dick, but don't take it personally. He's like that to everyone because he thinks he's a badass."

"I am a badass," I growl. Jude sits down beside her again, and they both pretend to ignore me.

"So how do you like to do yours?" Jude asks, grabbing a cookie and twisting it open. "I like to lick all of the cream off with my tongue before I shove the cookie in my mouth," he tells her, heavy on the innuendo.

"I dip the whole cookie in the milk until it's soft and mushy," she tells him, grabbing a cookie and doing just that. "Then I like to chug the murky milk after I eat all my cookies."

Seeing her like this is...strange after dealing with the uptight, stuck-up Page. I sit down at the table to watch more of this easygoing side of her.

"Double stuffed are the best," she tells my brother. He quickly agrees.

"Jude's gonna have to do *double* cardio tomorrow to work off this shit," I mutter, not letting myself give in to the delicious temptation, even though I have no idea how long it'll be before I can fight again.

"Why you always pissing all over my parade, Jax?" Jude grumbles. "You're such a Debbie Downer."

"He always such an angry pessimist?" Page asks Jude.

"Oh yeah. And he gets worse every year."

"Why do you think that is?" she inquires, while they both pretend like I'm not in the fucking room.

"I don't know. Probably because he's sad knowing he can never be as awesome as me."

"You think you're so fucking funny, don't you?" I ask, reaching to grab one of the fucking Oreos from the pack.

Cracking it open, I notice Page's gaze on me. I hold her eyes as I slowly run my tongue over one of the white cream sides. Those perfect lips of hers part as she focuses on my mouth like I intended, just to fuck with her. Trying to get a rise out of her is more fun than anything I've done in a long time.

"Let me know whenever you're ready to go home, Page," I tell her, making her blink and break the spell.

"Ah. Can't we keep her? Pretty please, Jax? I've always wanted my very own gorgeous, yellow-haired attorney," Jude begs, turning to me with clasped hands and big pleading eyes, making Page laugh. I don't like that he's the one eliciting such a sweet sound from her. "I promise I'll feed her and take care of her all by myself."

"Nice, I'm sure Page loves being referred to as a stray dog."

"Relax, Jax. I can take a joke," she replies with a snort, making my brother laugh. Hearing her use my nickname so familiarly causes that battering ram feeling against my chest that I try again to ignore.

"Relax? The woman who told me I could end up serving a twenty-seven-year prison sentence is telling me to fucking relax?"

"Holy shit! Are you serious?" Jude asks, his teasing and cookie in his hand forgotten.

"With our progress today, I'm feeling a little more confident about your chances," Page responds with a smile. "I bet you won't get more than thirteen years."

"That's not funny," I mutter.

JAX

"Thirteen motherfucking years!?!" Jude exclaims.

"That's the minimum I'll serve if I'm convicted on both charges, right Page?"

"Minimum, as in *the least?*" my brother asks. "Jesus, Jax. Why didn't you say anything?" He turns to Page. "What are the odds of him not getting convicted?"

"I'd say fifty-fifty at this point. That's why I informed Jax that if he's offered a plea to a lesser charge of just three or four years, he should consider it."

"Jax, you'd be crazy not to take that shit!"

"That's what I told him," Page responds to Jude, causing me to snap.

"Fuck you both! I'm not pleading guilty. Why is that so hard for you to understand?" I jump to my feet and yell at them. "It's because you still think I did that shit, right? Screw it. Jude can give you a ride home because I've had enough of you for one fucking day."

I slam the front door when I storm out of the house, and as soon as my car cranks, I throw it in reverse, peeling out of the driveway and heading for the gym. I need to burn off some serious stress and frustration. And yeah, maybe a part of me is disappointed that during the biggest fight of my life I don't have a single person in my corner.

...

Page

I yawn once again as I stare at my computer screen, working on direct and possible cross-examination questions for Jax. When my dad comes into my office, I swear I must have nodded off and am dreaming.

"Page," my father's voice booms.

"Yes?" I ask, trying not to show the hurt on my face from his words the night before.

"I owe you an apology. I'm sorry I assumed the worst. I didn't know you'd made so much progress on Malone's case so soon."

I almost swallow my tongue. My father, Miles Davenport, was apologizing to me? Jax really had scared the sushi out of him.

"Thanks."

"Keep up the good work," he says, before leaving as quickly as he came. A compliment and an apology in one conversation? It was turning out to be a red-letter day for the history books. But even that thought didn't lift my spirits for long.

I hadn't slept much last night after Jude gave me a ride home. I felt guilty about what had happened with Jax. I wanted to believe him, I really did. But a part of me...I just couldn't shake my first impression.

That reminds me.

I search through our firm's contact database, then as soon as I find the one I'm looking for I pick up the office phone and dial the number.

"Hi, Mr. Rhodes. This is Page Davenport, a lawyer in Silver Spring. I have a criminal client who'd like you to give him a polygraph."

"Oh, sure. How soon do you need it?" he asks.

"First available spot you have."

"I just had a cancelation, so how about this afternoon at four?"

"I'll have to confirm with my client, but that should work. Do I need to be there?"

"No, just him. But it'd be great if you could talk to him to formulate three or four questions and then email them to me, along with his charge sheets before the appointment."

"Sure. I've already got your email address, so I'll get that to you, along with the confirmation that he'll be there at four today after I talk to him. I'll have him bring you a check drawn on our firm's account to protect the report under attorney-client work product. Do you still charge a thousand?"

"Yes, and that sounds great. Thanks, Ms. Davenport."

I hang up but then hesitate before calling Jax. I need to give him as much notice as possible for the polygraph appointment, but what if he's still pissed? He might not even answer. That'd be good, and then I can just leave him a message. I take a deep breath and dial his number.

"Hello?"

Sheesh, he answered right away.

"Oh, um, hey, Jax. So I've got you a polygraph scheduled for today at four if that works?"

"Yeah."

"Okay, so I need to draft up the questions. Which ones are you confident you can pass?"

"Any of them. All of them. Whatever the fuck you want to ask." So he still sounds a little pissed.

"How about, *'Have you ever forcefully engaged in sexual intercourse with Christina Loftis without her consent?'*"

"Fine."

"And, then after that, *'Did you strangle Christina Loftis?'*"

"Uh-huh."

"And then the last one, *'Have you ever forced Christina Loftis to perform oral sex on you?'*"

Jax barks out a laugh on that last one. "Force someone to perform oral sex...what idiot bought into that bullshit?" he mutters softly, mostly to himself.

"All right, I'll send these on over to Mr. Rhodes and email you his address. You'll need to come by here beforehand and get a check to pay his fee. That way he's working for the firm and not you, assuring the results are protected in case you don't pass."

"Right," he grunts before hanging up on me.

After putting in the urgent check request with our bookkeeper, the rest of the morning I busy myself with formulating questions for other witnesses. After lunch, I get a surprise about as shocking as my father apologizing. *Elliott* apologizing. Of course he doesn't say the actual words, but instead sends a humongous vase of flowers with a note that says simply, "*Hope to see you soon, so we can move past this misunderstanding.*" That was as close as I'll ever get to an apology from the stubborn man.

A giggle slips past my lips remembering everything Jax said to him on the phone. I would've paid good money just to see Elliott's reaction in person. Jackson has a way with words and a way of getting everyone's attention right away. The fact that my father and Elliott, two of the most bullheaded, untouchable men I know, fear Jackson Malone is gratifying, to say the least.

Even after receiving the peace offering, I don't call Elliott. I'm starting to look at my life a little differently, and that means his place in it, too. Was I really willing to spend the remainder of my days on this Earth tied to that arrogant, self-important man?

For so long I've been told it's what I *needed* to do. *Should* do. That it's a great opportunity, and one day I might be the freaking First Lady. But what about what I want for myself? I don't yet know what that is, but I'm starting to think that whatever it turns out to be, it won't be a loveless marriage like the one my parents endure.

It's easy to pinpoint the cause of my sudden contemplation. I'm developing a horrible, probably incurable, case of hero worship for the one man I never imagined would come to my rescue, and who also happens to be the one man I absolutely can't have.

...

I've chewed off every single one of my perfectly shaped, manicured fingernails by closing time Thursday. No call from Jax yet, but I don't know how long those tests take. It's been an hour and a half, so I figured he'd be done by now. He didn't even stop in to say hello when he picked up the check before his appointment.

Ready to call the work day good, I turn off my computer and grab my phone and purse. Then it hits me. Jax doesn't have my cell phone number. Son of a...beach. Saving his number in my phone, I decide to send him a text, just a quick note to call me either way. Busy typing on my phone I step off the elevator and out the front door heading toward my car.

"Page."

"Sheesh! You scared the heebie-jeebies out of me!" I exclaim to Elliot, clutching the phone to my chest to keep my heart from leaping out onto the sidewalk.

JAX

"Get a grip, Page. And when the hell are you going to stop using toddler phrases and speak like an adult?" he asks.

It still amazes me that God would go to such trouble creating an exterior masterpiece, and then hand the man's soul over to the devil. Or maybe he traded his soul for all his millions.

Elliot's gray designer suit fits his impressive frame perfectly, and his ridiculous four hundred dollar politician haircut has his thick brown hair sweeping to the right in the exact formation of his many right-wing supporters, my dad making the top of the list.

"Oh, crap. I must have missed that adult speaking course in college. What was it, Proper Procedures in Profanity 101? Maybe there's a *Potty Mouth for Dummies* I can order online to catch up."

"What the fuck is the attitude about?" he asks, rocking back on his expensive heels with his hands casually in his pockets.

"Hold on, let me take notes," I say, pretending to type on my phone. "What the...was that f-u-c-k? I want to make sure I get this right. Here, let me practice using it in a sentence. What the fuck do you want?"

Elliot scoffs indignantly. "You're not going to thank me for the flowers?"

"Sure I will, as soon as you *actually* apologize. Go ahead, let's hear yours first."

"Jackson Malone is a bad influence on you."

A bark of laughter escapes before I can even try and hold it back. "And exactly how well *do* you know Jackson Malone?" I ask him, crossing my arms over my chest. His quick judgment pisses me off, even if I had done the exact same thing.

"I know he's an out of control meathead, and he's going to get what he deserves."

"You don't know *anything* about him! You're just jealous because he's the epitome of virile, and pissed that he was able to cut you, Mr. High and Mighty, down in a few sentences," I counter, walking past him.

"Where are you going? I came to take you to dinner."

"I'm not hungry," I mutter over my shoulder.

"Well, I am," he says, grabbing my arm to stop me. "Come on, Page. I've missed you. Let me take care of you tonight."

Oh, crap. He's looking at me with those sad, denim blue, puppy dog eyes. The look he pulls out right before he gets all charming and I can't help but give in every single freaking time. He's a good-looking bastard, and he knows it.

What was the old saying? If you can't screw the man you want, screw the one you're with? Tonight I need the reminder that my thoughts about Jackson Malone are stupid and pointless because he's definitely off limits. Maybe Elliot can help me accomplish that.

CHAPTER SEVEN

Jax

I watch Page hesitate on the sidewalk, but I already know the asshole isn't going to take no for an answer. I had overheard their entire conversation from the shadows of the parking garage and barely held back my laugh at Page's cattiness. I had no idea the woman had it in her, so maybe it was my bad influence.

I'd been here for ten minutes before she walked out, debating whether or not to go inside. I had the polygraph report in my pocket, but for whatever reason, I couldn't bring myself to show it to her. I wanted her to believe me without a fucking piece of paper to back it up.

"Fine, but *just* dinner," Page finally responds to the jerk. I admit that I'm shocked when she actually caves after how shitty he treated her yesterday. Why does she put up with this hateful fucker?

"You say that now," the asshole says, taking a step closer to her and reaching for her jaw. "But you know after a few glasses of wine you'll change your mind and want...dessert."

My teeth grind painfully against each other from the anger boiling up inside me at seeing him fucking touch her.

When Page doesn't protest the jackass leans forward and kisses her cheek before moving over to her lips. Her posture is cold and rigid at first, but after a few seconds she relaxes into him and presses her palms to his chest.

My own chest constricts, freezing my lungs just like getting slammed on the canvas during a fight. I've never felt anything like it before, and I have to say it sucks.

As much as I want to get back in my car and leave, I can't. My feet are cemented to the ground, forcing me to watch while I try to figure out what the hell is wrong with me. Whatever it is doesn't ease up. Not when he loops his arms around her waist, and definitely not when she willingly presses her body against his.

"My place or yours," he asks when he pulls his lips away.

"Yours," she responds, so softly I barely hear it from my hideout.

"Then let's go. I'll drop you off at work tomorrow," the dickhead says, grabbing her hand and pulling her around the building.

Still feeling somewhat numb, I get into my *impractical* car. For a few minutes, I consider calling one of the many women in my phone to get sucked or fucked, just because I can. I had missed calls from four different girls just today, but it's stupid to even consider doing something so risky. As much as I hate to admit it, Page is right about needing to lay low when it comes to women until all this shit is over. Besides, I don't really *want* any of those faceless women. So if I'm not going to fuck, I'm going to fight.

On the way to the gym, I'm surprised to get a text message from Page. One that says, *"Call and let me know how it went, either way."* And immediately after that, *"First thing tomorrow."* Because it looks like she was going to be busy tonight. *Fuck.*

I park and head inside what is practically my second home.

"Jax! What are you doing back so soon?" my head coach and manager, Don Briggs, asks as soon as I walk through the door.

Shit.

I'm not in the mood to talk to anyone, but I know he won't just give up.

JAX

"Nothing else to fu-reaking do," I say, catching myself at the last minute when I notice Coach's teenage daughter eating dinner behind the front counter with him. "How's it going, Sadie Hawkins?"

"Bored out of my fucking mind," the brunette *Annie* replies with an eye roll.

"Sadie!" Coach admonishes her. "You guys are bad influences on her," he says, scowling at me.

"Your fault for bringing her in here."

"Do you think I trust her to stay home by herself? Hell no. I'm not stupid. I know exactly what boys convince sixteen-year-old girls to do when they're left unsupervised."

"Dad!" Sadie covers her face and groans in embarrassment.

I shake my head in slight amusement and quickly go change in the locker room. I push the earbuds in and strap the iPod to my arm, turning the volume of the thumping bass up until it's at hearing damage levels. I consider running a few miles but know that will never do. I need to hit something. Hard.

After wrapping up my hands, I go straight to one of the hanging bags and start in, pummeling my fists into it like it's someone's face and body. Imagining it's the jerk that doesn't deserve an incredible woman like Page doesn't help as much as I thought it would. Probably because it's hypocritical to say he isn't good enough for her, knowing I'm certainly not either.

The longer I throw punches and kicks the worse I feel. I'm suffocating on the lack of control in my life. I can't fight. I can't get rid of these bullshit charges. And I can't fuck. Instead of my usual any-hot-woman-will-do policy, I'm starting to think it was now only-one-woman-will-do. And even if she didn't think I'm a fucking monster, and she wasn't engaged to an asshole, she's still off-limits. There's no way I'd risk her losing her license to practice law.

"Who you beating the shit out of?" Jude asks when he yanks one of my earbuds out.

"No one."

"Right." He laughs, wiping the sweat off his face with a towel. "You don't rock the bag like an eight-point-oh on the Richter scale unless you're seriously angry."

"I'm not angry."

"Um-huh. So it won't bother you if I tell you that last night after you left I threw your hot ass attorney in my bed and tried to make an earthquake with her-"

I have an arm around his neck and the other around the back of his knees, cradling and pinning him to the mat before he can blink. Thinking about Page with another man is one thing, but with my own brother...oh fuck no.

"Kidding. I didn't touch her! Damn. So why...are you...pissed?" Jude asks through gasps while I choke him and he kisses his own knees.

I eventually release my hold, allowing him to stretch out like a slinky back to his normal size.

"I'm not," I respond, standing up and going back to the bag.

"You are. You want Page, right? I mean who wouldn't, she is so fucking-"

"Shut the fuck up!"

"Let me guess... She did the unthinkable and turned you down? Did she finally manage to put a ding in your impenetrable ego?" he asks, as he finally gets to his feet again.

"She didn't turn me down because I didn't ask her out."

"Then what's the problem? You afraid she won't enjoy your rear naked choke hold?"

"Fuck you," I bark, nailing a few combo shots on the bag.

"Too soon for choke jokes? My bad."

"She's engaged to an asshole. Even if she wasn't, she can't fuck with clients or she'll lose her law license."

"Then get another attorney," he says simply.

"Hell no. I think she might be the only one that can keep me out of prison."

"Then suck it up and get the fuck over her," he yells before walking away. Easier said than done.

...
Page

What the heck was I thinking? I ask myself as Elliot drills himself into me over and over again, faster than a woodpecker on speed, and just about as annoying.

"Oh shit! Fucking amazing." *Slap.* "You know you missed it," he groans, followed by two more slaps.

On my hands and knees, I watch the headboard creep closer to my face, knowing I'll probably ram into it soon. Not that it would slow Woody Woodpecker back there down.

Thankfully he must be getting close to the end because the frequency of smacks to my ass is increasing right along with their intensity. When my eyes close in boredom, I can't stop myself from thinking about a different man from the one currently inside me. My mouth goes dry just thinking about his massive, chiseled body. The feeling of it pressed hard against my backside. Remembering his dirty words about screwing me so good, I'd forget what I was pissed about. Watching his darting tongue lick the freaking cookie, all hot and sensual. My insides clench when I imagine that tongue between my legs, licking me, teasing me into a frenzy. Elliot grabs a handful of my hair, tugging my head backward, but instead of him, I imagine it's Jax yanking on my hair, forcing my mouth up and down his long, hard length.

"Ah! *Oh God*," I moan in surprise when my body shakes with pleasure, radiating from deep inside me and spreading through my body in waves so intense I can't hold myself up any longer. I collapse onto the mattress and wait for Elliot to finish.

"Damn, Page. You came so fucking hard. I gave it to you good, didn't I?" he asks.

"Mmm," I reply and then pass out with sweet dreams.

...

It's early Friday morning, and I had just hung up with the prosecutor in Atlantic City when the receptionist buzzes me. I'm still distracted by the news that Jax has been indicted by the Grand Jury, and needs to be in court Monday morning unless he wants to get arrested again. Awesome.

"Jackson Malone is here to see you," Jamie says over the intercom.

Shit! I told him to call me this morning and let me know the results. Him showing up...did that mean he passed or failed? Am I ready to know the results, that he's telling the truth and is innocent, or that he's lied to me and is actually guilty? I'll still represent him either way, but I know the way I feel about him will change, and I'm not sure I can handle that.

"Page?" Jamie asks.

"Oh, um, go ahead and send him back," I reply, tidying up my desk and running my fingers through my hair to fluff it. Why do I do that? I have no freaking idea.

"Hey," I say, sounding out of breath when Jackson appears in my doorway. Broken-in jeans and a black tee have never looked so good on anyone. I try to judge his results from his expression. He looks a lot like the angry volcano I met that first day.

Oh God, he failed.

"Nice flowers," he says sarcastically as he eyes the vase from Elliot on my desk.

"Ah, yeah," I respond, annoyed he's talking about freaking flowers when he knows I want to hear the results.

Finally, Jax pulls out papers from his back pocket and throws them down in front of me. I quickly grab them up and open them to start reading.

On the polygrapher's letterhead, it begins with a narrative of what Jax has been charged with, followed by the three questions and his answers of "no" to each. I'm holding my breath when I get to the results. The polygraph shows with ninety-nine point nine percent certainty that Jackson has *not* shown any deception on any of the questions.

Holy shit, he passed!

"Don't look so fucking surprised," he snaps.

I'm not so much surprised as I am relieved. The man in front of me really is the good and decent person I've gotten to know this week. It would've crushed and disappointed me if he'd failed.

"What can I say? I'm a cynical person. I wouldn't have believed my own father if he had been in your place until I saw this," I assure him, holding up the report.

"So what now?" he asks while he remains standing. I guess that means he isn't staying long.

"Actually, it looks like we'll be heading back to Atlantic City. I just got off the phone with the prosecutor. The Grand Jury's indicted you-"

"What the hell does that mean?" he interrupts.

"It's nothing to worry about, it just came sooner than I expected. Felony cases have to be presented to the grand jury to determine if the State has enough evidence for indictment to Superior Court. That's where all felonies have to be tried. The grand jury almost always indicts since it's such a low threshold for probable cause. The defendant and his counsel are not allowed in the grand jury, so there's no one to say to them that all the evidence is bologna."

"So what does this all mean?"

"Monday morning you have your first appearance in Superior Court. You have to be there to waive the court-appointed attorney, and I'll make a general appearance on your behalf. Mostly you'll just be proving that you haven't skipped town and are not a danger to the community. There's a chance the prosecutor might try to make you put up another bond, but I doubt it."

"That's all that will happen Monday?"

"Pretty much. But get ready for the cameras. As soon as the court calendar hits the media's desk, they're going to be like vultures trying to talk to you and get pictures of you arriving and leaving the courthouse."

"You're going to be there, too, right?" Jackson asks.

"Of course. We probably should go on up Sunday afternoon and spend the night to be there by nine a.m. Monday. Unless you want to leave at like four-thirty Monday morning?"

"Let's go Sunday."

"Yeah, probably safer since you never know with traffic, and all those dang toll booths take forever to get through. I'm going to draft a letter to give to the prosecutor on Monday and include the polygraph, Jude's statement, a copy of the hotel video, still photos from the video, and the bitch's Facebook pictures in a packet. Basically, I'll be informing him of all the reasons why he shouldn't proceed with prosecuting this case."

"Okay. Do I need to suit up and shit for this thing?" he asks, making me smile. Jackson Malone in a suit? This I can't wait to see.

"Probably, just to show the prosecutor, judge, and media that you're taking this seriously."

"I can do that."

"So do you want me to make hotel reservations for you, too, or are you going to get your own?" I ask.

"I can make them for all of us. Jude and my dad will probably want to go even if nothing's going to happen. Taj Mahal okay?"

"Sure."

"Any required princess preferences for your room that I should know about?" he asks with a smirk.

"Ah, non-smoking is preferred. I'll also need Internet access, of course, a robe, whirlpool tub, a bar, oceanfront view, and thousand-count Egyptian cotton sheets, but only if it's not too much trouble," I joke.

"Right. I'll try and remember all that."

"And if not, just try and remember the non-smoking part since I can't stand that nastiness," I say with a shrug.

"Let's go tomorrow, or even better, tonight."

"Ah, what?" I ask him in confusion.

"To Atlantic City. Come on, when was the last time you had a vacation?"

"Well, I just got back from Paris about a month ago, Bermuda in April, and Hawaii in February."

"You really are a spoiled bitch."

"I'm kidding, and don't call me that," I snap. "I haven't actually had a vacation since I finished my undergrad three years ago."

"So are you going up with us today or not?"

"I don't know. Are you going to stop calling me a bitch?" I ask, crossing my arms over my chest.

"Yes," he says, looking at the floor like a little boy being scolded. "Sorry."

"When are you leaving?" I let him off the hook since he apologized.

"As soon as you're ready. It's not like my dad and Jude have anything better to do."

I consider it for a minute. Spending a whole weekend with this man and his easygoing family does sound like a good time. Throw in some gambling and the beach, well that just seals the deal. Was it smart? No, but I'm tired of being smart.

"Okay. Let me get this letter to the prosecutor done, and all the attachments ready so I won't have to worry about it this weekend. I'll need to go to my apartment and pack a few things, but I could probably be ready around noon."

"Good. Should we pick you up here or at your place?"

"Ah, here I guess."

"All right. See you at noon," he tells me as he heads for the door. "Oh, and, Page," he pauses before hitting me with his parting comment. "Don't forget your bathing suit."

...

A few hours later I'm sitting in my office, going over my checklist for Monday one last time when I'm kidnapped. Well, I'd agreed to go with them, I just didn't think it'd be over Jude's shoulder with my protest.

"Jude, put me down, so I can grab my things!" I whisper, to avoid drawing attention to us when he leaves my office.

"Don't worry. Jax is getting all your shit from that neat little pile you made," he says with a slap to my behind.

"Jude!" I yelp in surprise.

"Ah, Page?" I hear the unspoken *WTF* in my brother's voice while we wait for the elevator.

I twist my neck and flip my hair up out of my face to see my older sibling frowning down at me like usual.

"Hi, Logan. Have you met Jackson's annoying little brother, Jude Malone?" I ask. "Jude, this is my annoying older brother, Logan Davenport."

Swinging me around, so I can no longer see Logan, I assume Jude is shaking Logan's hand. "Nice to meet you. We're kidnapping your sister. She needs a vacation after working so hard on Jax's case this week. Hey, bro, have you met Page's bro Logan?"

Jax must've joined us, although I can't see him.

"Hi, how's it going?" Jax says to my brother.

"Good. Where are you going?" Logan asks.

"Atlantic City," I tell him from Jude's back.

"Oh, well, ah have fun, I guess. Do Dad and Elliot know you're leaving?"

"I'm a big girl now, Logie, and don't need their permission. Now run along and tattle on me, snitch, before you kill my vacation buzz."

"Ha, aren't older brothers such a pain in the ass?" Jude laughs, slapping mine again. Why do men like to abuse my bottom?

"Touch her ass again and I'll break both of your legs," Jax warns Jude, making me smile that he's so protective of my ass...pen.

"I'm not her client, so we can be as inappropriate as we want, right, Page?" Jude asks.

"Ah, right," I mutter, mostly just to annoy Jax when we finally make it onto the elevator.

"She has a fiancé, even though the cheap bastard didn't give her a ring."

JAX

"What? No way. The deal's not sealed unless there's a fucking ring," Jude argues. "She's a free bird."

"Put her down," Jax tells his brother.

"No thanks."

"Did you guys get my purse?" I ask. "My phone? Briefcase? Luggage?"

"Yes to all," Jax replies. "Did you pack a bathing suit?"

"Ah, yeah."

"Bikini?" Jude inquires.

I smile. "Maybe."

"Hell yes," he replies.

"Jax, were you able to get us rooms?" I ask.

"Yep. Sorry but all they had were smoking rooms."

"Ah, shit...ake mushrooms. I'll never get the smell out of my clothes," I grumble.

"Don't worry. We'll get you so drunk you won't notice the smoke," Jude promises.

"I don't drink."

"You do this weekend, princess. You need to loosen up before you give yourself an aneurysm," Jax responds.

Finally, we make it out of the stuffy office, and thankfully without running into my father. My feet touch down on the concrete sidewalk beside a black SUV.

"Your chariot to an awesome weekend awaits," Jude says with a wave of his arm to the vehicle, making me laugh as I climb into the back seat. He slides in beside me, and their dad is already waiting in the driver's seat while Jax puts my things in the back. Again I can't help but wonder about their mother. Maybe I can ask Jude sometime since I know he won't bite my head off for asking.

"Hi, Mr. Malone," I say in greeting.

"Hi, Page. Sorry my knuckleheaded sons dragged you out that way."

"Oh, it's fine. It's probably all the steroids making them so testosteroni," I tease.

"No, you didn't just say that," Jude huffs. Lifting his *Every time you masturbate God kills a kitten* t-shirt, complete with an adorable faced feline. Instead of a cat, I'm suddenly fixated on his tan, washboard abs. I have to swallow back the drool. "This is all years of hard work, baby, and nothing else."

"I beg your pardon, but I'd have to point out that it's also great genetics," his dad says with a smile from the front seat.

The guys have me cracking up the entire three and a half hour drive. The time seems to fly by. They are so different from my uptight family, and I love it.

Jude and I played toll tap, sort of like punch bug, but with toll booths instead of Volkswagens. Every time one of those bad boys came into sight you'd have to try and be the first one to tap the other and yell "Toll tap!" I'm sure my shoulder is going to have bruises on it, but I gave as good as I got.

Jax is the quietest during the trip. Looking out the window most of the time, he seems like he's a thousand miles away. I figure the idea of going to court Monday is probably getting to him, making the whole situation seem more real.

When we arrive at the hotel, Jax checks us in while me, Jude and his dad wander around the non-smoking side of the casino. I've already had two fruity drinks when Jax finds us to give us our room keys.

"They took your bags on up to your room already," he tells me when he hands over the plastic card.

"Aw, thanks," I say with a pat to his chest that may have turned into more of a petting. "You're so sweet, Jax. Even sweeter now that I know you're not an angry rapist," I blurt out, maybe a tad too honestly.

He smiles and looks over at his laughing brother. "Is she already drunk?"

"Ah, well, I didn't know she was such a lightweight," Jude tells him. "She's only had like two of those fruity things."

"Oh my God! It's Jackson Malone!" We hear a feminine squeal, followed by several more.

"Ah shit," Jax groans when three young and very pretty women head for him.

"Sorry, ladies," I say, turning around to stand in front of the big, sexy man to block their path. "As his attorney, I've advised Mr. Malone not to concur...confer with any females until such time as his case is over."

The women don't look very pleased at hearing that, so I throw them a bone. "Have you met his brother, Jude? He's so much nicer than Jax and looks just like him, see," I tell them, shooing them away in his direction. Jude looks like he's going to make a run for it.

"Thanks." Jax chuckles from behind me.

"All part of my job," I tell him when I turn around to face him.

"I didn't know attorneys also handled private security for MMA fighters," he replies.

"*Jax!*" came another feminine scream.

"Shit. I better head to my room."

"I'll go with you. Not to your room, but mine," I clarify. "I mean, you go to yours, and I'll go to mine. I need a shower and to change clothes. Might be time for that bathing suit."

"Let's go. And you shouldn't go anywhere this weekend by yourself. It's not safe for women to wander around alone in a wild and crazy town like this."

"Ironic advice coming from you." I snort, as I stumble forward toward the elevator.

Jax catches me around the waist but immediately let's go to grab my elbow instead. "I think you should probably go easy on the alcohol."

"Yes, father," I tease when the doors swoosh open, and we climb on the elevator. Luckily Jax knows which floor we're on and pushes the number eight on the panel. "I thought you wanted me to get drunk."

"That was Jude's plan, not mine," he mutters. "I just said you should lighten up."

On the way up to our floor, my eyes are glued to Jax, noticing how well his black shirt hugs his broad upper chest. Remembering from that day at the pool what his sculpted upper body looks like. Wondering if the length behind the fly on his denim jeans is as big I bet it is. I'm betting it's...well, yeah. My face warms either from arousal or the alcohol buzz, I'm not sure which. Thankfully the elevator doors open, interrupting my carnal thoughts.

"This way," Jax says, heading to the left so I follow. "Here's your room, eight-eighteen."

"Oh, thanks," I say, pulling out the card he'd given me. I stick it in the slot and get all red lights. I try it again.

"Here, let me." He sighs, taking the card from my hand and easily swiping it to get green lights on the first try. He turns the handle and pushes it open for me. "I'm next door."

"Thanks," I say, breezing by him into the room, trying to avoid dwelling on how good he smells.

The first thing I notice is the incredible ocean view. Then I see the big ass whirlpool tub beside the bed. Next to the kitchen is a bar, and hanging on the bathroom door is a big, plush white robe. Did he do all this on purpose? I'd been joking about everything except non-smoking, and this room also met that request.

I turn back to the door where Jax still stands holding it open, watching me.

"You didn't have to do all this. I was just messing with you because of your princess insults."

"It's nothing," he says dismissively. But it really is. He keeps surprising me, probably because I keep underestimating him.

"Yes, it is. Thank you," I tell him. "I can't wait to soak in the tub."

With only a slight shake in my hands, thanks to the liquid courage I'd chugged earlier, I start unbuttoning the bottom of my white dress shirt. I make it up to the third one, right around my navel, when he finally notices.

"What are you doing, Page?"

"Getting ready to take a bath," I reply. When he doesn't come any further into the room, I start back towards him. By the time I'm standing inches away, I'm on the top button. I want, no *need* to know if the real thing is as incredible as the fantasy of being with him. Screw Elliot and the rules.

I let my shirt fall off my shoulders to the floor. "You might want to shut the door," I warn, working on the back clasp of my bra.

"Page..." Jax starts, he swallows deeply as his midnight eyes lower to my lace covered breasts. "Don't."

My breath catches in my throat at hearing that one word.

"Sorry," he says swiping a hand over his face. "But...we can't. Client-attorney whatever, and you're engaged for Christ's sake."

"Right now it's just you and me here. No one has to know..."

"I'm not interested, okay?" he snaps. "So let's just pretend that this never happened." He slips out the door and lets it shut in my embarrassed face.

The man who admits to sleeping with any and all women doesn't want me. God, I'm an idiot for thinking he might, and now I've made a huge fool of myself.

I sit on the edge of the bed with my head in my hands. My dad was right all along. Just as he predicted, in one moment of weakness I've managed to completely screw up this case.

CHAPTER EIGHT

Jax

What the fuck is wrong with me? The woman I can't stop thinking about naked just started taking her clothes off in invitation, and I leave the room like a pussy?

In the moment, hell yes I wanted Page. But long term? It's not worth it. I'm not worth Page losing her law license, and I don't want to be her dirty little secret behind her asshole fiancé's back. And that's all I'll be if we don't want to get caught.

Then there's the long-term picture. I don't want to start something with Page and then get sent to prison for years. I have faith in her skills, but she's right. Convincing a jury I'm not guilty is going to be a hell of a feat.

After taking a cold shower, I don't know what to do with myself. Things with Page are going to be awkward now, and that's not what I want. Hell, I invited her to come for the whole weekend to spend time with her, and I just slammed a door in her face, literally and figuratively.

My cell phone rings, interrupting my wallowing. Jude.

"What?" I bark.

"What crawled up your ass?" he asks.

"Nothing."

"What room are you in?"

"Eight-twenty."

"What room is Page in?" he asks.

"Why do you want to know?" I inquire, although it's obvious.

"Come on, jackass. I'll find out eventually. I'm guessing hers is beside yours. So if I'm in eight twenty-two, I bet she's in eight eighteen."

"Don't even *think* of fucking with her this weekend," I warn him.

"Why? Because you are?"

"No."

"Then until you admit you want her, and actually do something about it, she's fair game, bro."

"Do I need to remind you again that's she's engaged?" Although, Page didn't seem concerned about that a few minutes ago.

"No ring means that dude is shit out of luck."

"Leave her alone, Jude."

I hear a repetitive thumping like a knock right next to my ear, coming through the phone and at the same sound right outside my door in the hallway.

"Yowza, Page! Nice bikini. You going down for a swim?" Jude asks, and I'm yanking my door open before I can stop myself.

Goddamn!

The woman is even finer than I thought underneath those stiff suits. With just a turquoise triangle covering her pussy and nipples, now I'm the one getting stiff. She's tall for a woman, taller than some men I know, and her long, lean legs are spectacular. I'm certain they'd look even better around my waist.

Natural perky tits overflow from both sides of the tiny bikini top, leaving her flat stomach completely bare. It's painfully obvious from her hard nipples that Page is cold, and my cock twitches just thinking about running my tongue over the tight buds that look hard enough to break glass. Or running my tongue down her cleavage, or around her belly-button, or between her legs.

My eyes finally make it back to her face, and her eyes are avoiding me. Thank God, because there's no missing the rock hard erection I'm now sporting. While keeping her eyes on my brother, she unties her low professional bun and then reaches up with both hands to pile her hair up messily on the top of her head. I'd love to see her let all that blonde hair down just once.

Jude makes a whimpering sound which echoes in my ear.

"Are you two talking to each other?" Page asks. I finally realize I'm still holding the phone to my ear, just like Jude.

"We were until you distracted us," Jude responds, putting his phone away in his pocket, and I follow suit. "So, pool?"

"Yeah. They've got a hot tub down there, too, right?" she asks, cocking one curvy hip. I missed a spot. I want to lick her *right there* in that little curvy dip too.

"Hell yes they do," Jude replies, walking backward to his room. "Give me two minutes to change and I'll go down on you...I mean, I'll go down *with* you." He glances at his t-shirt with the kitten. The one that was the poster child for all the kittens that apparently get killed when someone masturbates. "Okay, maybe ten. You coming?" he asks me with a smile and a punch to my gut that lands when he passes. I'd been too distracted to react and block a hit for the first time ever.

"No, I'm not going to kill a kitten," I reply. Well, not until later. "And fuck yes I'm coming with you to the pool."

Jude disappears into his room, and the awkwardness is back, multiplied tenfold between Page and me. Without another word, she slams her hotel door. Okay, I deserved that.

I go back inside my own room and change into my white boardshorts and flip-flops. Grabbing a baseball cap and some sunglasses to hide as much of my face as I can, I snatch up my key card and phone, then I'm ready. I'm not going to risk them leaving without me, so I wait in the hall.

Page comes out of her room first, with more clothes on. A gray

Georgetown Law t-shirt and tiny navy blue shorts now cover her smoking hot bikini, the strings of which are still visible around her neck. She looks down and types on her phone, still refusing to look at me.

Damn it, I shouldn't have walked away. Right now we could be rolling around naked, fucking every which way, my tongue licking every single inch of her incredible body. But no, I'd done the honorable thing for once in my fucking life, and now she won't even talk to me.

"Page..." I start, wanting to try and explain.

"Don't," she says, holding up her palm without sparing me a glance. "I was tipsy and had a momentary lapse in judgment that I now regret. You're definitely off limits, I get that. But Jude's not."

She could've kneed me in the nuts, and I would've been less staggered. Thinking about her and Jude together...

"You can't be fucking serious-"

Jude's door opens and closes down the hall before he joins us in nothing but blue boardshorts similar to mine. In that moment I think I actually hate my little brother for looking so much like me. It's not the first time in my life that I've hated him, but it has been a long time since I've had such a shitty thought.

"Ready?" he asks Page.

"Yeah, and I can't wait to find some more of those fruity drinks. You won't let me do anything too crazy will you?" she asks Jude with a smile.

"I will definitely watch out for you," he says to her, and then to me, "You trying to go incognito, bro?"

"Try being the key word," I respond, pulling the bill of my hat down while we wait for the elevator.

"I really don't want to deal with a bunch of cage cunts," Page groans, crossing her arms over what I now know in great detail is a very ample chest. She shocks the shit out of me by using the "c" word.

"It's an unavoidable occurrence with Jax. Even the rape charge won't slow down these hoes," Jude replies when the doors of the elevator open and we step inside with an older, gray-haired couple. The man and woman quickly retreat to the opposite side of the confined space from us.

"Do I need to remind you where my eyes are?" Jude asks Page quietly behind me, making her giggle.

"I'm sorry. It must be hard, trying to stay away from all the women who come on to you, unfairly treating you as a sex symbol," she whispers to him, her voice much more seductive than I care for. Actually, my carefully contained rage is boiling up inside me.

"It is really...hard to deal with," Jude answers, lowering his voice. "I could use some help easing the pain if you're willing to give me a hand...or even better a mouth."

Unable to take anymore I turn around to glare at them. The two are so close it takes all of my self-control not to deck my brother, especially when I see his hand covering his cock and Page's hard nipples showing through her shirt. I yank Jude by his arm and slam him against the opposite wall.

"It's okay, they're brothers," Page assures the couple. "Although I'm not sure why the older, angrier one is being such a dic...tator to the younger, sweeter one."

"Because I've warned him to keep his hands off of you," I reply, looking at my brother's smirking face while I pin him against the wall.

"I didn't have my hands on her," Jude replies.

"So you don't want me, but no one else can have me either? Is that it?" Page asks, and Jude's eyes widen in comprehension.

"*You* turned *her* down?" he asks me. "Why? I thought you-"

"She's my attorney and she's engaged," I remind her and him. "Even if he is an asshole."

The elevator ride from hell finally ends, and we all rush out of the cramped metal container, the older couple moving faster than the three of us.

When we make it outside to the patio, I go in the opposite direction from Page and Jude, needing distance before I do something I'll regret.

I keep walking until I'm on the beach, the sound of the waves drowning out the thoughts in my head. Well, most of them. Being jealous of my younger brother is nothing new. You'd think I'd be used to it by now since I've been putting up with the shit since the day he was born.

...
Page

"So, what the hell happened back there?" Jude asks me as soon as we submerge ourselves in the warm, bubbling water.

"Nothing."

"And that's why you're pissed at him? Because nothing happened instead of...something?"

I shrug in response.

"Well, let's hear it."

"There's nothing to tell. He said he wasn't interested in me...that way," I admit.

"Bullshit!" Jude exclaims, smacking his palms on top of the water. "He's lying to you and to himself."

"Even if that is true, then why would he lie?" I ask.

"He doesn't want to get you in trouble."

"No one would find out," I tell him.

"And maybe that's the problem."

After thinking that over for a few minutes, I decide to turn the tables. "So what about you? Why don't you date?"

"Because I don't have time for that shit. I train day and night. I stay in the gym more hours than some people work every week. When I finally get done for the day, I'm wiped out."

"You can't take a few nights off?" I ask with a smile, not buying his excuse. Jax has time for women. Lots of them, apparently.

"Not if I want to win, and I haven't been winning, so I need to train longer, harder."

"Uh-huh."

Since the topic's been broached, I couldn't help but ask the question I've been curious about. "Jax said he thinks you're still a virgin. He was just joking, right?"

When Jude turns his head away instead of giving me a dimpled grin, I know it's actually true. This incredible looking, truly sweet man has never been with a woman.

"Attorney-client communications are kept confidential," I tell him.

"Fine," he huffs and then winces. "Technically, yes."

"Oh my God, Jude! How is that even possible?"

"I don't know," he grumbles and shrugs. A reddish hue was even creeping up the tan skin of his neck. "At first, I just didn't want to screw around with girls in high school knowing I don't want or have time for anything more with them. Then after a while I figured what the hell, I've gone this long, might as well wait until I can be with someone I actually care about or whatever for the first time instead of some random slut. It's stupid, I know..."

"It's not stupid," I assure him. "She'll be a lucky girl, whoever she is."

"But she won't be you," he says as a statement, not a question. "I just like fucking with Jax to try to get him to own up to wanting you. And you are really hot."

"Thanks." I laugh. "So are you, and flirting is fun. Especially when Jax gets all pissed off."

"I swear I thought he was going to knock me out on the elevator." Jude chuckles.

"I'm an idiot," I say with a shake of my head.

"Do you love him? The dude you're engaged to?" he asks.

I snort at the thought of referring to Elliot as someone I love. "I can barely stand him most of the time.

"Then why the hell would you want to marry him?"

Because my dad told me to. Is that the best reason I've got?

"I don't know. I don't think I want to anymore," I admit.

"Well good for you, I guess." Jude smirks. "So that only leaves one small problem."

"Big problem."

"But the rule doesn't apply after he's no longer your client, right?"

"I don't know. I guess not."

"Then why not let someone else take over his case?" he asks.

"I want to be the one to try it. That is, if he'll still let me."

"But you want to try him, too." He laughs.

"Yeah, and he literally just slammed a door in my face when I took my shirt off."

"Wow. That was maybe the stupidest decision of his life," Jude says with a shake of his head.

...

We spend most of Saturday out on the beach. Jax and Jude went off together and ran what seemed like the entire New Jersey coast for their cardio workout. All I know is that they came back with sweat cascading over the rippling muscles of their bare chests, down to their nylon shorts.

When they left things were somewhat tense between the brothers, but when they returned they seemed back to their normal, playful selves. Well, as playful as Jax gets. I was relieved since I didn't want to be the cause of any sort of bad feelings between the two. Despite what Jax may think, I don't want his younger brother. Last night I just wanted to make him jealous, to take a little of the sting away from his flat out rejection of sleeping with me.

The guys are ready to hit the water after running their marathon and insist I join them. My pale skin is starting to get toasty, and although I enjoy their father's company from his seat next to me, I've missed the brothers' bantering.

"So how was your run?" I ask them as we waded into the water up to our knees.

"It was good," Jude answers, smiling behind his dark shades so I can't see his eyes. "We only got stopped, what was it Jax, maybe a dozen times or so by skanks?"

There was no ignoring the boulder of jealousy hitting the bottom of my stomach.

"Two dozen." Jax chuckles from the other side of me.

"So, Page, what are you up to tonight?" Jude asks after a good size wave crashes against us at waist level.

"Nothing that I know of," I reply.

"You should come with us to see the fights," he replies.

"Fights?" I ask.

"Yeah. In the Xanadu Theater, the one at the back of the hotel? It starts at eight. There's only one for a title, but there are ten other fights on the card. It'll give you a chance to see up close and personal what we do," Jude tells me.

"Sure, sounds fun," I say. "If you guys don't mind me tagging along."

"I could probably use your security services to run off the cage cunts," Jax teases, the first words he's spoken to me since I made a fool of myself last night.

"Maybe I could get some of that yellow 'Caution' police tape to form a circle around you. Although, it'll probably take some big bouncers to handle that sort of job," I joke. About that time a wave breaks right in my face before I can turn my head away. I end up spitting out a mouthful of salty sea water. Yuck.

"You okay?" Jude laughs. "It's easier if you dive underneath the waves instead of taking them on face first."

Jax must follow the same advice because he surfaces a good distance away from us in the calm part of the ocean. He swipes a hand through his dark hair, pushing it off his face as he turns around and looks for us. The motion makes the muscles in his chest and arm flex in the sunshine. God, he looks freaking edible.

"We talked about you," Jude says, lowering his voice.

"What about me?" I ask although I can probably guess. The embarrassment I caused myself yesterday.

"He wants you–"

I scoff.

"He does, and for the first time in his life he's actually making the decision to *not* carelessly fuck a woman."

"Yay me," I say, pumping both of my fists in the air.

"Because this time he cares. He doesn't want you to lose your law license because of him."

Of course, he's right. No stupid, silly fling is worth what I worked years in school for. But what's the harm when it's just us in the privacy of a hotel room?

"I also think he's scared," Jude says before ducking under a wave that splatters across my nose and mouth.

"Of what?" I sputter when he resurfaces.

"That you're more than a one-night stand, which is unheard of for him."

"Why are you telling me all this, Jude?" I ask in exasperation.

"Because all it will take is another little push or two from you and he'll break. According to him, he hasn't fucked anyone in like two weeks. That's ten times as long as his previous record. Flash a little tit and ass, flirt with him. Hell, flirt with other dudes, and I guarantee he's gonna snap."

"So you're saying I should keep making a fool of myself?"

"You're not making a fool of yourself. If he wasn't attracted to you and you kept at it, that would be sort of sad. But I'm telling you, Page, he's more fragile than glass when it comes to giving into you."

"Well, here goes nothing," I say to Jude with a smile when we finally reach Jax.

...

Jax

I watch as Jude and Page take their sweet ass time getting through the waves. Despite Jude's assurance this morning that there's nothing going on with him and her, I can't help that familiar jealousy from rearing its ugly head.

"It's nice out here," Page says when she's only a few feet away. She's close enough that I can see her bikini through the murky chest-deep water, a skimpy purple one today.

Jude goes into back floating mode, which is easy to do here where the water's calm.

Page ducks all the way under the water and surfaces, adjusting the cups of her bikini. Her hair is braided in two ponytails today, and rather than make her look young and innocent she's so fucking hot she could be posing for a goddamn Sports Illustrated swimsuit edition. My cock is throbbing painfully under my thin board-shorts. It's been so long for me, and she is just so fucking sexy.

I'm lost in my own head imagining running my tongue down her wet neck and in between her heavy tits when I'm hit with a face full of gritty saltwater. I swipe my palm over my face and look up to find Page laughing. I've been dying to get my hands on her, and she might as well have just sent me an invitation.

"You *can* swim, right, rich girl?" I ask her.

"Yes. I mean *no*. No, I can't." She shakes her head and lies unconvincingly while backing away.

I dive into the five feet of water and jerk her legs out from under her, pulling her down until her ass hits the sandy ocean floor. Page's hands shoot out, reaching for something to hold on to and finding my shoulders. She squirms and fights for a few seconds, pushing against me until she's back on her feet again.

When I resurface, I expect her to look pissed. Instead, she's actually smiling as she wipes the water from her eyes. I know it's a bad idea, and that I'm playing with fire, but I can't resist this. Flirting with her. Touching her. I'm a goner.

I lurch forward, scooping Page up in my arms. "Hey, Jude. Catch," I yell to him and then toss her in his direction. She lands with a squeal and a big splash right in front of him. Before she can get to her feet, Jude grabs her up and throws her back to me. She lands with such force on this fall that the back of her bikini comes untied. Two triangles of purple fabric float to the surface of the murky water, leaving her bare breasts behind. Now all that holds her top on is the strings tied at her neck.

I jump in front of Page, blocking Jude's view, as well as anyone else who happens to be watching from the shore before she flashes them. I'm only a foot away from her and can clearly see the outline of her pale titties even through the distorted reflection of the water. God I'd give anything to reach out and touch them. My hands would only need to move forward just a little bit. Oh, but then my mouth would be jealous and need a taste.

"Um, Page?" I say, unable to look away.

"What you jerk?" she asks with a teasing tone.

"Your top," I tell her.

She glances down and gasps before submerging herself lower into the water.

Why did I tell her? Oh yeah, because it was the gentlemanly thing to do, and I didn't want her flashing the entire Jersey shore.

"Crap! Will you retie it for me?" she asks, spinning around and presenting her back to me.

I reach for the two floating strings, and unfortunately, tug them back into a bow for her.

"Thanks," she says, swimming away out to sea like she's embarrassed. Honestly, it's not much more than what she showed me last night when she took her shirt off in her room.

"No one saw anything," I assure her.

"Saw what?" Jude asks when he swims closer.

"My top came undone," Page tells him.

"Well damn. How the hell did I miss that?" he whines.

Page shakes her head and flashes me a smile as she swims backward. She stops suddenly, belting out a scream before yelling, "Son of a bitch!"

Since the woman never curses it must be something bad. She starts swimming frantically back toward Jude and me. "Go back! Watch out! Fucking jellyfish!"

Oh shit! She must've been stung by one of the bastards.

"Where did it get you?" I ask when she makes it back to us, her face scrunched in pain.

"Lower back...and leg," she says between pants.

"Is it bad?" I ask although I know it's a stupid question as soon as it leaves my mouth.

"God yes."

"Are the tentacles still stuck in you?" Jude asks. I have no idea what the hell he's talking about. He must've seen some shit about jellyfish on the Discovery Channel or something.

"I don't know!" Page exclaims. "I can't see it!"

"She probably needs to go to an urgent care and get checked out," he says to me as we head back to the shore. "You gonna take her?"

"Damn right," I respond to his question, making it clear that I'll take care of her, and we don't need his help.

"Hey, I don't need to see a doctor! I'm fine. It's just a little burn," she says, and then she stumbles in the knee high waves, worse than when she was drinking the night before. "Okay a lot of burn, but I'm sure it'll stop hurting in a few minutes."

Jude and I exchange a look that says we're not convinced. I start to reach for Page to pick her up but want to avoid the area that's hurting. "Which side is the sting on?" I ask.

"Um, the right. Why?" she asks. Instead of answering, I simply show her by grabbing her up on the left side with an arm under her knees and the other around her upper back.

"Ow!" Page says with a wince.

"Did I hurt you?" I ask her.

"No, it just...hurts."

"You're not going to bitch and tell me to put you down because you can walk?" I ask her, as I head to where we've set up camp on the shore, and my dad is still sitting.

Page shakes her head no, and then surprises me when she snakes her arms tightly around my neck to hold on.

"Damn, then you must be in serious pain."

"It's better now," she says, and when I glance down she's smiling up at me, her face only inches away from mine.

"Jude, did she really get stung?" I tease, holding her bottom up higher for him to examine her back and leg.

"Goddamn!" he mutters. "That looks like hell, Page."

"Yeah, and it feels like it, too, thank you very much," she replies, actually sticking her tongue out at me.

"Apparently, it also makes you act like a five-year-old," I joke when we make it back to our chairs and towels. "Or maybe that's your braids."

"Here," my dad stands up from his lounge chair, grabs my black Baltimore Ravens hat from my pile of things, and says, "If you're going to touch her, at least try not to be so damn obvious."

I bend my knees so he can put it on my head, and then he slides my dark sunglasses on my face.

"Good thing you don't have any distinguishable tattoos to give your identity away," Page says, eyeing my chest closely like there might be a microscopic one hidden that she's somehow missed.

"Not a one. I'm scared of needles," I tell her honestly, making her laugh. "And that information better remain attorney-client privileged."

"You could easily kill a man with your bare hands, but tiny little needles scare you?" she asks with a smile. Just the thought of the damn instruments makes me shiver.

Once Page is handed her beach bag and my wallet's thrown inside it, I slip on my flip flops, and we start heading to the front of the hotel. I'm pretty sure there's an urgent care just right down the road. Doubt we'll even need a taxi.

"So what else are you scared of, tough guy?" Page asks after I carry her a few minutes in silence.

I debate whether or not to admit my other fear. But when I look down at her warm, cobalt blue eyes I know I'd confess anything to this woman. Well, almost anything. I sure as hell can't tell her that I want her too.

"I'm claustrophobic," I tell her. "I can tolerate elevators as long as they're well ventilated, you know, not hot and stuffy. But if it's only a few flights, I'd rather take the stairs. Nothing worse that tiny boxes being held by a fucking string."

"Oh God. I'm sorry, Jax," she says in understanding, burying her face in my neck. I'd almost swear I felt her lips press against my skin.

JAX

The woman is trying her best to break me. "Was it really bad? Those days you were in jail?" she asks.

I shrug, refusing to admit I'd freaked out like a pussy. "The county lock up back home wasn't so bad, but the one here? Nasty and hot as fuck. Instead of sleeping on a mat laid out on the grungy floor I slept standing up against the wall all night. Well, what little I did sleep. Thankfully I was only there for one night, and my dad posted my bond the next morning."

"No wonder you were so angry that afternoon," she says softly, and I assume she means the day we met. "And you *really* don't want to go back, do you?" she asks as I cross a street, now only a block away from the urgent care on the corner.

"Fuck no I don't. That's why I've got an incredibly smart and very expensive attorney."

"What if I let you down? Maybe we should bring someone else on until Ryan's trial finishes up. He said he could be tied up a few more weeks."

"You're not going to let me down," I tell her, and watch as she chews on her bottom lip with unnecessary worry. "That's maybe the only thing in my life that I'm actually certain of."

"But-" she starts.

"But nothing," I interrupt her, and then pull open the door to the clinic. I carry Page in and sit her down in a plastic chair while I go to the front desk to check her in.

"Hi," the young woman in scrubs says to me with a smile while blatantly ogling me. I've kept my glasses and hat on to cover at least part of my face. "We normally require shirts, but I think we can make an exception to that policy for you."

"Ah, thanks. We were just out swimming in the ocean when she got stung by a jellyfish," I explain, nodding over to Page.

"Oh," the nurse says, her facing falling when she sees the beautiful woman I just carried in. "She'll need to fill out these forms, and then the doctor should be able to see you soon."

"Thanks," I say, accepting her offered clipboard that holds a stack of papers and has a pen attached with a metal string.

"Here, they need you to fill all this out," I tell Page, handing it off to her.

She nods and takes the forms to start completing them. I look over her shoulder and see that her birthday is December twentieth, which is about the crappiest time for one. She's allergic to penicillin and mold. She had her tonsils taken out when she was eight-years-old, and she takes anti-anxiety and antidepressant medications every day. So she really has been diagnosed as being high strung. Once she checks all the little boxes and signs her name fifteen times I take the forms back to the lady at the front, and then we wait.

Every few minutes Page continues to wince like she's in pain while we sit in the hard plastic chairs. I'm about to go bitch about them taking forever when they finally call her back. As soon as I stand up beside her, she holds out her palm. "I'm pretty sure I can walk that far."

I motion for her to go for it, walking slowly behind her. It's the first chance I've had to get a good look at her sting, and it's something else. Red wavy whelps cover a section of her lower back and around her side, with more of the same under her right butt cheek, that yes, I also checked out. *Damn.* No wonder she's in pain.

After they confirm with her that she doesn't mind me tagging along, they check her blood pressure, which is a little high at one-twenty-eight over ninety. The nurse assures us it's probably due to the pain. Page's temperature is normal, and she weighs a hundred and twenty-six pounds.

Page lays flat on her stomach on the exam table after the nurse leaves us alone in a room. With nothing but her tiny strings holding up her top, and the small triangle covering her perfectly curved ass, I'm about to lose my shit. I sit down in the plastic chair and apply pressure to my rising cock, doing more harm than good. Now it's just springing back up looking for more attention.

Unable to take the temptation any longer, I jump out of my seat. Under the pretense of looking at her injury, I stand right beside her ass and trail my fingertips along the sting imprints, careful not to actually touch them. Page squirms and cold chill bumps raise under the tips of my fingers. "Cold?" I ask her.

"No," she replies. She doesn't tell me to stop touching her, so I don't. Hell, I *know* she wants my hands on her, and it's a goddamn shame I can't take things further. Well, maybe a little further won't hurt anything.

...
Page

Oh for the love of all that is holy, what is that man doing? I mean, not that I want him to stop. I'm barely suppressing my groans because the skin to skin contact feels so good, but I'd also like to know what the heck he's doing. Is this what Jude meant? That I'm finally wearing him down?

Jax has been acting differently today. Not in the weird, *this is awkward because I turned you down* way either. No, it's more like a sensitive side to him I've never experienced. And I was shocked to find out that this normally tough, arrogant, angry man is scared of needles and small spaces. Now I have even more motivation to make sure he's not found guilty by a jury so that he won't get an active prison sentence.

Pushing those unhappy thoughts aside, I close my eyes to savor this amazingly intimate experience. Jax's massive lethal hand gliding a path so soft and gentle along my spine and down my leg. He knows exactly what he's doing to me. But wait. He said he didn't want me. Is he just horny and I'm the only available option?

Ugh. I don't like that thought at all. I don't have much time to ruminate on that, though because Jax finds a way to distract me. On an up pass, his feather-light touch moves to the inside of my thigh, and I almost hyperventilate.

"You're leaving a wet spot on the table," he says.

"Huh?" I ask. Am I so aroused it's leaking out? I look down at the white paper covering the exam table. Of course, he's referring to my still soggy bathing suit. "Haha," I mutter, relaxing my body back down.

Jax's finger is grazing along the outer seam of my bikini bottom when there's a knock on the door. He jerks his hand away like I've managed to sting him.

"Miss Davenport?" a woman's voice asks.

"Oh, um, hey," I say, starting to get into a sitting position.

"No stay where you are, so I can get a good look," she says, and I hear the snap of gloves. "I'm Dr. Bailey, and...Well, hello there."

Of course, she's checking out Jax.

"Hi, how's it going?" he asks, and she giggles. The doctor, a woman who spent years in medical school, is actually giggling like a little girl. You'd think he asked her to strip down naked instead of offering a neutral greeting. It reminds me of Joey from *Friends* being able to just say *"How you doin'?"* to make women swoon.

I yelp and jump out of my skin when the woman actually touches the sting!

"You okay?" Jax asks when he comes to stand up by my head.

"Uh-huh," I answer. And, oh yes, he's a very nice distraction from the pain. I'll just memorize the indentations of his six pack of abs while the doctor pokes and prods me. Ah, and those lovely cuts of muscle that travel down underneath the low waistband of his board-shorts forming a V. I want to follow those two beautiful lines home.

Jax squats down so that he's eye level with me, resting his forearms on the exam table. I reach out and pull his sunglasses off, wanting to actually see his midnight eyes. His gorgeous face is even better than his sculpted muscles.

"Now you just ruined my secret identity," he tells me with a wide, panty-wetting smile.

"I think you're safe from all your fangirls in here," I respond. "Mostly."

"Well, it looks like there aren't any tentacles left behind," the doctor says. "I'm going to apply some vinegar, and then we'll need to use a razor to shave the area, making sure to remove any remaining nematocysts."

"What the fuckocysts?" Jax asks, making me and the doctor both laugh. "And you won't have to use any, ah, needles will you?"

"No needles and nematocysts are the jellyfish's poisonous cells that activate their venom," she says before she opens the door and gives instructions to the nurse. A few minutes later vinegar is poured on my back and upper thigh. Then the sadist runs the razor with no shaving cream over the raised stings!

"Ah God," I groan and press my forehead against my folded arms. I feel Jax's palms rubbing up and down them before he squeezes my hand. I hold onto him while the evil woman works her dull blade all the way down my burning lower back and side, to the skin below my bottoms. When I feel liquid poured over it again I assume it's over, thank goodness.

"All set. You may need some hydrocortisone cream to rub on the areas once or twice a day until it heals."

"Great," I say sarcastically.

"Give this to them out front and they'll take care of you," the doctor tells us quickly, papers rustling. "You might want to stay out of the ocean for a few days." The door opens and then quickly shuts again.

I move into a sitting position, letting my legs dangle off the side of the table before trying to ease my weight down on the sore area near my upper thigh.

"Frick," I huff as I finally accomplish my goal. I'm about to jump down, but then Jax is suddenly there in front of me. His big warm hands spread my legs apart to wedge his body between them. I gasp when I feel his hard, thick length press between my thighs. Only two very thin pieces of fabric keep us from finding out how well his enormous key will fit into my throbbing lock. Oh and I bet he'd slide right in, even if it would require a minute to adjust to all of his size.

My greedy hands automatically reach for his sculpted stomach while his continue sliding forward on the top of my thighs. When I look up into his beautiful face, his dark eyes are filled with need. Need for me or just...any woman?

Before I can ask, his lips part and dip down to capture my bottom one between his two. They move to do the same to my smaller top lip before his tongue sweeps in and brushes mine, making me moan. I'm desperate for more and tangle my hands in his hair to tell him so. In response his palm reaches up to cup my jaw, tilting my head to the side allowing him a better angle at which to dominate my mouth.

God, the man kisses even better than he looks. As if his seeking tongue isn't enough to turn up the heat, melting me from the inside out, one of his thumbs on my inner thigh wanders over and presses against my pulsing clit through my thin, damp swimsuit.

"Mmm." I shudder and moan with pleasure, urging Jax onward.

Between the incredible kiss and the applied pressure of his thumb, it doesn't take long before my body starts to shake. While I'm gasping for air and convulsing, Jax's mouth moves down my chest. His tongue snakes underneath one of the triangles covering my breast and flicks against my nipple before his hand jerks the material out of the way to grant him unrestricted access to suck on more flesh. The cold air and my arousal have my nipples beaded and sensitive. My fingers continue to thread in the back of his wet hair, holding him in place.

Once I have some of my wits back, I realize Jax is still hard as a rock between my legs, needing his own sweet relief. I let go of his hair with one palm and reach down between our bodies to caress his cock.

"Ah fuck," Jax mutters around his mouth full of my tingling nipple. He keeps his hands busy weighing and taking measurements of both of my breasts.

I like the feel of his long thickness in my grasp, but I want to touch his skin and run my fingers over every vein and every single inch of his length. Sliding my hand underneath his waistband, I finally get my hand around his velvety smooth, hard as steel shaft.

On a groan, Jax goes completely still a second before his hips began to thrust, slowly at first and then becoming more frantic, telling me he's getting close. He's a lot to hold on to, but I try and cover as much ground as I can with my small hand.

Jax's teeth nip my breast before his mouth returns to mine, his tongue plunging possessively in and out of my mouth in time to my quickening strokes. He growls low in his throat and shudders when his warm release pulses all over my fingers. The pressure of his lips on mine ease up as his body gradually relaxes.

"God...I needed that," is the first thing he says. That snaps me back to reality quicker than you can click the heels of your ruby slippers. He said he "needed that," meaning the orgasm, not that he needed me or even wanted me.

"Because it's been a long time?" I ask, quickly losing the last wave of the ecstasy that had felt as strong as a tsunami just moments ago.

"Well, yeah," Jax replies, moving away from me to grab some tissues from the opposite counter. He offers me a wad, which I accept to clean up with.

"How long?" I ask, keeping my eyes lowered.

"Huh?" he asks. "I haven't fucked anyone since the night before I got arrested."

"So you'll what? Screw around with me because it's convenient for you to get off, even though you're not 'interested' in me?" I ask, hopping off the table. I try not to let my face show the pain that shoots through my leg and back.

When my cold feet hit the tile floor, I also realize I'm screwed. I don't have any shoes because the big jerk carried me. Forget that, I'd rather take my chances with tetanus. Maybe I can get a booster shot before I walk out of the office.

I grab my beach bag and head for the exam room door after I make sure my girly parts are all covered back up. I eventually find the front of the clinic, walking as fast as my sore leg will allow.

"Page, wait," Jax says behind me, but I ignore him. He's horny. I'm here and throwing myself at him. It doesn't take a genius to figure out what just went down and why.

I smile at the woman behind the checkout counter when I hand her my paperwork, although I'm the furthest thing from being in a cheerful mood.

"That'll be one-fourteen," the middle-aged brunette says unenthusiastically.

A hundred and fourteen bucks to pour a dollar bottle of vinegar on me and scrape my sore skin with a fifty cent razor? Wow, what a rip. I hand over my debit card, which is when Jax catches up to me.

"I was going to take care of the bill," he says.

I didn't miss the sudden flurry of females suddenly converging and crowding around the small checkout desk. There're more open mouths gawking at Jax than the blow-up doll section in a sex shop.

"That's ridiculous. It's my back and leg, so why would you take care of it?" I ask him.

"Because it's my fault you're here this weekend in the first place."

"Right," I say at the reminder that I'm supposed to be here on business. I'm his attorney. I just gave my client a freaking hand job. After he got me off while he had his mouth on my breasts.

Awesome.

I can imagine writing that up for the State Bar Ethics Committee. *Well, members of the committee, I didn't fuck him, I just stroked his cock until he came. No, I didn't clearly conflict myself out of his case. I can represent him without remembering what it feels like to have his tongue in my mouth and on my tits while his hand is between my legs.* Gah!

"Page, wait!" Jax yells after I take my receipt and walk out the front doors. "You don't have any shoes on. Let me at least get a cab."

"I'm fine," I say, already feeling tiny pebbles embedded into my heels. I hope it's pebbles and not say, pieces of broken beer bottles or dirty syringes?

"Hard-headed woman," Jax mutters behind me.

When we reach the hotel, I go straight to the elevator banks and smack the up arrow, hoping Jude and their dad will bring my flip flops and towel in with them.

"I'm sorry," Jax says when we're alone in the small metal box. Those two words make me feel about the same amount of inches tall. It's exactly what he'd said last night when he rejected me. "I crossed a line I swore I wouldn't with you, and it won't happen again."

"Good to know," I say, crossing my arms over my barely covered chest.

"Hey, this is all your fault-"

"My fault!" I exclaim.

"You can't keep flaunting your ass and tits in front of me and expect me to keep my hands off of you! But from now on that's *exactly* what I'm going to do."

"Yes, I think you've already made that perfectly clear, you big jerk."

I pull my keycard out of my bag before the elevator doors open, so I can quickly escape this infuriating man. After I slam my room door practically in his face, I pull off my sandy, wet bathing suit and take a warm shower, which burns the fire out of my stings.

If my mood isn't shitty enough already after making a fool of myself and being extremely unprofessional, when I unplug my phone from the charger I've got three missed calls from Elliot, two from my dad, and one from my mom. Wonderful.

Elliot has also taken the time to send me a few sweet text messages to let me know he's thinking of me. One says, *"Where the hell are you?"* and another later one says, *"You're fucking him, aren't you?"*

That's it! As soon as we get back to town Monday I'm calling it off. I'm tempted to break up with him via text message, but that's the wimpy way out. This is something I need to say face-to-face.

Feeling brazen I simply type in a response of *"XOXO you, too"* and hit send before turning my phone off and slumping backward on the king size mattress. My eyes are heavy from exhaustion after the day's excitement, so it takes no time at all for me to fall sound asleep.

...

I wake up to a knock on my door, or on one of the rooms next door. Sitting up I glance over at the alarm clock beside the bed and see that it's six-thirty. I've been asleep for over two hours. There's another knock, definitely on my door. I only have a towel around me from my shower but say screw it. Checking the peephole first I see that it's Jude in a black *Havoc* logo tee and cargo shorts.

"Hey, Jude," I say when I open the door.

He winces before looking up and down the hallway. "Thank goodness no one heard you," he says on an exhale. "Appropriate greetings for me are 'Hi, Jude' or 'What do you want, Asshole' but never 'Hey, Jude.'"

"Why?" I ask. "The Beatles?"

"Yeah. You have no idea how many goddamn times I've heard that shit."

"Got it. So, what's up, Jude?" I ask him with a smile.

"Much better. And I've got your shit," he says, holding out my flip flops and towel.

"Thanks," I say, taking them while struggling to keep my towel secured around my nakedness.

"Nice outfit but they may not let you in to eat wearing just that," he says.

"To eat?" I ask.

"Yeah, we're gonna grab dinner at Hard Rock before the fights. You're still going, right?"

I glance next door to his brother's room, certain he'll be there. I need to suck it up and pretend like nothing happened so that we can try and get things back to normal.

"What happened with him?" Jude asks, instantly killing that hope.

"Doesn't matter."

"How's your back?"

"It's okay, not hurting nearly as much."

"Well, hurry up and get dressed. We've got a seven o'clock reservation, and I'm starving."

"Yeah, yeah. Keep your panties on." I smile.

"Speaking of panties," he says, tilting his head to the side and checking out the bottom of my towel. "I'd take a guess and say you're not wearing any, are you?" he asks with a wide grin. Of course, Jax's door opens at that moment, probably because he'd been eavesdropping through the thin walls.

"Ugh," I groan before shutting my door on them both.

"What'd you do to her?" I hear Jude ask his brother.

"Nothing. Mind your own goddamn business," is Jax's harsh reply.

I quickly blow dry my still damp hair before pulling it up into a high ponytail. I decide to slip on a short, casual navy blue sleeveless dress with a brown leather belt and matching wedges. After I brush my teeth, put on a little mascara, eyeshadow, and lipstick I'm ready to go. I grab my purse and open my room door to find all three Malones standing around waiting patiently for me.

Where the heck is their mother? Even though I've been tempted, I'm scared to ask in case something horrible happened to her, like she passed away. I don't want to be the one dredging up a tragic history. Martin Malone is a pretty upbeat guy, although there does seem to be a sadness about him, noticeable by his frown lines.

Tonight their dad is dressed like Jude in a plain green tee and khaki shorts. And even though Jax is outfitted just as casually, he somehow wears his relaxed fit jeans and snug navy blue shirt like they're worth a million bucks. How cute, the two of us match all the way down to our toes. He's even got on a brown leather belt low on his hips and dark brown *Sketchers* on his feet. When I finally work my way up to his face, of course, he's smirking down at me with his cell phone in his hand.

"Oh look how sweet, the Bobbsey Twins coordinated," Jude says before he and his dad start laughing at us.

"I can go change," I say, turning back to my room, but Jude grabs my arm and tugs me along toward the elevator.

"You're not changing. I'm starving," he says while we wait for the elevator.

When it finally comes we all file on. For whatever reason, I can sense that Jax is the big warm body standing behind me in the corner. When I feel a breeze like my skirt is being lifted, I certainly *hope* it's him and not his dad. Jude's completely innocent since he's standing next to me.

"Why are you sneaking a peek under my skirt?" I snap, pressing my skirt down as I spin around to face him.

"Oh please." Jax huffs and buries his hands in his front pockets to appear innocent. "I was looking at your stings."

"You could've just asked."

While I'm fussing at Jax, a group of people crowds into the confined space with us. I'm nudged forward so that I'm now chest to chest with Jax. I expect him to smirk or make a comment about me trying to touch him, but he doesn't. Instead, he presses his back against the wall and lifts his face to the ceiling, sucking in deep, open-mouth breaths.

Of course! The man's claustrophobic. All the other times we've been on the elevator together it was just us or one or two people, never crowded like tonight. It probably doesn't help that it's hot as Hades with an exorbitant amount of strong perfumes, colognes and hairspray clogging up the air. We only have a few more floors to go, but it seems like it's taking forever, stopping on each and every one.

"My older brother, you met him yesterday, Logan? He's terrified of cats," I tell Jax softly to distract him. "Even kittens."

He looks down at me with a tightly clenched jaw and a raised eyebrow, silently asking me to keep going.

"When I was ten or eleven I found these three really cute little black and white kittens out near the dumpster behind our church. They couldn't have been more than a few weeks old, so tiny and meowing like crazy with no mama cat around. Of course I wanted to keep them but noooo. I remember when I picked one up and ran over to show my parents Logan screamed like a little girl in front of everyone. The whole congregation was still standing around the parking lot gossiping after the service, so they heard him screeching before he ran back inside. He was sixteen or seventeen at the time."

The last sentence makes the corner of Jax's lips raise, coming close to an actual grin.

"So you didn't get to keep any of them?" he asks, as the elevator jerks like we're moving again.

I shake my head. "Nope. Logan waited at the church while we took them to a vet's house. Afterward, I remember telling my parents I wanted to be a vet and rescue animals when I grow up so I could actually keep all the kittens and puppies. They told me I was too smart and pretty for such a disgusting job, and that my choices in life were marrying a wealthy man or going to law school."

"So you didn't want to go to law school?" he asks with a scrunched forehead.

"No, but I was still single when I finished my undergrad degree in just three years."

"What'd you major in?" Jax asks as I hear everyone filing out of the elevator on the first floor.

"Biology" I laugh. No one ever asks me that, it's just a given that I was probably Pre-Law with some major like Political Science. "Even though I had a 4.0 GPA, with that major I probably just barely squeaked through admissions at Georgetown because I was a legacy."

"Why didn't you just go to veterinary school?" he asks. We both inhale deep cleansing breaths when we make it into the open floor of the high-ceilinged lobby, escaping the cluster of people.

"Because my parents wouldn't pay for it and I didn't have any money," I say with a shrug when we catch up to his dad and Jude.

"I'd pay your tuition," he says.

Wait, what does he mean by that?

"Pay what tuition?" Jude asks when we approach.

"For veterinary school."

"Huh?" Jude asks, echoing my thoughts again. I look back over my shoulder at Jax in confusion.

"You know I have more money than sense," Jax says.

His dad mutters a "Got that right."

At the same time, Jax asks, "What does it cost, a few hundred thousand?"

"Don't be silly, Jax. I'm not going back to school, and even if I were, I definitely wouldn't go back on your dime for *a few hundred thousand.*"

He clearly must be joking because otherwise...it's too preposterous to wrap my head around.

"Now that we've cleared that up, can we please go eat?" Jude whines.

"Lead the way," I say with a sweep of my hand since no one's moving and things are uncomfortable after Jax's extremely unexpected but generous offer.

"Thank fuck," Jude says as he takes off ahead of us, continuing to grumble about delays. "Everyone's taking their sweet ass time."

"Scared of *spiders*," Jax says to me, nodding toward his sibling's back. He says the last word louder than the rest.

"Ah! What the fuck?" Jude screams after he does a little hop that brings his knees up to his chest. "Where's a spider? Is it a big one?"

"You stepped on it. I'm pretty sure it's dead," Jax teases Jude, which causes him to have a full body shiver.

"So what are you afraid of?" Jax asks me while we walk toward the Hard Rock Cafe.

"Failure," I admit, since he'd been honest with me. "And snakes."

"Huh, really?" Jax asks, scratching the side of his head like I've noticed he does whenever he's thinking. Bending down next to my ear, he whispers so only I can hear him, "I don't remember seeing you flinch earlier today. You wrangled that python in my pants like a pro."

An embarrassed laugh escapes me at the same time cold chills race down both arms from feeling his warm breath against my ear.

"Guess yours is the exception," I respond, unable to help my smile.

∼

Dinner is uneventful and mostly quiet as the men shovel food in their mouths the entire time. I'm talking appetizers, salads, entrees, *and* my favorite, dessert. After Jax, Mr. Money Bags insisted on paying the check we went over to get our seats at the Xanadu Theater.

I end up sitting between Jax and Jude, with their dad on the other side of Jude, in the front freaking row! We can almost reach out and touch the huge metal octagon.

"How'd you guys manage to get such great seats on short notice?" I ask. "And how much do I owe you for my ticket?"

"Nothing, they were free," Jude says.

"Free? You mean you got four front row tickets for free?"

"Yeah, princess, you didn't know? You're with MMA royalty," Jax chuckles.

"Ha! That's hilarious." I can't help my giggle. I may be a little looser than normal after the two girly drinks I had at dinner.

"Seriously, Jax was named the first ever IFC *King of the Cage*. He has more wins, more knockouts, and fewer losses than any other fighter in the entire worldwide league," Jude brags proudly on his older brother. "Actually, he has no losses."

Wow, that's...impressive.

"They probably stripped that shit from me, too, because of that fucking slut. I'm gonna have to fight to earn my championship title back," Jax tells us.

"That's BS," I reply. "What happened to innocent until proven guilty?"

"The IFC cares more about the sponsors' opinions than the truth since they don't want to lose a penny."

The lights dim and loud music comes pouring over the speakers, Ludacris's "Move Bitch." The crowd starts clapping and cheering so I do the same, even though I don't see anyone or anything happening.

"What's going on?" I ask the guys.

"The first fighter just came out and is getting cleared by the ref to enter the cage," Jude explains, nodding to a curtained area. "This song is what he picked for his intro, you know, to get hyped up."

"Oh," I say, then after thinking it over, ask, "What songs do you guys use?"

"Sick Puppies' *'You're Going Down'* is Jax's, and mine's Macklemore's *'Can't Hold Us.'*"

"Nice," I tell Jude. Familiar with both songs, I can see how they fit each man's personality.

Finally, I spot the mostly naked little guy when he climbs up the steps and steps into the cage. Tight, black spandex shorts, small red gloves, and a red mouthpiece is all he's wearing. A rock song comes on and then the second fighter goes through the same procedure.

Once both are in the cage, the ref goes inside and locks the door. While the two men bounce in place on their feet, the announcer tells us their names, weight, and records. These are flyweight fighters, weighing in at a whopping one hundred and twenty-five pounds. I actually weigh more than these scrawny guys.

Even though they're small, they come out brutally swinging. By the second round, I'm pretty sure blood's sprayed us from the geyser pouring out one of the dude's nose. I cover my eyes until the crowd roars because someone is deemed the winner.

"What happened?" I ask.

"There are three ways to win; by knockout, by submission, or by decision," Jude explains. "If both fighters last all three rounds or five rounds in a title fight, then the judges decide who wins by a point system. If all three judges agree, it's called a unanimous decision. If it's two against one judge, it's a split decision. If they all score it even with no clear winner, it's a draw."

"Okay. So that guy won by a submission?"

"Yep," Jude responds. "A knockout is when the other guy is unable to continue fighting or is no longer defending himself, sometimes because they're actually unconscious. A technical knockout is when the ref or a doctor says a fighter is too injured to go on. A submission is when a fighter taps out in defeat."

"Wow, this is scary. I can't imagine seeing one of you up there getting hit over and over again."

"I *don't* get hit," Jax says.

"Never?" I face him and ask skeptically.

"Never."

"That explains how you still have such a pretty face," I tease him with a smile.

"Pretty?" Jax scoffs.

"What about you, Jude? Your face is still pretty too. Don't you ever get hit?" I ask.

"Hell yes." He laughs, rubbing his jaw likes he's having phantom pain from a past fight. "Jax is what we call a striker or a heavy hitter, meaning he wins by knocking guys out with his fists. I just try and dodge my opponents' punches and kicks until I can take them down since I'm better on the ground. You know, with wrestling and submissions."

"Jude is a helluva lot better than me at the ground game when he doesn't get knocked out beforehand or submit," Jax responds.

"Nothing's worth breaking an arm or leg," Jude replies. "And I've never been knocked out, asshole. Well, except by you, but that doesn't count since those weren't officially sanctioned fights."

I'm caught off guard when a cameraman suddenly appears right in front of our faces. I hear the announcer say Jax and Jude's names which are immediately followed by deafening applause and cheers. Nice to know the fans are still behind Jax while his case is pending.

The two take the attention in stride, Jax with a lazy, carefree nod of his head, and Jude with a fist pump and smile.

The rest of the night is a blur of punches, kicks, and bloody, sweaty guys before Jax walks me back up to my room. I think watching two men beat the crap out of each other will take some time to get used to, but it had been fun to see the fights with the guys. I don't want to say goodnight, but I worry about what I'll do if I don't turn in now.

"You sure you don't want to come play poker with us?" Jax asks, leaning a muscular shoulder against the wall beside my door.

I shake my head while pulling my key from my purse and sliding it in the slot. "Thanks, but I better head to bed."

"Okay, suit yourself." He shrugs. His dark eyes lower to my lips, making me think he's considering kissing me. Of course, he just pushes off the wall and starts for the elevators with a quick over the shoulder, "See you in the morning."

Oh, and I can't help but notice that the man's firm backside is like none other.

"Goodnight," I call back. "And, Jax?"

"Yeah?" he asks, turning around to walk backward with his hands in his pockets.

"Thanks for everything...you know earlier today?"

"Everything?" he asks with a cocky grin. Of course, I know right away that *he's* referring to what happened in the doctor's office.

"That, and your, um, offer," I say, my cheeks burning from the embarrassment of actually talking about it. "That's probably the second nicest thing anyone's ever done for me."

"Oh yeah? What's the first?" he asks, coming to a stop in the hallway.

"Well, this one time a guy answered my phone and set my hateful father and jerk fiancé straight with just a few stern words. I think they may have actually pissed themselves, which is pretty freaking hilarious."

"Sounds like they were assholes who deserved that shit," he says with a widening smile.

"They did. But now I'm all confused. A man I just met shouldn't treat me better than the two men who are supposed to love me unconditionally."

"Being more decent than those two isn't a hard thing to accomplish, even for a jackass like me."

"Guess not," I agree sadly.

...

Jax

Heading back downstairs in a thankfully empty elevator, I'm still thinking about Page. The damn woman is making me go soft. I never

JAX

expected her to say she didn't actually *want* to go to law school. What kind of parent doesn't let their kid choose their own career?

Hearing that makes me thankful that our dad's always been so supportive. Most parents would hate having not one but two sons that fight for a living. Not him. Dad's always encouraged us to do what makes us happy, even more so after he became a single parent.

While Jude and I are trying to relax and gamble a little in the casino, women keep approaching us, practically shoving their tits in our faces or rubbing their asses on us. I've never understood until now how Jude resisted the constant temptation. After meeting Page and getting charged with rape, I see the sluts for what they are; faceless, brainless bodies to fuck for a few minutes, only to be forgotten seconds afterward. What a waste.

Page is classy and beautiful, so damn smart, unintentionally funny and an OCD perfectionist. And kissing her in that damn doctor's office? I don't think I've come that fast since I was a horny teenager. I swore to myself that shit wouldn't happen again. So now I'll only have the memories of the sexy sounds Page made, and how good it had felt having her hands on me to haunt me like nightmares. She's got me wishing for things I can never fucking have. It's like being trapped in hell while staring into heaven. It's so fucking close but always just out of reach.

God, I want more of her. Since when did I become a rule follower anyway? Probably since I met someone worth keeping them for.

...

The next day we all hang out around the pool since none of us want a repeat of yesterday's angry attack of sea life. The salt water would probably burn Page's stings like a motherfucker, too. She stays unusually quiet, not just with me but with Jude and my dad as well. I think they notice her withdrawal since no one seems very talkative. After the last few days, she's sort of become a part of our family, and it's been nice actually having a woman's presence mingling with the three of us for the first time in seventeen long years.

"So what's the plan for tonight?" Jude asks. "*Ego?*"

"He has the biggest," Page mutters softly, nodding to me. She's sunbathing next to me, lying on her back with her dark sunglasses covering her eyes.

"Yes he does, but I was actually asking if you want to go to *Ego* tonight. You know, the nightclub here?" Jude asks.

"You kids have fun shaking your asses," Dad says before he gets up from his lounge chair. "I'm turning in early."

"Can I drown in fruity drinks and gamble there too?" Page asks after my dad walks off, getting to a sitting position in her lounger. Today's cock tease consists of a black and hot pink polka dot material that barely covers the four gorgeous areas of her body.

"Sure can," Jude assures her.

"Then I'm in," she says. "Although, we should probably go soon and turn in early since we have court tomorrow."

Goddamn, I hate the reminder of that fucking guillotine blade hanging over my head.

"So we'll go at seven? Call it a night maybe around eleven?" Jude asks, looking between Page and me.

"Why do you even want to go?" I ask him. "It's not like you're gonna pick up any women."

"I can't go hang out and have fun with my brother and his attorney?" Jude scoffs. "Page will dance with me, won't you?"

"Sure, although, just to warn you, I have the rhythm and coordination of a newborn baby fawn," she tells him with a smile.

Screech.

That was the sound of my teeth meeting at the thought of his or anyone else's hands on Page.

"No way." Jude snickers. "I bet you're more like a baby giraffe since you're so tall."

"I'm in," I agree. If I'm there, no one will touch her, not even myself.

...

An hour later the three of us are sitting at the bar in *Ego* ordering a round of drinks. When I'm training for a fight, I usually avoid alcohol, but since I'm not and have no idea how long before that may ever happen again, I decide to go with a bottle of *Budweiser Select*. Page is throwing back drinks as quick as the bartender sets them down. Jude's staying sober, because, well he's only twenty.

"Woohoo, let's dance!" Page exclaims, sliding off her barstool and heading for the dance floor. It's early, so there's not a lot of people on the floor yet. Page doesn't seem deterred by that or act intimidated by all the attention on her.

"This should be fun," Jude says with a smile before he follows her.

I'm working really hard on trusting my brother on the whole Page issue, but it's still not easy to see the two wrapped around each other like pretzels, grinding to the beat of the loud music. The woman lied, she can dance, or at least she can move her hips in a way that's sexy enough to make me pant from a hundred feet away.

Tonight she's wearing a white strapless dress that makes her glow under the black lights of the dark club. She doesn't go unnoticed by the guys in attendance, either. That would be impossible with her perfect curves and long, gorgeous legs. Her blonde hair is styled in one single braid that falls over her right shoulder, and I'm sure I'm not the only one thinking about how I'd like to wrap it around my fist and yank on it while fucking her from behind.

With her back to me, I can tell that Jude's at least keeping his hands above the belt, so I probably won't break them. Page's arms are wrapped around his neck, reminding me of how'd they'd felt yesterday when they were around me.

The longer I sit at the bar, the more I wonder why the fuck I'm torturing myself. I should just go back to my room and...what? The fact that I'm less miserable here, watching the woman I want but can't have dance with my brother than I would be if I weren't here, is disturbing. If I leave, I'll drive myself insane wondering who she's dancing with, how they touch her, and if she's going back to some random guy's room with him. Her fiancé seems to be far from her mind. The thought shouldn't make me as happy as it does. The asshole doesn't deserve her. She hasn't mentioned anything about him this weekend, but she's bound to have heard from him. Does he care that she's here? Is she going to wise up and end things with that asshole?

While I'm arguing with myself, Jude walks back up, swiping at the sweat running down his forehead.

"Can I get a water?" he asks the bartender.

"Where's Page?" I ask, looking back out on the floor.

"Chill, she's in the bathroom, probably mopping up her own sweat," he replies. "Did you see the woman's moves? She was trying to kill me."

"Mm-hmm," I mutter, unable to stop myself from seeking her out anyways.

After Jude guzzles half of his glass of water, he turns to me, and asks, "So, you just gonna sit here all night like a bump on a log?"

"Maybe."

"Well, don't expect her to...uh-oh," he gasps.

"What?" I ask, following his gaze across the room.

"I'm not sure, but...is that Page?" he asks.

"Where?"

"On top of that table?"

On a table? What the fuck?

A sexy woman in a white dress is dancing provocatively on a mini-circular stage off to the side of the dance floor. I don't know whether I want to jerk her off there and throw her over my shoulder, or, well...keep watching. Knowing I'm not the only one watching is what seals the deal on my decision.

I take off in her direction, pissed at her for letting other guys see her this way, and incensed that I even fucking care. Why does this woman affect me like this? Is it because I'm just horny and want to fuck her? No, it's more than that. As I watch her gyrate several feet up in the air, I realize that she means more to me than a quick fuck. I'm driven by this unfamiliar need to just be near her and take care of her. And hell, in return I think I actually want her to take care of me. Not that I'd ever admit that shit to anyone.

It's becoming clear from my viewpoint that Page either isn't wearing any panties, or they are minuscule since her ass is practically hanging out. I can't help but wince when I see the jelly sting welts.

"What happened to your sweet little ass, baby?" the jackass next to me asks Page loud enough to be heard over the music.

"Jellyfish," she yells back.

"I bet I could kiss it and make it better," the Jersey Shore wannabe says.

"I bet I could leave you permanently disabled before you can blink," I warn him.

His eyes widen when he finally faces me. Page is taller than this shrimp. Without another word, he turns and leaves.

"Go away, Jax," Page shouts without turning around, her arms still moving above her head, her hips fucking hypnotic.

"Page," I yell over the music, trying to get her attention. "Page!"

No response. I thought we could do this the easy way, I'd ask her to get down, she'd agree, and we'd be good. I should've known better after the three drinks she downed in the span of five minutes.

"Page, get your ass down!"

"No!" she shouts. "Stop scaring guys away, you big jerk!"

Fine, if she won't come down then I'll go up since I can't yank her down by her ankle without hurting her. I grip the edge of the small stage, pulling myself up on it, and then get to my feet.

Finally doing what I've wanted to all night, I grab Page's hips and pull her flush against me, wedging my knee between her legs.

"W-what are you doing?" Page stutters or slurs as her body stiffens up.

"Dancing with you," I whisper against her ear.

"Why?" she asks. "So no one else can?"

"Yes."

Finally relaxing, she wraps her arms around my neck.

Page

The room feels like it's spinning around me, but I'm not sure if it's an effect of alcohol or Jax's close proximity.

His warm, hard body is pressed tightly against mine, and he smells so freaking good. Even though I have no clue why he decided to climb up here and dance with me, I take advantage of the moment and lay my head on his shoulder. Jax's arms around me tighten in response like he approves. I never know with him. This whole weekend has felt like a crazy, emotional roller coaster. At the moment I can feel us teetering at the top, right before the sudden drop-off.

"I like the braid," he says against my ear. "But I'd give anything to see you with your hair down."

I'm taken aback and not sure how to respond to his statement. There's no doubt in my mind that I'm deep into conflict of interest territory. I haven't told Jax yet, but tomorrow I'll go to court with him and give a limited notice of appearance just for his arraignment. After that, I have no choice but to bow out and let another attorney take over his case. I'll still help out, doing what I can, but I'm not capable experience wise or emotionally to represent him in his trial. I have another small reason for withdrawing, although I'm not getting my hopes up that anything will happen between us once I'm no longer representing him.

"I'm thinking about turning over your case to someone else," I eventually get my nerve up and tell Jax. He goes still, and I brace myself for his reaction.

"No."

I wait for more, but nothing else follows. That's it? Just no?

"Um, yes, I am."

"No," he says pushing me back to see my face. "I need you to get me through this."

"But-"

"No buts," he says, cutting me off. "Don't even think about it."

"There's a conflict, Jax-" I start and he interrupts.

"Look, Page, *nothing* is ever going to happen between the two of us, so there's no reason for you to quit."

Whoa! His words are like a slap to my face. "Then what the heck are you doing up here with me? I'm not an idiot. I know what a hard cock feels like."

"That-that's just biology, plain and simple. And maybe I'm up here with you because I don't want to see my attorney get hammered and then fucked over by some asshole the night before I have court."

I gasp at his insinuation that I would do something stupid to jeopardize his case. That's why I'm trying to get out of it.

"Screw you, Jax," I say, even as my eyes start to sting. I turn around to sit on the platform and jump down to the dance floor. I can't stand to look at that infuriating man another second.

"Whoa, Page, what's wrong?" Jude asks as I storm past him and head for the elevator bank. I dive into one just before the door shuts, but Jude's right behind me and strong arms it open to slide in at the last second.

"I really wish you didn't look so much like your brother," I tell him before a stupid tear trickles down my cheek.

"Sorry," Jude says. "I put the blame completely on our parents."

Ignoring the three other people on the elevator with us, he pulls me in for a hug and a few more tears escape.

"What'd my pain in the ass brother do now?" he asks.

"He doesn't want me, even if I get out of the case," I say softly into his shirt.

"I find that very hard to believe," he replies. "He never takes his eyes off of you. I'm telling you, Page, he's seconds away from slamming you against a wall and fucking you."

"Jude!" I exclaim before apologizing to the other hotel guests. I'm more than thankful when we get off on the eighth floor.

"It's true," he says as we walk down the hall to our rooms.

"Only because he's horny and I've been throwing myself at him."

"Ha!" He barks out a laugh. "Okay, I know my own brother. If Jax were horny, he would've been fucking women all weekend. Last night he turned down so many I lost count."

"He did?" I ask in surprise. "Well, I'm sure it's because of his trial. He's trying not to get caught in any more drama."

"Do you really think that would stop him? I don't. He's hung up on you, and no one else will do. I can tell by the way he completely ignores other women. That's not Jax. Usually, he'll size up every room he enters trying to decide who he wants to fuck. There are always more choices than Baskin Robbins, but lately, it's you and only you."

I shake my head and stop outside my door to pull my keycard from my cleavage.

"That was a really awesome thing to witness," Jude jokes. "Now go get some sleep and then tomorrow act like you could care less about him. It'll drive the arrogant bastard crazy. Watch and see, I'll bet you a pack of double stuffed Oreos that I'm right," he says with a smile.

"You're on," I agree. "Goodnight, Jude."

"'Night."

CHAPTER NINE

Page

After a weekend of drinking, sunbathing, and gambling, all while enduring the presence of the hottest man on the planet telling me he doesn't want me, I can't wait to go to court and get this over with.

It's early Monday morning, and I'm ready right on time. I grab my keycard and shoulder bag, then head for the lobby to meet up with the guys to head to the courthouse. I'd just pulled my room door shut when I hear my name.

"Page?" Jax says from behind me, causing me to jump.

"Sheesh, you scared me!" I tell him, turning around to face the man who had just given me a freaking heart attack. No, wait, I think seeing him in a dark suit, crisp white dress shirt and blue tie might be what actually does me in. The man is gorgeous in jeans and a tee, but in a suit, *Lord have mercy*.

"Goddamn," Jax mutters, his eyes roaming over my sleeveless cerulean dress that's a little more slutty than professional, but I want to look good for all the judgmental talking head pricks. Oh, and how cute, the two of us match yet again.

"I'm about to be broadcast and talked about across the country," I explain, running my fingers through the long curls that took me forever to get just right. I didn't wear my hair down for him, I just wanted to do something different with it.

"Were you going for the Instant Boner Professional Chic look?" he asks, making me laugh. "If so, you nailed it."

"Funny, but that's enough, Jax," I warn him. "You've got to stop looking at me like that, too. Cameras are going to be watching your every little move today."

"And how exactly am I looking at you?" He stalks forward like a hungry predator until he's only a foot away from me.

"I don't know, just ...*that* way," I say, gesturing in the general direction of his face.

"What way?" he asks innocently, contradicting that notion when his tongue wets his bottom lip. "Like you're a berry flavored *Tootsie Roll* pop, and I want to yank your...wrapper off to find out *exactly* how many licks it takes to get to your center?"

My breath whooshes out of my lungs, and my blood is boiling. I'm so hot I'm melting from the inside out.

"Um, yeah, I was thinking more along the lines of you licking the bottom of a *Ben & Jerry's* container but your, ah, *Tootsie* pop analogy works pretty well too," I ramble, pushing my hair nervously behind an ear and keeping my eyes on the carpet instead of on his liquid lava pools. "Either way, you need to um, stop because it's...inappropriate, and the, ah...the paparazzi will flip out..."

"Then we better do something about it before we get to the courthouse."

I lift my head in confusion, and his heated stare fogs up my brain even more arousal than his naughty words.

"Ah, what?" I ask.

I gasp when my back suddenly hits the room door. Jax's massive, carved from granite body is pressed deliciously against mine before I even notice he'd moved. His erection pokes all thick and hard into my abdomen, and I barely suppress a needy whimper. My traitorous arms wrap around his back, pulling him even closer to smell his clean, masculine scent.

"I'm thirty seconds away from finding out just how many licks of my tongue it'll take to get you off. If I can do it in less than fifty, you're going to fuck me. Less than forty, you're going to suck me. Deal?" he asks while brushing his lips over my ear. I can't think with him rubbing both of his warm hands slowly up the back my thighs, underneath my dress, and I realize I've been holding my breath.

"Yes," I moan in an exhale when a shiver causes my body to undulate against his, pulling a groan from Jax that I feel rumble out of his chest.

"Key?"

"What?" I ask uncomprehending.

"Come on, Page. I need your room key now before I drop to my knees and go down on you right here in the middle of this fucking hallway."

"Oh," I reply in understanding with another shiver, then reach into my briefcase to pull the plastic card out with a shaky hand. Jax jerks it from me and does it himself when I take too long. A second later my feet leave the floor, and he's carrying me inside my room, the door slamming shut behind us.

"Wait," I say flattening a palm to his heaving chest. Jax freezes but then puts me down. My bag falls from my shoulder to the floor, forgotten. "I thought...you said you weren't interested..."

"I'd fail that polygraph because I was lying like a motherfucker," Jax says.

"I don't want to just be a means to an end because you're horny," I tell him.

"I'm desperate for you and only you, princess," he replies, making my knees even weaker. Picking me back up he doesn't stop again until he's lowering me to the bed, his lips crashing down on mine an instant before our tongues caress each other's, hot and urgent. One of his hands goes under my dress, yanking my panties down and flinging them to the floor.

"Start counting," he says when he slides down my body and spreads my thighs wide open.

The first lick of his wet tongue on my flesh has my hips levitating off the mattress and a cry of pleasure escaping my throat.

"Count or I'll have to stop after each one to do it for you," he warns.

"Wh-one," I force myself to say so he'll keep going. "Oh God, two. *Three!* Yes!" I'm about to combust from the incredible ecstasy pumping through my body caused by his rapidly swirling tongue. "Four, five, six, *ohhh seven!*" My entire body shakes from the building pressure. It's almost too much for me to handle, but the tight grip of his hands on my thighs hold me captive.

"EIGHT! *Oh, fuck!*" I yell to the ceiling and thrash when his fingers penetrate me while he keeps lapping at me. It's too good. Too much. "Nine! *Oh Godddd, nine.* TEN, eleven, twelve! Ah! Thirteen! Four... AH YES!" is the last coherent thought I have when my orgasm tears through me like a hurricane, leaving nothing but complete destruction behind. Instead of stopping, Jax keeps right on going. It's like he's finally speaking the native tongue of my pussy, the one it's been craving and needing my whole life. The next time I come I yell out Jax's name in praise and gratitude rather than a number.

"Oh shit, I can't move a muscle," I tell him when I can speak again. My thighs have fallen open, all modesty forgotten, and my arms are lying limply beside me.

"All I need is your mouth to move," Jax replies, his voice deeper than normal. Oh yeah, that was the other part of our deal and not one I mind accommodating at all.

I tilt my head to the side and watch as he stands up, unzips his suit pants and pushes them and his boxer briefs down in one shove. Holy moly, I'd forgotten how huge his cock is, protruding in my direction like a dangerous weapon.

I look up at Jax when he cradles the back of my head and brings it toward his body. My eyes stay on his as I lick my lips and open wide for him to shove his cock into my mouth.

"Ah fuck!" He groans when my lips seal around his length, sucking as I pull away.

I roll to my side and prop myself up on my elbow to find a better angle to take him deeper. Holding his cock by the base in a loose fist, my other hand drops down to caress his balls.

"Fuck, Page," he growls when I take him as deep as I can go. No sooner do I pull back than he's pulling my head forward again. I hum my approval as he works my mouth faster on his cock. "That feels fucking incredible," he says, and then he can't hold his hips back any longer. They thrust forward in contrast to the direction of his fingers tangling in my hair, forcing himself down my throat and making me moan with my mouth full.

"*Ahhh, God!* That's enough," he grumbles. "Page, stop." I look up at his face. His eyes are pitch black, his jaw clenched tight like he's that volcano again, about to explode. I give a slight shake of my head, indicating my intention. "Damn, woman...you're a fucking saint," he says, running his fingertips gently along my jaw while I continue to fill my mouth with his length. His entire body locks up a second before a choked off "*Ah, ah, ah*" sounds come flowing out of his mouth at the same time the thick, warm liquid runs down the back of my throat.

When I pull my mouth off of him, Jax sinks down to his knees beside the bed and reaches for me, pulling my mouth to his, weaving both of his hands through my hair. There's nothing gentle or soft about his tongue forcing its way into my mouth. It's a hot and possessive kiss, showing me how much he wants me.

If not for the knock on the door, we probably wouldn't have stopped until Jax was inside me.

Reality slams sharply back into focus. Shit...ake mushrooms, we have to get to court! What the hell was I thinking? Did I regret what we'd just done? Heck no, but it was still stupid all the same.

When our lips pull apart, Jax gets quickly to his feet and starts redressing while I sit up on the side of the bed and try to order my legs to hold me up when I stand. Even knowing I need to rush, I'm too relaxed and happy from the orgasms to get upset.

"Yo, Page?" Jude calls out from the other side of the hotel door. "Didn't you say we had to leave by eight-thirty? And have you seen Jax? We don't know where the fuck he's at. He was supposed to meet us downstairs, and he's not in his room or answering his phone."

Knowing it's just Jude makes me feel a little more at ease. I pick up my panties from the floor and duck into the bathroom to let Jax deal with him. I need a moment to put myself back together after having my world rocked.

...

Jax

I zip my pants and quickly tuck in my dress shirt before jerking Page's room door open.

"Oh," Jude mutters in surprise, his eyes widening when he stumbles backward a step. He's cleaned himself up a little nicer than his usual sweats, wearing a pair of khakis and a white polo shirt for court and the cameras. "Here you are. And damn, I have to say that pink is really *not* your color. Maybe try some red, it'll go better with your dark skin and hair."

"What the fuck are you talking about?" I ask, and unfortunately, I still sound like I just ran a few miles. I guess that's to be expected after Page just blew the fuck out of me. I almost groan aloud thinking about how sexy the woman was looking up at me while her mouth was full of my cock.

"I'm talking about your lipstick choice, bro. I know you want to look good for the cameras and all, but that's taking it a little too far, don't you think?"

"Shit!" I exclaim in understanding, glancing around for a napkin or tissue. I snatch some up from the hotel dispenser and head for the mirror over the dresser.

Son of a bitch. How much of the shit was Page wearing, and how come I didn't notice? There are probably pink rings around my cock too. I quickly dismiss that thought before all the blood can rush back down to investigate.

Jude follows me around the room, and I know he's waiting for an explanation. Tough titties.

"What time is it?" I ask him while I scrub my face. It's going to take some water to get this mess off, so I go back over to the kitchen sink to wet a towel.

"Eight-forty."

"Fuck!" I exclaim. "Page, we've got to go!"

"Shouldn't you be in a better mood? You know, after getting it in?" Jude asks.

"Watch your fucking mouth, and I didn't get it in," I bark, which is technically true since he interrupted before I could fuck her. Satisfied that all the lipstick is finally gone, I toss the napkins in the trash.

"Bullshit." Jude laughs. "You'd have me believe that you both lost track of time for something as important as *court*, and all you were doing was what...*kissing?*"

"I'm serious, Jude. Shut the hell up, and don't say a goddamn word about it outside of this room!"

"I know that, and I won't so calm the fuck down."

The bathroom door opens, and Page finally steps out. Other than her face being a little flushed, she looks just as perfect as she did before I attacked her. God, she's so fucking sexy, all that long, blonde hair streaming down over her shoulders while rocking that killer dress.

"Wheeewwww," Jude whistles. "Hot damn, Page! Now I know *exactly* why you two are running late. And you owe me some Oreos."

Oreos?

Pages smiles shyly as she moves through the room. "I know, double stuffed," she says to him, grabbing up her briefcase from where it hit the floor. "Ready?" she asks, finally making eye contact with me for the first time since before we were interrupted.

When she starts to turn away, I grab her waist and hold her in place so I can lean down and brush a soft kiss on her cheek. "You look gorgeous."

She blinks her big blue eyes up at me a second in surprise before she smiles and says, "So do you."

"All right, people, let's go!" Jude huffs at the delay.

After what we just did together...I don't want Page thinking it's just sex between us. That I just wanted to get off. She deserves more than that, and for the first time in my life, I actually want more than that.

"Yeah. Let's go," I agree, leading the way out the room to the elevator and hitting the down arrow.

"Are we okay?" Page asks softly to Jude. "Can you tell?"

"Other than your cheeks being a little pink, his lips looking redder than normal, and my cock being hard as a rock, we're fine."

"Thanks." She laughs as we step into the elevator and head for the lobby.

"Where's Dad?" I ask.

"He was getting the valet to bring the car around, so we should be able to leave as soon as we get down."

"Good."

When the door opens, we walk quickly to the front where our ride waits. At least the courthouse is only a few blocks over.

After Page climbs in the back, I shove Jude toward the front so I can sit with her.

"Really, Jax?" my dad grumbles as soon as everyone's in and all the doors shut.

"What?" I ask innocently.

"You know exactly what," he replies, maneuvering the car away from the curb. "You both better be damn careful."

"Remember, don't make any comments to the media, and let me talk if the judge or prosecutor asks any questions," Page says to me. It's impossible to look at her luscious mouth now without thinking about my cock in it. Her dress is riding up her thighs, and all I want to do is throw her down and fuck her until she screams my name again.

"Don't look at me," I tell her, adjusting the growing bulge in my pants.

"What?" she asks, glancing down at my hand on my cock.

JAX

"When I look at you...I can't help thinking about...earlier."

"Geez," my dad mutters, putting the signal on for the courthouse parking lot. I try not to stress about all the media vans lining the street.

"Oh God, everyone's going to know," Page mumbles, covering her face with both hands.

"Just forget about the polygraph and go back to treating me like I'm an angry asshole who is guilty."

"Yes! Okay, I'll try to do that." She nods.

"And I'll go back to treating you like a spoiled, elitist bitch."

"Hey!" she exclaims, whipping her head in my direction indignantly.

"This can work, see? You're such a pampered princess, thinking you're better than everyone."

Her eyes narrow at me when the SUV comes to a stop in a parking spot. "And you are a stubborn jerk who won't consider a plea deal even though it's your best chance of getting out of jail before your thirtieth birthday," she responds.

"I'm not fucking pleading!"

"Yeah, this is much better." She exhales. "We might be able to do this after all. You ready?"

Even though she just managed to royally piss me off, I still have to stop myself from reaching for her hand in comfort. Instead, I take a deep breath and open the car door.

I'm instantly greeted with cameras, microphones and questions being hurled at me faster than an MLB catcher.

"Excuse me," I say as politely as possible as I push my way through toward the courthouse entrance. I don't wait for Page, figuring it's best to keep my distance. When some of the reporters yell Jude's name to ask him questions, at least I know he's right behind me.

After we make it up the steps and through the front doors things calm down. There are more reporters roped off at the entrance, but no cameras allowed thankfully. My dad catches up with us, and we have to empty our pockets and go through a set of metal detectors. On the other side, I finally turn to find Page.

Talking to the horde of vultures she looks confident and composed with her shoulders squared and chin raised. She's so damn sexy it hurts.

"Look away," Jude mutters quietly beside me. I know he's right, so I turn my back to her.

"Let's go," Page says a minute later, not slowing down when she walks past us, her heels clicking loudly on the hard floor with her sure and purposeful stride. Of course, I follow her, right down the hallway and through the double doors of the courtroom. It's filled with people in every row, plenty of which seem to be fans who had actually made posters and shit. Huh, quickly reading a few of them, they all think I'm innocent. That's good to know.

Page finds some room for us on one of the front reserved rows and sits down with me beside her, and Jude and my dad on my other side. I can feel everyone's stares on the back of my head, or more likely on Page.

The raised bench where the judge usually sits is empty, but a man I assume is District Attorney Franklin begins yelling out a roll call of some sort.

"I'll answer for you," Page whispers under her breath.

I notice some of the people speak for themselves, others have attorneys who stand up and respond on their behalf.

Finally, he gets to the middle of the alphabet and calls, "Malone, Jackson."

"Present and represented by Page Davenport today," she says, and then retakes her seat.

"Today?" I ask since it sounded like she meant it might be someone else tomorrow.

"We'll discuss it later," she snaps under her breath, barely moving her mouth.

Damn right we would. She isn't bailing on me just because we'd gotten each other off.

Apparently, typical court administrative procedures are boring. After what feels like hours have passed, Judge Bray comes in, and DA Franklin eventually calls my name again.

"Let's go. Don't speak unless I okay it," Page reminds me before heading through the gate at the front of the bar, right up to a table on the left side. Page stands behind the first seat, so I stand behind the other one.

"Mr. Malone, you've been indicted by the Atlantic City Grand Jury on charges of First Degree Rape and Assault by Strangulation. Have you been informed of your right to counsel?" the judge asks.

"Yes, your Honor," Page barely mutters under her breath, and I repeat it.

"And have you retained your own counsel, or do you wish to have a court-appointed attorney assigned to your case?"

"I've retained my own counsel," Page coaches softly, and I echo.

"Your Honor, my name is Page Davenport of Davenport & Davenport, and I've been retained to represent Mr. Malone. If your Honor pleases, I'd like to give notice of my limited appearance on his behalf today."

Limited? Does that mean what I think it does?

"I beg your pardon Ms. Davenport, but I'm ready to proceed with Mr. Malone's arraignment today. I don't usually allow a case to go forward until the defendant has secured counsel ready to make a general appearance. So either you make a general appearance today, or we'll appoint counsel for Mr. Malone."

I don't know what all that means, but it must have freaked Page out because I hear her gasp, although probably no one else notices.

She looks down at the table for a second before her confidence returns. "Yes, your Honor. Then I will offer my general appearance on the record today so that we can proceed."

"Thank you, Ms. Davenport. Your appearance is noted for the record. Now, Mr. Franklin, we're ready to hear from the State."

"Yes, your Honor," Franklin, the District Attorney, says when he stands up at his table beside ours. "The defendant, Jackson Malone, has been indicted on charges of First Degree Rape and Assault by Strangulation. The Grand Jury found probable cause to believe that he did forcibly engage in vaginal and oral sex against the victim's will, and with the assistance of a dangerous weapon, more specifically, overpowering the victim using his superior strength to strangle her with his bare hands."

Holy shit that sounds bad.

"Does the defendant understand the charges as they have been stated against him?" Judge Bray asks.

"Yes, your Honor," Page replies.

"And at this time, how does the defendant plead?"

"He pleads not guilty, your Honor, and would like to proceed with a jury trial," she answers.

"Very well," the judge replies and then glances down in front of him. "Let's go ahead and calendar the case for the July seventh term of court. Any objections from the defendant or the state?"

"No, your Honor," Page responds.

"No objection, your Honor," District Attorney Franklin answers.

"Motions will be due two weeks from today, on June sixteenth, and all responses to motions are due three weeks from today, on June twenty-third. We'll have a hearing on any motions or allow for a change of plea on June thirtieth at nine a.m. Mr. Franklin, does the state wish to ask for another detention hearing?"

"No, your Honor. The defendant has already posted a fifty thousand dollar secured bond, and voluntarily appeared today, so at this time the State will not request detention."

Page lets out a breath, so I take that to be a good thing.

"All right. Let's move on. Mr. Franklin, call your next case."

Before I know it Page is already walking off toward the swinging gate without me. I follow, and she nods toward the back when she looks over at Jude and my dad, which I take to mean we're leaving. Thank fuck. This shit is stressing me the hell out.

When we step out into the hallway Page turns to me. "Go ahead on to the car with your dad and Jude. Don't talk to anyone or make any statements."

"What are you going to do?" I ask.

JAX

She digs in her briefcase and holds up a manila envelope. "I need to drop this off by the DA's office, then I'll meet you out there."

"You sure you'll be okay by yourself?" I ask.

"Yeah, it won't take but a second."

"I'd rather wait for you."

"Fine," she says through clenched teeth, then she takes off down the hall.

"Whew, glad that's over," Jude says from beside me.

"I'm sorry it was so goddamn stressful for you," I respond sarcastically.

"Both of you hush," Dad hisses. "Eyes and ears everywhere."

"Page will be right back then we can leave," I tell them.

"Incoming," Jude says before a herd of women converges on us with loud squeals and more *OMGs* than a teenager's text message log.

"I am such a huge fan," one of the blondes at the front says to me as she invades my personal space. "I know you're innocent, and the slut is lying about all that shit. Can I have your autograph?"

"Um, sure," I agree with a polite smile.

Handing me a black marker she holds out her shirt on which I scribble my name quickly across the bottom.

After her, they come one right after another wanting pictures or autographs. A few even give me phone numbers and offer to fuck me. It isn't unusual, but now it just feels...inappropriate. Every few seconds I scan the growing crowd of people until I finally spot Page. Annnd...based on her narrowed eyes and pursed lips, she looks pissed.

"Thank you all for your support," I say as I walk away from them, moving toward her.

"Ready?" I ask.

She narrows her blue eyes and turns away, starting toward the exit without a word.

"Jude!" I yell for him, and he extracts himself from a group of women. Hell, even my dad is talking to two older ladies.

I brace myself for what waits just outside and walk quickly through the parking lot, looking forward to getting away from this place and being alone again with Page. After we're in the car pulling away, I finally can't hold it in any longer.

"What the hell was that about?" I ask her.

"It doesn't matter. I'm stuck representing you now," Page replies, staring out her window. "And I told you to stay away from women, especially in the freaking courthouse!"

"Stuck representing me? That's nice fucking phrasing. You were trying to get out, weren't you?"

"I should withdraw. I *need* to withdraw. I'm clearly conflicted out."

"If you get out then I'm fucked," I tell her.

"I could still help with the case, just not try it. Ryan should be the one to try it anyways. I don't know what I'm doing, and I'm going to screw it all up," she says with a shake of her beautiful head.

I finally give into the urge and reach for her hand.

"There's no one that can do this better, so stop trying to bail on me."

"Then don't do this," she replies, pulling her hand out from under mine.

Motherfucker. She's gone back to ice princess mode. Screw that.

I hold my tongue on the way back to the hotel, through the lobby, and on the elevator. I don't say a word while I wait for Page to pull out her key card. Then it's on.

I press my body against her back and hear her gasp. Wrapping one arm around her waist, I run the other one up the front of her thigh, heading underneath her dress. Her entire body shivers, but she doesn't protest.

When the lights on the door finally flash green, I pull on the handle and lift her forward into the room to get us out of the hallway. As soon as her feet hit the floor, I yank her panties down and off so I can cup her bare pussy.

Her head falls back against my chest, and she moans when my fingertips graze along her slit. Feeling her wetness is almost enough to bring me to my knees.

I let go of her waist to work on the zipper running down her back, peeling the dress off of her, leaving her in nothing but a strapless bra and blue heels. The bra I quickly discard, but the heels, oh the heels can stay.

I rub my erection that's protruding angrily from my pants against her bare ass while filling my hands with her pussy and breast. She's getting closer, and my cock is about to bust its way out of my fly.

Page's body convulses and she whimpers through her orgasm before she goes limp. My arms are all that keep her upright.

Now that I have her good and relaxed, I know she'll be much more agreeable to keeping this two person party going. I pick her up and lay her down on the bed so I can get myself undressed.

With a faraway look in her eyes she watches my every move as I lose my suit jacket and shoes, then my pants with boxers, before finally ditching the hundred button dress shirt. I crawl up on the bed beside her, expecting her to second guess this and be timid. I've never been so happy to be wrong.

Page climbs on top of me, kissing me for all she's worth. My hands grip her ass greedily, grinding her against my hard cock until the fighter in me can't stand being on my back any longer. I flip our positions, putting her underneath me, and spread her thighs wider by wedging my knees between them.

"Please, Jax," she moans against my lips.

"Please, what?" I ask while moving my mouth down, tasting her delicious neck. Of course, I know what she wants, I just want to hear her say it.

"Fuck me," she says softly. "Please fuck me."

"Oh, I'm going to fuck you so damn good, princess," I assure her. "But only on two conditions. Look at me, Page," I order, waiting for her eyes to open. She finally blinks her cobalt blue eyes up at me. "Promise me that this," I motion my finger between the two of us, "isn't going to stop just because of the case, and promise me that you're going to be the one to take my case to trial no matter what."

"Jax..." she starts, avoiding my eyes like she's going to argue, but I know a way of persuading her. I slide down her body and nuzzle her pussy with my nose, making her squirm. I kiss her flesh softly with just my lips before letting my tongue snake out to wet her.

"Oh God!"

Hearing her cry out I go to work on her clit, easing two fingers inside of her at the same time. Just like this morning, her hips go wild, and her moans almost sound like she's in pain when she finally comes. Reaching down she tries to pull my body back up hers.

"I promise. Now fuck me, damn it!" she exclaims.

Smiling in triumph I head for my pants to grab the condom out of my wallet, and Page starts freaking out.

"Where are you going? I need you in me," she says, raising up and grasping my bicep with both hands, her expression almost frantic.

I can't help but cough out a laugh, seeing her so damn horny. "Can I get a condom first?" I ask.

"Oh. Okay," she says with an exhale and lets me go. This is going to be so fucking incredible.

After I have the condom from my wallet, I lay back down on the bed and offer it to her between my two fingers.

"Put it on, then saddle up and ride me, princess."

She tears the wrapper and places the latex circle on the tip of my cock to start rolling it down. The look of intense concentration on her face is almost comical, and I have to hold back my chuckle so I won't piss her off. When the condom is finally to her satisfaction, she throws her leg over my hips, straddling me. My sense of humor is lost when she holds my cock upright and eases her tight pussy down on it. The only thing sexier than a pissed off Page is a naked Page riding my cock like a cowboy's wet dream.

Unable to keep my hands off of her any longer I reach up and grab two handfuls of her breasts. Suddenly it's like a switch is flipped. The woman freezes before she starts scrambling off of me.

"What's wrong?" I ask.

"I can't do this," she says, climbing off the bed.

No, no, no. What the hell happened to my eager, horny Page?

"What are you talking about?" I ask, sitting up on the edge of the mattress.

"Why did you want me to fuck you like *she* did? In the same freaking hotel?" she yells, and then I curse when she pulls her dress back on. Wait, what is she talking about? *Oh shit*!

"Page, calm down and talk to me for a second, okay? I want to fuck you any way I can. With you on top, I can see your gorgeous body while we do it, that's the only reason I suggested it. Damn it, I didn't even think about her or the similarity because there is *none* between you and her."

"This is a bad idea," she mutters with her back to me.

"No, it's not. Stop overthinking things, take the dress off, and get back in bed with me so I can fuck some sense into you."

"Maybe after your case is over..." she starts, but I'm not going to let her pull away from me any further.

Coming off the bed, I launch myself at her, silencing her with my mouth so she can't talk any more nonsense. I jerk the damn dress off again and then I pick her up and carry her back to bed, covering her body with mine when I lay her out on the mattress.

Intertwining my fingers with hers, I pin them both above her head, holding her smaller ones with just one of mine. She spreads her thighs wider so I can fit against her body, and since I still have on the condom, I ease into her tight warmth.

Her back arches while her hips thrust against mine and she moans into my mouth. Pretty sure I've ended her doubts, I still want to know for sure.

"You okay?" I pull back to ask.

"Yes, don't stop," she says quickly before lifting her head to cover my mouth with hers again. Her legs lock around my waist, and when I feel her heels digging into my lower back, I start pounding into her with more force. I reach down and cup her ass, squeezing it while driving into her clenching pussy.

"Jax, oh shit, yes!" she breaks our kiss to throw her head back and moan, making me smile. The woman never says a single swear word until she's getting off.

"You close, baby?" I ask, not sure how much longer I can last. She feels too damn amazing.

"Yes!"

Letting go of her hands, I grab her thighs and press her knees to her chest, changing the angle and making her tighter.

"Oh fuck, Jax!" she exclaims when she squeezes my cock. I thrust my tongue into her mouth and shove deep inside her pussy to feel her walls quiver with her orgasm.

Page's arms go around my back holding me tightly while her body writhes underneath mine, and I lose it.

"Ah...ah, God!" I groan when every muscle in my body tenses on my next thrust and then shudders with pleasure. "Fuck, Page."

My hips rock slowly forward a few more times, trying to milk every last drop of ecstasy from my cock. I kiss her neck between pants, before moving down to her collarbone and then to one of her heavy breasts. I tongue her hard nipple and suck her soft flesh into my mouth, content and happy after finally doing what I've fantasized about so many times.

"Mmm, that was incredible," Page says softly, running her hands up and down my back. "Just like this morning."

"Hell yes, it was," I agree with a satisfied smile. Moving back up to her eye level, I like seeing all of the markings my mouth and beard have left on her pale chest and neck.

"Don't we have to check out in like," she raises her head to get a look at the clock. "Crap, five minutes?

I reach over to pick up the landline hotel phone and press zero without moving off of Page.

"Front desk," a woman answers.

"Hey, this is Jackson Malone. Can I keep the four rooms in my name for another night?" I ask while admiring Page's beautiful, flushed and very satisfied face below me.

"Sure, Mr. Malone. That won't be a problem since Monday's are our slowest occupancy day. I'll make the reservation for you right now."

"Great, thanks," I say, and then hang up the phone. "Nope, we don't have to check out until tomorrow at noon."

Page laughs underneath me. "So now what?" she asks.

I reach for the phone again and dial Jude's room number.

"Hello?" he answers.

"We're staying another night. Let Dad know."

He chuckles on the other end of the line. "And why would that be? So you can practice the rear naked choke hold with Page? Ask her if I can watch, you know for training purposes. Oh but, wait, you're probably just kissing each other, right?"

I hang up on him.

"Now we're going to stay here in this room for the next twenty-four hours. Shit!" I exclaim when I suddenly remembered something important. "Okay, after I grab some condoms we're going to stay right here, and I'm going to fuck you at least once on every surface in this room. You decide where you want it the next round, and I'll be right back." I reluctantly stand up, throwing away the used condom to start getting dressed.

"Jax, wait," Page stops me, sitting up on her elbows. "Maybe you ought to have Jude buy them, you know with the charges and all, and the media being so greedy to get dirt on you?"

"Hell, you're probably right." I grab my cell phone from my pants pocket to call him on his, this time in case he's already left his room to find Dad.

"Why are you calling me instead of mounting a beautiful blonde right now?" he answers.

"I need a favor. Can you go buy me some condoms?"

He laughs. "And what if I refuse?"

"Then I guess I'll have to, but we're trying to avoid bad press."

"I'll think about it."

"Jude!"

"Kidding. I'll go," he huffs.

I let out my breath in relief. "Thanks. Box of Magnum Thins. At least a dozen, not a skimpy three pack."

"TMI, man, and you're going to fucking owe me for this."

"I know," I respond before hanging up and climbing back into bed with the gorgeous, naked woman watching me.

"A dozen?" Page asks with a smile. "A little optimistic of you, don't you think?"

"I know three wouldn't be enough. Six probably won't be either," I assure her. "Are you hungry? I can call in something."

"Not for food," she says, reaching down to stroke my semi-hard cock back to life. I brush my lips over hers and kiss her softly, holding myself back from entering her by only a thin thread until there's a knock on the door.

"Finally," I say. Jumping up I grab a towel from the rack in her bathroom and wrap it around my hips before yanking the door open.

It's not Jude.

"Oh, um, they told me this was Page's room," Elliot, the bastard, stammers in surprise.

Holy. Fucking. Shit.

Other than his eyes widening in surprise, he looks the same as he did out in front of Page's office a few nights ago. He smooths his hand nervously over his brown, side sweeping politician haircut.

"Well...it was. But, um, her whirlpool didn't work so we switched," I quickly come up with the lie. "She's in the next room over now, eight-twenty." I give him my room number.

"Really?" he asks, looking over my shoulder into the room. I know he can't see the bed from this angle, thank fuck. I can tell by the narrowing of his eyes that he wants to call bullshit and storm past me into the room, but he won't because he's a pussy. Or he's just smart because he knows I'd kick his fucking ass for even trying.

"Yeah, but after we got back from court, I think she went down to the spa to get a massage or some shit," I further the lie to try and get rid of him before he pushes the issue and I fuck up my pretrial release with a new assault charge.

"Oh, right. I'll try to find her there," he says, and then thankfully, he heads back to the elevator bank, rubbing the back of his neck and looking up and down the hall.

As soon as the door shuts, Page is up and dressing. "Crap, crap, crap. Quick, go get your things and bring them in here, and then give me your key."

There goes the most awesome day of my life, right down the motherfucking drain.

"Here, they gave me two," I tell her, grabbing one of the keys from my pants pockets and offering it to her. "Are you going to tell him to leave?"

"I'm going to try. He can't find out about us, or he'll turn me in!" she exclaims while grabbing her bags, that were thankfully already packed since we'd planned to check out when we got back from court. "Hurry!" she instructs me.

Fucking son of a bitch.

I throw my clothes back on then start the room swap, grabbing my bags from the other room and dragging them to the new one.

I should've told the bastard I'd just fucked his fiancée and been done with it, but Page was right. If she pissed him off, he'd rat her out to the State Bar.

After Page is gone to settle in her new room and wait for the asshole to return, I sit on the edge of the rumpled bed and look around, wanting to break everything in this damn room in anger and annoyance. Then Jude actually knocks on the door. I go yank the door open and let him in without a word.

"You sure do have a lot of clothes on to be fucking."

I walk back over and sink down on the unmade bed, my elbows digging in my knees while I cover my face in frustration.

"Where's Page?" he asks.

"In her new room, which is my old one."

"Oh-kay?"

"Elliot just showed up."

"Who the fuck is Elliot?" he asks.

"Page's fiancé."

"Ohhh."

"I opened the door, thinking it was you. Thank God he didn't see her in here."

"So I guess you won't be needing these?" he asks with a smirk, holding up the brown bag.

"I need to punch something."

"Wanna head to the gym?"

"Might as well," I agree with a sigh. "Just give me a second to change."

CHAPTER TEN

Page

I quickly shower and then dress in some cotton shorts and a t-shirt. I scatter a few of my things around Jax's room to make it appear like I've been here more than five minutes. I can't help but notice that his room is not nearly as nice as mine. Then there's nothing for me to do but wait for the inevitable.

I've just pulled my laptop out and sat it down on the desk to look busy when there's a knock on the door. Here we go.

Yanking it open I pretend to be shocked by his presence. "Elliot? What are you doing here?"

"I thought I'd surprise you. I was driving back through from my meeting in New York and figured I could give you a ride home. When's check out?"

"Oh, well we decided to stay another night."

"Why?" he asks, and I don't miss the tick in his jaw.

Think quickly. Think quickly. "To talk to one of the employees, a potential witness, who doesn't come into work until tonight."

"Oh." I'm pretty sure he bought my lie.

"So I bet you're in a hurry to get home. You don't have to wait for me."

"Not that big of a hurry," he says, reaching for my hip.

I quickly swat his hand away. After I've slept with Jax, he deserves to know the truth. Well, a partial truth. "Elliot, I've been thinking, and um, I don't want to do this anymore."

"Do what?" he asks.

"This. Us. I'm not...I don't want to marry you."

"What the hell are you talking about?" He walks past me, moving farther into my room and looking around, so I let the door close.

"I don't want to be with you anymore," I say softly to his back.

"So what, you're breaking up with me?" he asks when he whirls around, his voice growing louder, his face turning redder. "What the hell is going on, Page? Is fucking around with your client that damn good?"

"I didn't fuck my client," I lie with as much conviction as possible.

"Bullshit!" he yells before jerking down the collar of my shirt, exposing my breasts. "Where'd all those fucking marks come from, you lying bitch?"

"Elliot, stop. You...you need to leave," I stutter, trying to pull away and get his hands off me.

The next thing I know my left cheek is stinging painfully, and he's forcing me backward, down onto the bed, his hands wrapping tightly around my neck.

"Is this what he does to you? Is this what you like now?" he growls as his face contorts above mine in anger. My hands start clawing at his, my nails digging into his flesh while I bring my knees up to my chest trying to keep him off of me. He doesn't budge.

Realizing I'm completely powerless to stop Elliot I do the only thing I can think of.

"Jax!" I scream his name, hoping I'm loud enough for him to hear me through the thin walls. Then the room starts darkening, and I feel myself drifting off, my body going limp.

When I come to again Elliot's hands are gone from me. I cough and gasp lungs full of desperately needed oxygen. I finally manage to sit up and find Jax on the ground, on top of Elliot, hitting him over and over again while Jude tries to pull him off. My hearing finally starts coming back to the sounds of flesh meeting flesh, and Jax's loud cursing.

"Jax!" I try to yell, but my voice is too hoarse. And I had to say, after what just happened, it is kind of satisfying to see Elliot getting beat half to death. Finally, Jax eases up and lets Jude pull him away.

Chest still heaving, Jax stands up and comes around the bed to my side. He rubs his thumb gently over my sore cheek and then his fingertips trace down along the sides of my neck. "Are you okay?" he asks, his dark eyes still sizzling like hot lava after his eruption. I nod, and he pulls me against him, his arms going comfortingly around me. I let myself melt into his warmth for just one peaceful second.

"Camera. Record now," I say softly against his chest. Reaching into his pocket, Jax pulls his phone out with one hand and brings up the video application, hitting record. Keeping the phone out of sight he holds it against his leg.

"What the hell is wrong with you?" Jude asks with a kick to Elliot, who's still on the floor. "Were you trying to fucking kill her?"

Elliot sits up, his face bloody, glaring daggers at me or Jax, maybe both. "You're fucking done, Page! I'm reporting your ass to the Bar, and you'll never practice again."

"You do what you think you need to do," I say calmly for the recording. "And I'll do what I need to do, get a warrant against you for attempted murder. It'll be really hard for you to win elections from prison."

"No one will believe you."

"Look at her fucking neck!" Jax yells at him. "Your handprints are still on it!"

"I'll tell the police it was you. That you choked her, and she lied and blamed it on me because she was fucking you!"

"Jude and I just had to pull you off of her because she was passing the fuck out. It'll be the three of us against you."

"I've got better lawyers," Elliot replies, swiping a hand over his oozing lip and staring down at the blood. "She's fucking you, and he's your brother, both worthless witnesses."

"What if we hadn't been next door and heard Page scream for help? What if I didn't have a key to get in? Would you have killed her, then blamed that shit on me, too?"

"Probably," Elliot finally admits.

"Well, then it's a good thing we've got your confession recorded," I tell him.

"What the fuck are you talking about?" he snarls.

"Say cheese motherfucker, you're on candid camera," Jax tells him, showing him the phone. "And damn, I fucked your face up. If you ever lay a hand on her again you won't walk away. They'll have to carry your ass off on an ambulance, probably to the morgue."

"Did you just threaten me on video?"

"Yeah I did! You could've killed her, you dumb son of a bitch. If you're not smart enough to learn from this lesson then the next time you'll pay for it. Now get the fuck out of this room, and if you say one goddamn word to *anyone* about her or me, this video goes live for all your constituents to see."

Pulling himself up on the foot of the bed, Elliot finally gets to his feet, cupping a hand over his still bleeding nose. "This isn't over," he warns before finally leaving.

"Jesus Christ!" Jude exclaims, coming over to examine me closer. "This is what fucking being strangled looks like right after it happens." He and Jax both take pictures of my neck with their phones while it's fresh.

"You alright?" Jude asks. "You sure you don't want to call the police?" I nod, even though my eyes begin to water. The reality of the situation is finally starting to hit me. "I'll head on out. Let me know if you need anything, okay?" he says. I nod again.

After he's gone, Jax stretches out on the bed and pulls me against his chest. I can't hold it in any longer. My tears turn into messy, embarrassing sobs on the front of his shirt, but Jax doesn't comment, he just tries to comfort me.

Everything is going to hell, all because I crossed a line I shouldn't have.

"Shhh. It's okay," Jax says against my hair. "That was some seriously scary shit. All I keep thinking about is that Jude and I were about to leave. If we hadn't...if he'd...God, I hate that bastard so much."

I nod my agreement.

"Look, he's not going to say anything, you know that, right?"

"Yes. But someone will," I tell him "Eventually. And we won't have blackmail on them."

"Then we'll be careful," he assures me.

I shake my head. "It's too dangerous."

Jax loosens his grip to pull back. "What are you saying?"

"Can we just stay here and hideout until my neck heals? I don't want anyone seeing it and accusing you of doing this. Then we can go home, but this stops until after your trial."

"I want more than that, but I get it. If that's what you want then... okay. But I'm going to try and change your mind over the next few days," he says with a smile.

CHAPTER ELEVEN

Jax

Page is sitting at her desk across from me in her office, asking me a million questions. They're basic questions we know the prosecutor will likely ask me at trial, and Page wants to work on my "attitude."

"How many women have you slept with?"

"Huh?" I ask, lost in thought remembering how damn good it was to sleep with the woman in front of me. "He can ask me that?"

"Maybe. I'd like to know for curiosity's sake," she says with a shrug and a blush.

"A lot. More than a lot. I don't exactly keep a running tally."

"God, Jax! That's...that's disgusting!"

"Hey, I didn't hear you complaining."

"Definitely regretting that slip in my judgment," she mutters under her breath.

"Hey!" I scoff.

It's been weeks since I last woke up with Page in my arms, both of us naked, going at it before our eyes ever open, more times than we could count. It had been the best few days of my life, being able to get to know Page and just be together. Her dad had called and left a few messages, which I could tell upset her. So one afternoon while Page was in the shower I'd listened to the messages. Her dad bitched about her breaking up with Elliot and how she needed to make amends with him. I called Miles Davenport back on my phone and informed him that the asshole almost killed Page and then sent him the video as proof. Page still hasn't figured out why her father is suddenly sweeter than honey to her, even though he has to know what the two of us are up to and how it could end Page's career.

So yeah, I'd been on top of the world sharing every second with an incredibly gorgeous woman. A woman I'm pretty sure I'm falling in love with, something I didn't think was even possible. But then we had to return to the real world where attorneys and their clients can't fuck. That brief taste of heaven was just enough to drive me insane, desperate to have it again.

"If the prosecutor asks, give a vague answer like, 'a couple a month for the past few years.' Nothing more specific," Page says, bringing me back to our trial prep.

"Got it," I reply with a wink. "So, princess, how many guys have you been with?"

"Just four," Page says to me on an exhale.

"And those four include the jackass senator and me?" I ask in surprise.

"Uh-huh."

"Wow." I laugh.

"Hey, I'm proud of the fact that I'm not a whore."

"Unlike me?" I offer.

"You're not really a whore since you don't get paid. So you're more like a manslut."

"Oh, well, thank you for that distinction, princess."

"Just trying to be accurate. So, moving on, tell me about your childhood."

"Why do you need to know about that shit?" I snap. I realize I've probably been more caustic than necessary when Page actually flinches in her seat. The topic is just not one that's up for discussion.

"The prosecutor will want to know if you got into any trouble when you were a juvenile. Any sort of sexual act or violence in your youth might be deemed relevant. I don't want any surprises."

"I can assure you that my juvie record consists only of assaults. On other boys."

"Why'd you get into fights with other boys?" she asks with a tilt of her head.

"Because they said shit that pissed me off."

"What'd they say?"

"That's none of your fucking business!" I snarl.

"What the heck, Jax? You snap like that in the courtroom, and you're going to end up behind bars!" Page exclaims, standing up from her desk and pointing to the door. "Get out of my office, and don't come back until you can go more than five minutes without being a complete jerk!"

I stand up and start for the exit, telling her over my shoulder, "Then you probably won't ever see me again!"

I know I'm more cranky than usual. It's been two weeks since I laid a finger on Page, after getting to fuck her rocking body seven ways to Sunday for five long days in Atlantic City. The withdrawals are only getting worse instead of better. There's only one other way to burn off the horniness - hit the gym and hit it hard.

After I change into a pair of shorts, I go find Jude. He's always at the gym.

"Cage?" I ask when I find him hitting a long bag.

"Hell yes," he answers, rolling his shoulders back. Other than the heavyweights, he's the only one that will go at it with me. Pussies.

Hands wrapped up, gloved and ready, Coach Briggs is all set to ref for us. Basically, he just tells us what we suck at. "Alright, I want a good, clean fight. Touch gloves, then on my signal."

We bump gloved fists and then it's on like *Donkey Kong*. My baby brother is a fast son of a bitch, so I have to swing twice as many times as

I do with other guys to actually hit him. Fortunately for me, if you swing enough times you'll finally land one. Sometimes one is all it takes. Not today. Jude takes the body shot in stride. He lands a few painful leg kicks on me since he's always been better at those, but eventually I sweep his feet out from under him. Once I mount him, he doesn't have anywhere to go, and since I outweigh him, that means he's left taking a face full of my fists, one right after the other. He tries to block them for a while, but when he can't hold his gloves up in front of his face any longer, I call it quits.

"You're done," I tell him through the mouth guard.

"Bring it!" he responds. He always was a glutton for punishment.

"I would have called it anyways, Jude. You weren't protecting yourself worth a shit," Coach tells him. "You should've tried to get Jax off his feet from the get-go."

I stand up, leaving Jude laid out on the canvas.

"Who's next?" I yell to the other boys in the gym.

"You and Page have a fight?" Jude asks once his mouth is free of plastic.

"No."

"Yeah you did. What'd you do this time?" he asks, still flat on his back.

I yank my mouthpiece out to respond. "I may or may not have yelled at her."

"And let me guess, she didn't deserve it?"

"No, of course not. Then she kicked me out of her office. Told me not to come back until I can go five minutes without being a jerk."

"I guess you'll never see her again." He laughs.

"That's what I told her."

"How's the whole, not fucking her until after the trial thing going?" he asks.

"Absolutely awesome."

"Sounds like it."

"Not that you'd know anything about that, right? Still carrying your V-card, little bro?"

JAX

Jude finally gets to his feet but still looks worn the fuck down with his shoulders slumped in defeat. He has to curl his gloved fingers around a hole in the cage just to keep himself upright. I've told the boy he spends way too much time in this damn gym. He needs to get a life outside of this place.

"You know, maybe if you didn't make everything about fucking, Page might tolerate you a little more."

"Actually, if I didn't make everything about fucking, the woman wouldn't have anything to do with me. Getting her all worked up is the *only* way she tolerates me."

"Then maybe she needs some 'working up' to get through the next few weeks with your dumb ass," Jude remarks. "That or a million dollars might be enough compensation for having to put up with you."

"We can't go out in public," I remind him.

"Oh, that's right," he says with a face-palm to his own forehead. "Because out in public is where everyone goes to fuck. Go to her place, you dipshit."

That's a hell of an idea. If I show up at her place, will she slam the door in my face or let me fuck her? She'd said not to come back to the office unless I wasn't a jerk, but she didn't mention staying away from her apartment. And if I stopped by with flowers or some shit asking her to forgive me, hopefully, she'd get over being pissed off. Then I have another idea.

"There is this firefighter fantasy she told me about while we were in Atlantic City that I could play on if Jack will let me borrow one of their uniforms."

"TMI!" Jude yells, covering his ears. "Shit, now I need to go home. Bastard," he says, shoulders hunched, moping off to the locker room.

Once I put in a call to my buddy Jack, I swing by the firehouse before heading home to shower and suit up. The damn yellow jacket, pants, and black rubber boots are heavy as fuck. I could wear this mess instead of weights to workout at the gym.

After I get off the elevator on Page's floor, I put on the helmet and unzipped the big yellow jacket, revealing my bare chest and stomach covered only by the thick black suspenders. Taking a deep breath that she won't slam the door in my face, I knock. It feels like forever before the door finally opens. Page's mouth is wide ass open as she looks me up and down, her cheeks reaching second-degree burn status.

"Jax...what the...Oh. My. God," she stutters. Finally closing her mouth, she glances over her shoulder into the apartment, then back at me. "Um, now is not a good time," she tells me softly, almost a whisper.

"There's someone else in your apartment?" I ask with barely contained rage.

"Yes-"

"What the fuck, Page? It better not be the fucking Senator or so help me, God, I will go get an ax and chop off his-"

"Page? Who's at the door?" a feminine voice asks from inside, to which Page slams the door in my face.

Well damn, that hadn't turned out as I expected.

Shaking my head before hanging it in defeat, I about face to the elevator. I hear a scuffle in Page's apartment, then the door is yanked open again. When I turn around, a forty-something woman is sticking her perfectly coiffed blonde head out the door. Her eyes widen when she sees me.

"Are you here to see Page?" she asks.

"No," Page quickly responds from the other side. "He had the wrong apartment." Her denial stings.

"But he looks familiar. Oh, I know! Are you that Jackson Malone fellow?" she asks, stepping out into the hall to reveal a cream colored, trendy skirt suit that probably cost more than my motorcycle.

"Yes, ma'am, I am," I respond.

"Kill me now," Page mutters.

The woman comes down the hall, examining me with one raised eyebrow. "Well, don't be shy. Come say hello, Mr. Malone. I'm Page's mother, Cindy Davenport."

Oh shit. I could make a run for the elevator, which I'll have to stand and wait for. I could hit the steps, or I could turn around and go back.

"Come on, dear. We haven't got all night."

JAX

Oh fuck a duck, this can't be happening.

Shoulders slumping in embarrassment I walk back to the apartment.

"Oh my," her mother says. "Aren't you a treat?"

"Mom!" Page exclaims. "Weren't you heading out?"

"But I haven't had a chance to talk to Mr. Malone. How are you, dear? Such dreadful lies causing you all this trouble."

"I'm doing pretty well, Mrs. Davenport."

"Mom, I'll talk to you tomorrow, okay?" Page says, gently pushing her mother down the hall, past me, and toward the elevators.

"Should I go, too?" I ask, still pissed that she didn't want me to meet her mother. Is she ashamed of me, or does she just not want anyone else to know about us for her license's sake? It's not like her own mother would report her to the Bar.

"No. You can stay. We have those cross-examination questions to practice and all," Page tells me, and the majority of my anger fades away.

"Good to see you so hard at work after hours on his case, dear," her mom says with a smile before the elevator thankfully whisks her away.

Page closes her eyes, rubbing a hand over her face and sighing.

"Bad timing?" I ask. Nothing kills arousal like mothers.

Squaring her shoulders, Page seems to collect herself and her confidence when she walks towards me. She surprises the shit out of me when she actually jumps on me, wrapping her legs around my waist and her arms around my neck. My reflexes are quick, so I grab her ass to hold her up at the same time our lips meet, hot and hungry.

Easily carrying her tall, lean weight, I make it inside her apartment and shut the door with my foot before clothes start flying. The fireman's hat and jacket are first, then Page's shirt and bra. The rest are all below the belt and will require us separating.

"Bed?" I ask against her lips.

"Anywhere," she responds, sounding like she's ready to throw down right where we're standing.

"But I didn't even get to use the line I had ready for when you opened the door," I tell her when I lay her down on a bed I assume is in her room.

"Doesn't matter," she says, her hands trying to figure out how to get my fireman pants off.

"So you don't want to hear about how I've got a long ladder to use to save your pussy," I ask.

"No." She laughs. "That's horrible."

"You're so hot I need to cool you down with my hose?"

"Stop talking and get naked fireman," she responds. "I'm in desperate need of your...hose, even if it has been in thousands of fire crotches."

"Hey!" I scoff, but then her hand finds its way into my pants, fisting my hard shaft. I have those heavy pants off a second later, retrieving the condom in the pocket before tossing them along with her shorts and panties out of our way.

I flip Page over like a pancake to take her from behind. After tearing the condom wrapper with my teeth I start multitasking, rolling the condom down with one hand while the other estimates her readiness. Hot damn, she's dripping wet, and she immediately starts squeezing the fuck out of my fingers. I barely touched her, and she came for me.

"Damn, princess. You miss me getting you off the last few weeks?" I ask, pulling her hips back and lining my cock up to slide inside her.

"Yes," she moans.

"Then why didn't you just ask for it?" I'm sheathed all the way inside her wet heat after one deep shove.

"Oh God, Jax!"

"Is this what you needed?" I ask, my hips pumping like they can't go fast or hard enough.

"Yes!"

"Then we're lifting...the goddamn... no fucking...sanction," I tell her, leaning down to bite her shoulder.

"Please," she almost sobs that one word.

"Please, what?" I ask through clenched teeth. Sweat is already running down my face while I try to last. "You want me to fuck you...until your body shakes underneath mine?"

"Yes, God yes!"

"You going to let me fuck you all night?" I ask, my hands tightening on her hips to pound into her harder with each word. "Every. God. Damn. Night?"

"Please, Jax!"

I press my chest flush against her back to reach around underneath her. My fingertips circle her trigger point and with one last deep shove her sexy body tenses and shakes, her moans music to my ears.

"*Ahhh*," I groan with the explosion of my own release. After she milks every last drop from me, I pull out and flop over onto the mattress beside her. Page continues to lay limply on her stomach, face buried in the pillow. "You still alive, princess?" I ask with a poke to her ribs.

"Mmm," comes out softly when she squirms. Finally, she turns her head to the side to face me, hair in her eyes, a fuck-drunk smile stretched across her face.

"You fuck me so good they can have my license," she mutters, making me laugh.

"Have you noticed that you only swear during sex?" I ask.

"Well yeah, that's the only time I'm not able to think before speaking."

"Makes sense. Guess you didn't miss that profanity class in college after all," I joke.

"Huh?"

"I was there that night Elliot showed up outside your office. I was about to come up and see you with the polygraph results."

"Oh. So you heard that?"

"Yeah. You were funny. Until you agreed to leave with him."

"Oh yeah," she says, rolling to her side to face me with a smile. "That night I was thinking about you while he was screwing me. When I came, he thought it was his doing. Idiot."

"You thought about me that night?" I ask in surprise. But wait, that was before she knew I'd passed the polygraph. And she wanted me anyway?

"Uh-huh. More specifically your tongue."

"Well, now you know exactly how many licks it takes me." I laugh, pulling her to me.

"Yeah, I do," she says, and then goes quiet for a few minutes. "I think I know why you got so upset in my office earlier."

"Oh really?" I ask, hoping she's wrong.

"Your mom's name was on your birth certificate, so I did some research on the court database and online..."

Fuck.

"I don't want to talk about that shit, Page," I tell her, getting up and quickly escaping to the bathroom.

CHAPTER TWELVE

Page

As soon as Jax closes the bathroom door, I'm up on shaky legs, grabbing his heavy fireman pants and jacket and hiding them in the wardrobe closet in my spare bedroom. If he doesn't have any clothes, he can't leave.

I barely dive back into bed before he comes out with his angry mask back in place.

"What are you looking so smug about?" he asks with dark, narrowed eyes.

"Nothing. Come back to bed," I say, lifting the covers to climb underneath them. I'm soaking wet between my legs, but I don't want to leave his sight for a second to even go to the bathroom. I know he'll try to make a run for it.

"There won't be any heart to heart talks if I do," he warns.

"Okay," I agree.

As soon as he's back in bed next to me, I cling to him. "You don't have to talk because I already know," I tell him. His entire body tenses and I wait for him to push me away. "It's okay, Jax."

"No, it's not fucking okay."

"What happened to her?" I ask. Yeah, I read the articles, but after a few weeks, there wasn't anything new reported.

"Fuck if I know."

"You haven't seen her or talked to her since then?" I ask in surprise.

"Nope, and I don't want to."

"Why not?" I ask softly.

"She fucked a boy in her and my dad's bed!" he yells. He tries to push me away, but I hold onto him tightly.

"I know. It's okay, Jax."

"It is anything but o-fucking-kay."

I climb on top of him, straddling his hips, so he can't get up and leave without throwing me off. God, I hope he doesn't actually do that. It's anyone's guess since the volcano from the first day in our office is back and brewing in his dark eyes.

"Talk to me. Please," I beg, leaning down to brush my lips over his.

He throws a big, muscular arm over his eyes, keeping me out. I'm about to give up when he finally says, "It's all my fault."

"What?" I ask, pulling back in confusion. "You were only a little boy, right?"

"I was ten."

"Then how's it your fault?"

"I caught them," he mutters quietly.

"Your mom, and the, ah..."

"Boy in her class? Yeah. They...believe me, you really don't want to hear this fucked up shit, Page!"

"Jax, you can trust me," I assure him, peeling his arm away from his face. "Attorney-client privilege," I say, combing my fingers through the front of his jet black hair, the same color as hers in the photos from the articles. "I just want to know because I care about you."

His face softens, the volcano simmering, temporarily at least. His hands start moving soothingly up and down my back before he blows out a breath in resignation.

"I went to baseball practice after school at the Y like every weekday in the spring, but that day my coach was sick, so they canceled it. I walked home like usual, just...earlier. Jude was eating cereal out of the box and watching *The Lion King* in the living room. He was only three-years-old."

He pauses, and I'm not sure if he's going to keep going, so I reach for his hands and intertwine his fingers with mine. After a big exhale he keeps going. "I heard...noises coming from down the hall. My parents' bedroom door was shut, and I didn't know what the hell was going on. Only my mom's car was home. It sounded like she was screaming so I went in and just...stood frozen trying to make sense of it. There she was with this kid on top of her, both of them naked. I remember saying something like, 'Get off my mom' and the boy laughs, telling me she liked it. My mom yelled at me to get out, so I did. A few minutes later she came into my room and screamed at me to keep my mouth shut and not to say a word to anyone about what I saw, especially my dad. I think she even threatened to take away my *Gameboy* and shit if I told anyone."

"I'm sorry," I say during his pause, even though it's completely insufficient for what happened. "Did you tell someone? Because you should have. It was unfair of her to ask you not to."

"Sort of. That night I was still all fucked up and didn't want any dinner. My dad must've known something was up because I was always eating everything in sight. He offered to play catch with me in the backyard, and eventually he asked what was wrong. I didn't say anything about her, but I just asked him what sex was, since I thought, you know, that might have been what I'd seen them doing. He gave me the *'You're too young to worry about that'* speech. But then later that night he must have told my mom I'd asked him about it. I heard her start screaming at him, asking if he was going to believe a lying kid over her. My dad wasn't stupid and knew if she was freaking out it must be something bad. He came to my room and asked me if there was anything I wanted to tell him. I told him that mom told me not to, and he said 'Moms and Dads shouldn't ever tell their kids to keep something from the other.'"

"So you told him?"

"Yeah, with her in the room with us, screaming the whole time. My dad told her he was done. He was going to get a divorce and was going to the police. She started crying, begging him not to do that to her. She asked him to let her pack a bag and leave town before the police came looking for her. My dad caved. Told her to never to come back. She left in tears, yelling at me, telling me it was my fault. That when Jude cried and wanted to know where she was for me to tell him I was the one that sent her away from him. That it was my fault he wouldn't have a mother. She said she'd miss him..."

"God, Jax," I say when I see the moisture in his dark eyes, wrapping my arms around his neck and laying my head on his chest. What an evil woman to hurt a little boy in such a cruel way.

"After that, all hell broke loose. She left town but took the sixteen-year-old student with her. It was a huge scandal. Two other boys came forward and said she'd sucked them or fucked them when they were students in her math class. Everyone knew she was a fucking whore, even the kids in my class. They probably heard their parents talking about it."

"Is that why you got into fights?" I ask, having already figured as much.

"Yep. Because I was pissed at her, pissed off at the mess she'd left behind, pissed off at all the shit everyone said. God, my dad was so torn up, and Jude...*Fuck*. He cried all the damn time for her the first few weeks."

"Which made you feel guilty, even though it shouldn't have."

"Hell, I was even angry at him because he made me feel like shit whenever he asked about her, and I was so fucking jealous. She loved him and not me."

"She didn't deserve you or him. Or your dad."

"Whatever."

"What happened to her?" I ask.

"As far as I know the police never found her or the boy. I guess they're off living their own happily ever fucked up after."

JAX

"Thank you for trusting me enough to tell me," I say with a kiss to his neck.

"Thanks for not kicking me out when I showed up as a naughty fireman. Can I stay the night?" he asks.

"Yes. I thought there was some sort of promise made about f-wording me all night," I tease him with a smile trying to lighten up after all the heavy.

"That was before you had to bring up old shit that killed my cock."

"Ah. Well, sleeping with you is just as nice, and I've missed waking up with you," I tell him. After I clean up in the bathroom, I climb back in bed naked and get into the spooning position. "Good night," I say to him, and he reciprocates with his arm holding me to him. I timed him, and not even fifteen minutes later Jax was back on top of me, making good on his promise.

CHAPTER THIRTEEN

Jax

I hurry into Page's office after her text that said *come in ASAP*. I figure it must be important since she didn't just call and tell me what was up.

"Oh, Mr. Malone," the receptionist calls out to me when I start walking back to Page's office. I'd done the same thing for almost a month now.

"Hey, Jamie."

"Page and everyone else is already in the conference room."

"Oh," I mutter. Page didn't mention a meeting with anyone.

Instead of her office, I head in the other direction. I wasn't expecting to see my dad, Jude, Coach Briggs and some guy in a suit sitting at the table with Page. When her eyes quickly lower I know exactly what's going on. It's a fucking intervention.

"I'm not pleading!" I yell. How many times do I have to tell them that?

"Jax, just sit your ass down and listen to what they have to say," my dad snaps.

I force myself down into one of the chairs with my blood pressure climbing through the damn roof.

"Jax, let me tell you about it before you yell or say anything, okay?" Page asks softly.

"Let's hear this bullshit yet again."

"This time, we have a real, legitimate plea offer from the prosecutor. You'd plead to one count of misdemeanor assault on a female. Even though with your clean record you would normally be in the low end of the sentencing range, the prosecutor insisted on a maximum sentence of ten months active that would be transcribed. So that's the exact sentence you would get. No more. Then you'd be on supervised release for two years after that."

"With only a misdemeanor you might even be able to fight again, Jax," Coach adds.

"No," I say without hesitation.

"Jax..." almost everyone at the table starts in on me.

"I didn't do anything wrong, and I'm not going to be locked up in a shitty fucking prison for ten months when I'm innocent!"

"Page said she's been over the maximum sentences with you if convicted, correct?" the suit asks.

"Yeah, a shitload of years."

"Right. Going to trial is a huge gamble," he says. "You could win big and walk out, or you could lose big and end up spending twenty some years in prison on felony convictions. When you get out as a convicted felon, your employment options will be seriously limited. This plea is a guarantee of only ten months, and it's only a misdemeanor."

"I'm sure from each of your points of view the plea looks like a no-brainer. But none of you will have to stand up in front of the world and say 'I'm guilty' of something you didn't fucking do, or be locked away in a concrete box for ten months. So, however great it looks on paper, I'm not signing that shit."

"Then we'll need you to write 'rejected' in big letters across the front page of the plea and then sign and date that notation," the suit says, passing me the paper and a permanent marker.

"Wait!" Page exclaims. "Can you all give us a minute?"

Everyone stands up and leaves the conference room so she can try and convince me one-on-one.

"Page, don't waste your time," I warn. Ignoring me, she comes around the table and climbs on my lap, wrapping her arms around my neck and kissing me. "You can't fuck me into submission," I tease her, but when I pull back, I see the tears running down her cheeks.

"I don't want to lose you," she says softly.

"I know, and I don't want to have to spend years locked up away from you," I tell her, wiping away her tears. "But you can't ask me to do this. This, pleading guilty, will break me, more than serving a sentence from a conviction will. I need you to support me on this. I've got faith in you and the system that I'm going to walk out of that courtroom a free man."

"But what if I let you down?" she asks, pressing her wet face to my chest.

"You won't let me down. That's one of only two things in my life I'm certain of."

"Are you sure? Because I'm not so sure," she mutters through sniffles.

"I'm sure."

"What's the other thing that you're certain of?" she asks after a moment.

"That I'm truly, madly and deeply in love with you."

She laughs and tightens her arms around my neck. "I love you, too, you pain in the ass."

After a shaky breath, she pulls away and turns around to grab the plea agreement. "Here, reject it so we can get back to work preparing for trial."

"Hell yes," I agree. With the fat permanent marker, I write the word "Rejected" in huge letters then sign and date it.

"There's one other thing that as your attorney I need to discuss with you. Just don't yell at the messenger," she orders, standing up from my lap.

LANE HART

"Okay." I already know I'm not going to like what comes next.

"Ryan mentioned that sometimes these cases go away, as in getting dismissed, after a civil settlement."

"Let me stop you right there, because if you even *suggest* that I should give this bitch a fucking dollar, I will go ballistic."

"I don't think you should, no. But as your attorney, it is an option that has to be discussed with you."

"Never. I'd write a check giving away every penny I have to charity before I let that whore have any of it."

"Good. Let me get them back in here just so Ryan can be another witness that you don't want to engage in civil settlement negotiations," she say, grabbing a tissue to wipe her face.

"Then can we go back to my place?" I ask. As what feels like the doomsday clock ticks down I want to spend every waking minute with Page.

"Your place?" she asks in surprise. "So I finally get to see your bachelor pad?"

"Yeah," I respond, trying to find the courage to tell her what I've been thinking about more and more lately. "And if you like it then I hope you might consider sharing it with me after I'm found not guilty."

"Really?" she asks with a smile, one that quickly fades. "But then everyone will know..."

"Can we just not worry about that until the time comes?"

"Okay," she agrees.

...

Page

I'm nervous and excited as I park my Mercedes in the lot of Jax's apartment building. He'd given me directions before leaving the office, and now here I am looking up at what appears to be a brand new tower, standing moderately high in downtown.

Heading inside I climb in the elevator and hit the number twelve to begin the ascent to the top. When the door opens, I wonder which way to go, but soon realize there's only one apartment up here - Jax's. After a quick knock on his door, he pulls it open and smiles in greeting.

I can't help but look past him into the big open room behind him.

"Wow, this place is really nice, Jax."

"Thanks," he replies as he steps aside to let me in.

The glass ceiling and entire wall of windows make the already massive space seem even larger, handy for a man that doesn't like small spaces. There are various beautiful potted plants and shrubs around the wooden deck that juts out over the city. The double balcony doors are open, so I head out them to get a better look. A patio set of chairs with thick cushions and a long bench seem like perfect places to sit and relax, along with the hot tub. More doors further down the way are open, leading into the bedroom and kitchen.

The entire place is so serene, done up in whites, creams and a touch of gold. It's not at all what I expected for the tough, angry man, but it makes sense that he'd want a calming fortress when he's not fighting. A place that's the opposite of the metal cage.

I know without a doubt that I can't let him go to prison. That place will take the man I'm in love with and make him bitter, and so angry that I'll lose him forever. I'll just have to do whatever it takes to make sure that doesn't happen to him.

"What do you think?" Jax asks when he comes up to the balcony ledge beside me. The sun's starting to set, painting the sky with streaks of orange, pink and purple.

"It's beautiful," I tell him.

"It is," he agrees as he turns to face me, "But after three years it's never really felt like home, until now."

His sweet and sincere words tighten my throat.

"Why don't you show me your bedroom so I can start plotting how to take over all the closet space?" I say with a smile.

"You can have it all, princess," he says before capturing my lips with his.

∽

LANE HART

The summer is flying by, and it's hard to believe it's already the Fourth of July. Maybe it just seems to be passing quickly because I'm counting down what might be Jax's last few days of freedom. We've spent almost every second together during the days and nights. Trial preparations are all but wrapped up. We have a strong case but...I just don't know if it's strong enough to win because of those damn pictures.

"Page, did you get a chance to talk to Coach Briggs the other day in your office?" Jax asks, interrupting my incessant worry. "He grew up around here with your dad."

"Not really," I say, holding out my hand out to the very large man with a round belly.

"Thanks for all your help with Jax's case, Page," Coach Briggs says with a smile. "And thanks for coming."

"Thanks for the invitation."

Jax explained that every year all the gym guys get together for a July Fourth cookout at the coach's house since he has a huge in-ground pool in his backyard. Apparently being an MMA coach/manager pays *really* well. Or maybe it pays well because he has Jax fighting on his team.

"Page, this is my daughter, Sadie," the man says, referring to the small girl beside him. Underneath the dark makeup and goth-ish baggy clothes, you can tell she's a very pretty girl, and she seems to be entranced by the mostly naked buff men running around her backyard. She stands beside us in awe, twirling one of her long brown braids.

I feel her pain since I'm the only other female having the pleasure of viewing this overload of hotness.

There's a ton of ripped men with more guns than a military base. These aren't just alpha males, these are the alphas that can beat the shit out of most other alphas. I follow her line of sight and, oh yes, out of all the available eye-candy she's staring at the very sleek and sexy Jude Malone.

"So, Sadie, how old are you?" I ask when the two men are distracted talking about tonight's pay-per-view title fight or whatnot.

JAX

Her green eyes, hidden behind thick glasses, finally blink over at me. "Huh?" she asks.

"Hi, I'm Page, Jax's girl...attorney," I try to quickly catch the slip.

"His girl attorney? Does he have a boy attorney, too?" She laughs. "Don't worry, I get it." She's a smart and very perceptive girl.

"So how old are you?" I ask.

"Sixteen."

"Ah. Then, unfortunately, you're a little on the young side for him."

"What? For who?" she asks.

"Hey, Jude," I yell in greeting, effectively setting off a horrible rendition of The Beatles' song by several deep, off-key voices. After splashing the guys and then flipping them off with both hands, Jude looks over and smiles. The girl beside me gasps at the six feet of gorgeousness headed our way.

"Page!" he says with his dripping wet approach. "How many times have I told you, 'Hi, Jude' is an acceptable greeting, and so is 'Sup, Jude,' or 'Hey, Jackass.' *Anything* but 'Hey, Jude.'"

"Sorry." I laugh. "Lesson learned. I wouldn't want to hear that God-awful singing, either."

"How's it going, Jude?" I'm surprised when the girl beside me bravely speaks up.

Jude shivers and looks around for a towel, grabbing one from a nearby lounge chair to use to dry off. "Hey, Sadie," Jude responds, barely acknowledging the doe-eyed teenager. "So, Page, you all set for trial?"

"As ready as we can be," I reply. I hate seeing the worry and fear that clouds his normally upbeat expression. "You ready to testify?"

"Oh yeah," he says with a smile.

"Try and keep the sex sounds as tasteful as possible," I remind him.

"Hey, I'm going to answer accurately and honestly, so if the judge doesn't like it, he can kiss my ass."

I sigh and shake my head when my eyes go back to Jax and his coach, still deep in discussion. "So who's fighting tonight?" I ask Jude.

"Mike Jacobs is the idiot who agreed to take on Linc Abrams this year," Sadie says right away. "Linc's the current world welterweight champion, and he defends his title every July Fourth. He's won by first round knockouts the last three years in a row."

Jude looks over at the girl in surprise like she'd just magically appeared.

"Linc?" I ask. "That's an unusual name. It sounds like he's really good."

"Yeah, and he's *really* hot," Sadie replies, to which Jude scoffs.

"All the more reason to watch tonight." I laugh. "Aren't you a welterweight too, Jude?"

"Uh-huh."

"He's ranked fifth in the country," Sadie speaks up for him.

"Really, Jude?" I ask, and he nods. "That's awesome!" I exclaim, but he just shrugs modestly.

"Does Jude have a nickname?" I ask Sadie, figuring she'll know.

"Yeah, um, *The Matrix* because of how fast he moves ducking and dodging opponents' swings and kicks," she says. The girl is like a walking, talking MMA encyclopedia.

"And because of how fast he dodges women," Jax adds when he joins our conversation, slipping an arm around me, to which I side-step. Even if everyone here probably knows we're together, we can't risk it in public.

"Too bad you didn't learn that skill, bro," Jude counters.

"If I hadn't been a player, then I wouldn't have gotten charged, and then I never would've met my incredibly beautiful and smart attorney that's going to keep me out of prison."

"I really hope you're right," Jude says sadly.

The pressure on my shoulders is almost too much to take. I'd been meeting with Ryan, our state court criminal defense attorney, several times a week since he's still too swamped to second chair Jax's case. He thinks we're ready, but I'd feel better if he was there in the courtroom with us, making sure I don't screw up.

CHAPTER FOURTEEN

Page

Each day is more stressful than the last as we get closer to the trial date. Jax is sleeping less and less each night, and I would know because I'm usually awake beside him in his bed. Whenever he realizes I'm not able to sleep either he makes love to me, both of us losing ourselves in each other to try and fight off the worry.

The night before the first day of trial I barely slept more than an hour or two in the hotel bed. I was ready to get it over, but in a way, I just wanted to hide out in our room instead of go to the courthouse.

It takes hours to pick a jury since everyone had seen or read something about Jax's case due to all the media coverage. At last, we agreed on a dozen jurors, and much to my satisfaction, seven were female. I knew Jax could persuade them to his side.

The men weren't too bad either. Two were young, in their twenties, which I thought would work in our favor since they would be able to put themselves in Jax's shoes. Another man was in his thirties and seemed to be a conservative accountant. One was a father who had me the most worried, and the last one was a retired gentleman. I had no idea which way he'd go.

The first witness for the State, Detective Shaw, was the officer that initially interviewed the bitch when she went to file the report late the next day...plenty of time to manufacture the bruises on her neck. I didn't have many questions for him since he was only reporting what she told him.

Next up, we finally got to hear from the alleged victim. I hate to admit that she's really pretty, wearing a white suit with her dark hair swept back in a chignon like mine. The prosecutor went through his many questions with her on his direct while I took notes, preparing for what to hit her with on my cross-examination. After a quick recess, it was my turn to question her.

"Give her hell," Jax whispers against my ear, making me smile.

Judge Bray comes back in and calls court back to order, then the bitch went back up to the witness stand.

"Ms. Davenport, your witness," the judge says to me. Getting to my feet, I start toward the lying whore with a stack of our exhibits.

"Ms. Loftis, I'd like to ask you to identify what has been marked as Defense Exhibit One. Your Honor, may I approach the witness?" I remember to ask, making me feel like I'm in a game of *Mother May I*.

"Yes, you may," Judge Bray replies.

I proceed to the witness box and hand her the first document. "Please identify that document for the jurors."

"Um, it looks like a phone bill," she says. Her amber eyes slightly narrow at me, and her lips are pursed tightly together like she's just waiting for me to give her a hard time.

"So it's a record of phone calls?"

"Yes."

"This is Mr. Malone's phone record for the night of May twenty-fourth. Do you recognize your phone number in the call log?"

"Yes," she answers after a second.

"Tell the jurors about those entries that contain your phone number."

"The first one was a missed call at nine-forty-three p.m. and the second was an outgoing call at eleven oh-one p.m. that lasted ninety-eight seconds."

"So based on your recollection and this document, is it correct to say that you initially called Mr. Malone and that he was simply returning your call?"

"Yes, I believe so."

"And do you remember leaving Mr. Malone a voicemail?"

"Yes."

"Your honor I'd like to play Defense Exhibit Two, an audio recording, and ask the witness to identify it as her voicemail to the defendant on May twenty-fourth." I hate calling Jax a defendant.

"Any objection from the State?" the judge asks. When the prosecutor didn't object, Judge Bray lets me play the disc that contains the recording over the courtroom sound system.

"Hey, sexy, it's Christina. I just saw you on TV at your brother's fight, so I know you're in town. Give me a call if you want a replay of last time."

"Was that your voice Ms. Loftis?" I ask when the recording of her voice stops.

"Yes."

"And when you said 'a replay of last time' you were offering to let Mr. Malone have sex with you?"

"I just meant that I wanted to hang out with him while he was in town again."

Riiight.

"And what did happen when he was in town previously?"

"We started talking after one of his fights, and he asked if I wanted to go back to his room-"

"He asked you, or did you ask him if you could go back to his room with him?" I interrupt to set her straight.

"Oh, um, I'm not sure."

Lying bitch.

"What happened after you arrived in Mr. Malone's room that first night?"

"He slammed me against the wall and um, had sex with me," she responds, trying to sound like a delicate little flower.

"Was that before or after you performed oral sex on him?"

Her mouth opens then closes. "After."

"Right, and did he initiate the oral sex or did you?"

"I don't remember."

Lie, lie, lie.

"If I told you that Mr. Malone says that you were on your knees before the hotel door closed, and you were the one that unzipped his pants without his prompting, would that be accurate?"

"Objection," the prosecutor jumps in.

"Overruled. You may answer Ms. Loftis," the judge gives her the go ahead.

"It was so long ago I'm not one hundred percent sure."

"But you do admit to performing oral sex on him on that occasion?"

"Yes."

"And then you had sex with him?"

"Yes, twice that night."

"And all of that occurred with your consent?"

"Yes."

"Okay, going back to the night of the *alleged* incident, had you been drinking before you arrived at Mr. Malone's room on the night of May twenty-fourth?"

"I think I may have had one drink at the bar downstairs."

"Just one?" I ask.

"Maybe two at the most."

After playing *Mother, May I* again with the judge, I take a receipt up to show her. "Does this look like your receipt from a bar at the Taj Mahal on May twenty-fourth?"

"Yes."

"And that's your signature from paying with your personal credit card?"

"Yes."

"And how many drinks are listed on there?"

"Five, but I was with friends," she says quickly.

Bullshit.

"So what happened when you arrived in Mr. Malone's room?"

"He attacked me."

"Describe in detail how he 'attacked you.'"

"He just came at me and then threw me on the bed. I tried to get him to slow down and he wouldn't. He held me down with his hand around my neck and told me to...perform oral sex on him."

"Did you physically protest?"

"I tried, but he wouldn't stop."

"So let me make sure I understand your answer. You're saying that Mr. Malone's delicate and sensitive penis was in your mouth full of teeth, and you decided not to do anything but suck on it?"

There're snickers from the gallery, and I'm almost sure one of them is Jude's.

"I was afraid he'd hurt me if I...tried to hurt him."

"Okay, then what happened?"

"Then he...forced his penis into me. He kept choking me until he finished inside me."

"What did it feel like when he was choking you?"

"It hurt."

"Could you explain to the jury in detail what it feels like to have someone's strong hands around your neck?"

Hell, I can do that better than her.

"I-I couldn't breathe."

"And is it true that you weren't wearing any panties when you arrived at Mr. Malone's room?"

"I, uh, I don't remember. I may not have."

"Why would a woman not wear panties to a man's hotel room unless she's going to have sex with him?"

"Yes, I wanted to have sex with him, but I didn't want him to hurt me," she finally admits. I try not to visibly celebrate that small but very important victory.

I go through a few other questions to which she gives bullshit answers, and then I start asking her to identify the pictures of Jax from her Facebook page. I put those mouthwatering bad boys on the overhead projector so that there's an entire wall showing the sexiest man alive in little to no clothing.

"Is this your Facebook account?" I ask.

"Yes."

"And did you post this picture on May twentieth of Mr. Malone?"

"Yes."

"And could you read the comment you posted."

"Even yummier in person and tastes divine."

We went through several other photos with similar comments.

"So, Ms. Loftis, would you admit that you were a pretty big fan of Mr. Malone's?"

"Yes, before he attacked me."

"And did you get upset when Mr. Malone ignored your texts and calls after the first occasion you had intercourse?" She had already identified the call log of the six different times she'd called him and he didn't answer. And I'd happily put her five desperate text messages on the overhead. The ones asking Jax variations of what he was doing and when he was coming back to Atlantic City.

"No."

"No? You weren't upset that a man had slept with you and then wouldn't talk to you?"

"No."

"So all this, your false accusations of rape, aren't the result of being a woman scorned?"

"Objection," the prosecutor said.

"Sustained," Judge Bray says, preventing her from being able to answer, which is fine since it was the question that was important.

Here goes the fireworks finale that will probably land me in hot water with the judge, but the benefits of the jury hearing it would be worth it.

"Ms. Loftis, would it come as a shock for you to hear that Mr. Malone passed a polygraph on all of your false accusations?"

"*Objection!*" the District Attorney stands up and yells. "Your Honor, the State moves to have defense counsel's last question stricken from the record."

"Sustained, and motion granted. This is a warning to be careful, Ms. Davenport. Court reporter, please strike the last question from the record. Jurors, please disregard the last question and do not consider it during your deliberations. Ms. Davenport, you may continue, and I advise you do to so cautiously."

"No further questions, your Honor," I respond, swiftly heading back to my seat. I hope I made my point. Since I can't offer the polygraph into evidence, I've put the jurors on notice that he took one and passed.

Jax has a slight smirk on his lips, and I know he's trying hard to conceal his expression.

"Next up is the doctor and then the nurse that examined her," I whisper to him.

Unfortunately, the doctor's testimony doesn't go so well for us. He said it was possible that Ms. Loftis's injuries wouldn't show up immediately, which screws us on the video and eyewitness saying she didn't have any marks on her neck when she left that night. I knew from experience the doctor was full of shit, but I couldn't very well explain how I knew.

On the second day of trial the DNA expert testified that the DNA was a ninety-nine percent match to the mouth swab sample collected from Jax, which sucked, and we couldn't come up with an explanation for that except that she must have taken his condom. That's just too gross to believe. After that, the State rested their case, and it was our turn to put on evidence.

I still called the valet and the hotel security guard to identify the video and show the bitch's clear neck. Then I called Jude to the witness stand and asked what he heard through the hotel wall. There were snickers again after his imitation.

Lastly, I called Jax and let him go through his whole story, contradicting hers wherever we could with the evidence again. He did great and kept his cool even during the prosecutor's cross-examination.

Even though everything had gone as well as I'd hoped, including my closing argument, I was still freaking out. I just don't know if the jurors will believe the lying bitch or Jax. That night while we waited hours for the jury to deliberate, I barely resisted the urge to throw myself into Jax's arms for comfort. I could tell he was nervous, but trying to hide it from me and everyone else. He barely spoke, and he kept staring off into space.

Media people began pouring into the courtroom the longer we waited, and by the time the jury came back with a verdict it was almost midnight and the place was filled to capacity.

I tried to read the jurors faces when they filed into the jury box. After they all avoided eye contact with Jax and me I began to worry even more.

"Has the jury reached a verdict?" Judge Bray asks the jury, and a hush fell over the courtroom.

"Yes, your Honor," the accountant stands up and says proudly. He must've been selected to be the foreman by the other jurors.

"All right, Mr. Malone, please stand. Mr. Foreman, if you will now read the verdict."

My entire body is shaking as I stand beside Jax, who somehow remains as solid and unemotional as a tree.

"We, the jury, find the defendant...not guilty of the first count, the charge of First Degree Rape."

Oh, thank God!

"With regards to the second count, the charge of Assault by Strangulation, we, the jury, find the defendant...guilty."

What!

Guilty?

No, no, no. How is that possible?

"Order in the courtroom!" the judge yells with a slam of his gavel after the gasps and muttered whisperings grow louder. "Thank you, Mr. Foreperson. We'll now proceed with the sentencing of the defendant."

Oh no. Sentencing? I can't handle this. Everything seems to be running on fast-forward, and I'm pretty sure my legs are turning to Jell-O.

"Calm down, Page. It's okay," Jax says softly. The man who is about to be sentenced is telling me to get a grip. I meet his gaze that seems too calm for the circumstances.

"I'm sorry," I tell him, blinking back tears.

"Shh," he says. "You were great. You did everything you could."

"Mr. Malone, after a finding of guilty of the charge of Assault by Strangulation, a Class H felony, and in consideration of your prior clean criminal record, I hereby sentence you to serve six months in the Department of Corrections, followed by two years of supervised release. Bailiff if you would please take the defendant into the custody of the State."

Oh God, they were taking him *now*? No! I don't know what to do, but I can't just let them take him away.

"Your Honor," I start. "The defendant would...request that he be given a reporting date...in order to get his ah, finances and everything in order before serving his sentence."

"Your request is denied. Bailiff?" Judge Bray answers right away and nods to the sheriff deputy.

Jax won't look at me, and it's either to keep from giving away any emotion to the media vultures or because he's pissed at me. Likely the latter since he trusted me to get him through this, *without* an active prison sentence, and I failed him.

"Your Honor, the defendant hereby gives his notice to appeal the verdict of the jury," I say quickly. "On the basis of ineffective assistance of counsel." I try to think of anything that might keep Jax out just a little longer. "Counsel requests a stay of his sentence until the appeal."

"Request denied, but his appeal is noted for the record. And I have to say, Ms. Davenport, an ineffective assistance of counsel claim is unlikely to be founded."

Shit!

I can't let Jax go off to prison, I just...can't! He's innocent! There's only one thing left for me to do to try and save him.

"Then your Honor, I hereby admit to the court that I proceeded with the representation of Mr. Malone after a clear conflict of interest in violation of Rule 1.8 of the New Jersey Rules of Professional Conduct."

That has the judge's eyebrows raising.

"Page, what the fuck are you doing?" Jax asks, grabbing me by my elbow.

"Whatever I have to do," I meet his dark, questioning eyes and tell him.

"Ms. Davenport, are you admitting in open court to engaging in an inappropriate sexual relationship with your client?" he asks. The entire courtroom gasps, including Jax beside me.

"Yes, your Honor."

"No!" Jax exclaims at the same time.

"Then I suggest you retain your own legal counsel and surrender your law license to the court immediately."

Shit, he's still not going let Jax stay out.

"Yes, your Honor."

"Page, no! God, why did you do that?" Jax asks. I watch in horror as the bailiff handcuffs his wrists in front of him. A tear escapes and runs down my cheek when they take him away.

"Court is adjourned," the judge says, and the courtroom erupts.

I stand paralyzed, not knowing what to do without Jax. I'm going home, and he's...

"Page," Jude says when he appears beside me.

"I'm sorry," I tell him. "I'm so sorry."

His arms go around me as the tears pour out. "Hey, don't you dare blame yourself. You did great."

"I let him down," I sob.

"No, you didn't. He loves you, and I know he doesn't blame you. He blames that bitch for lying about all this shit."

"I'm going to try and go see him." I need to talk to him, one on one without a room full of people and cameras. Oh God, I just admitted to sleeping with him in front of all these people! The whole world knows what an unprofessional whore I am.

"Page! Page!" I hear my name being called. Turning around, I groan when I see my brother. I don't need his shit right now.

"Save the lecture, Logan. I know I screwed up. Disown me for all I care," I tell him, not in the mood to deal with him or our father.

"Come on," Logan says, yanking on my arm to pull me away from Jude.

"What are you doing?" I ask, jerking away from his grip.

"I've got an idea to save your ass and your law license," Logan says, surprising me.

"Y-you do?" I ask.

"Yes, now let's go through the back hallways to avoid the crowd," he says, heading for the exit to the judge's chambers only attorneys can use.

"I'll call you," I yell to Jude and he nods.

Swiftly we walk through the dark hallway, down the stairs, and out the back door of the courthouse to head for the jail entrance across the street.

"Would you marry him?" Logan asks once we're on the dark, quiet street.

"What!" I exclaim, coming to a dead stop.

"Were you just fucking him or do you love him enough to marry him?"

"I-I don't know. Why?"

The idea of marrying Jax doesn't send me into a full-blown panic attack like the thought of marrying Elliot always did. Actually, the thought of spending the rest of my life with Jax was nice. More than nice. Living with him, having him always be the first person I see every morning and the last person I talk to every night? That's maybe the easiest decision I'll ever make. But Jax...he's terrified of marriage after what his mother did to his father...

"Jax wouldn't..."

"If he agreed to marry you, would you?" Logan asks.

"Yes."

"There's a loophole in the sex with client rule. Marriage. The husband-wife confidentiality trumps attorney-client."

"You think that will really work after the fact? But what about his appeal?"

"He can still allege ineffective assistance of counsel, that you were clearly conflicted, and then have another attorney take his case to the Court of Appeals. But the Bar won't be able to discipline you for it if you're married. Jax wouldn't be *required* to testify against you, but as it is, they will force him to testify now, and hold him in contempt if he refuses."

"Holy crap, Logan. I think you might be a genius! But what if he doesn't agree. He probably won't, and I'm not going to make him marry me just to keep my license."

"It won't hurt to ask him, right? And there's always a magistrate on duty at the jail. I'll ask Jax and see if he'll actually agree instead of just going along with it in front of you. If so, then we'll get it done."

"You mean, now? Like we'd...we'd get married tonight?" I ask.

"The sooner, the better."

"Oh God. Dad's going to kill me, isn't he?" I exclaim, covering my face when more tears fall.

"Yeah, he is. It's a good thing he's scared shitless of your soon-to-be husband."

CHAPTER FIFTEEN

Jax

Don't freak out. Don't freak out.
Despite how many times I repeat my new motto, I'm on the verge of freaking the fuck out. Everything is happening so fast before I can wrap my head around any of it. I can't say I'm entirely surprised by the verdict. Page had warned me all along that I could get convicted because of those goddamn pictures of her neck. But having it happen and now dealing with it is a different story.

I'd had to surrender all of my possessions, including my clothes except for my boxer briefs and socks, which I only got to keep after the guard conducted a cavity search. I shiver at that unpleasant memory. Now I'm back in an orange fucking jumpsuit like I wore while I was waiting to make bond a few weeks ago. Even if the bright color is going to make me go blind, I have to admit it's pretty damn comfortable. The flip flops under my socks are another story, and the handcuffs continuously dig into my wrists, making even the simplest maneuvers difficult.

Of the long list of unpleasantries, the smell is the worst. That familiar aroma of piss, shit and despair have my stomach rolling, and I haven't even made it past the administration stage yet.

Despite how fucked up things are in here, I can't stop worrying about Page. How upset she must be, wrongly blaming herself. Hell, I'd give anything to be in bed holding her. And now she's fucked up her career because of my dumbass. If I were pissed about anything, other than the bitch lying to cause all this drama, it'd be that Page went and screwed herself over to try and help me.

"Malone, let's go," one of the older sheriff deputies says, indicating I should stand up. Shit, I guess this is where they seal me in behind the bars with some lovely new roommates.

In a tiny, cramped space.

At least they'd finally ditch the handcuffs.

"Your attorney wants to see you," the deputy says when we start down a hallway.

Thank fuck! I need to see Page and try to talk some sense into her if it's not too late.

"In you go," he says, opening a big heavy door that leads to a small room with a metal table and two metal folding chairs.

And definitely not Page.

I start to say to the deputy that he has the wrong guy when I realize the blond, clean-cut man with bright blue eyes looks familiar. Page's brother?

"Logan?"

"How are you doing?" he asks, his expression full of pity.

"Awesome," I respond. "Where's Page?"

"Waiting outside. There's something I need to talk to you about first."

"Okay?"

"Do you love her?" he asks, sitting down in one of the chairs, so I follow suit.

"Yes."

"Enough to marry her?" he asks, and my mouth falls open.

Marry her? Where was this conversation going? Of course, I've

JAX

thought about it, and hell wanted it, but I knew it was a long shot because then everyone would assume we'd slept together while I was her client.

Being with her for the past few weeks...I can't imagine my life without her now. Thinking about having to go just six short months away from her is physically painful. I never want to be separated from her. I want to spend the rest of my life with that woman.

"I'd marry her in a heartbeat."

"Great, so should I get her and the magistrate to come on in?" he asks, standing up to leave.

"What the fuck? You mean like get married right now? *Here?*" I exclaim in confusion.

"Like I told her, the sooner, the better. If you're married, I think there's a chance that she might be able to keep her law license."

"Well in that case, hell yes! Go get them." Relief washes over me. She might still be able to practice and hadn't thrown it all away on me.

He smiles and nods. "I appreciate your enthusiasm, and you agreeing to do this for Page."

"I'd do anything for her."

"Then she's lucky to have you," he says.

After Logan bangs on the door, a deputy opens it, and he disappears.

I stand up and pace, waiting. I ask myself if I'm sure this isn't crazy. I can't find a single shred of doubt or second guessing. After how my parents' marriage ended, I never thought I'd want anything to do with the fucked up institution. But I want Page to be mine. Forever.

The door finally opens again, and Page is the first one through. The sadness on her face hits me like a punch to my gut. And then the tears are enough to bring me to my knees. She heads for me, and I have to lift my cuffed hands over her head to hold her, pulling her to me and tucking her under my chin.

"Hey baby, don't cry."

"I'm sorry." She sobs against my chest.

"Me too. I'm sure you never imagined your wedding day quite like this."

"Are you sure about this? You don't have to," she says, looking up with her watery, blue eyes and red face. "It might not even work."

"I want to," I assure her. "I'd marry you for no other reason other than to just make you my wife. If it helps you keep your license, all the better."

"I love you," she says softly through her tears. "And I'm not just doing this for my license."

"I know, and I love you, too. *Goddamn it.*" I groan. "I don't even have a ring. After all the shit I talked about that son of a bitch being too cheap to give you one."

"Don't worry, our wedding bands are on the way. Hopefully. I called Jude and your dad."

"They're going to let them in?" I ask with a smile, and she nods.

"Logan had to pull a few strings to get us a license backdated so we can avoid the waiting period," she tells me.

Five minutes later the six of us are squeezed into the small room.

"Congrats, bro," Jude says with a pat on my shoulder. "I did the best I could on short notice. I thought you might want to start with this one. You know, do it right."

He drops a small diamond ring into my cuffed hands.

"Thanks. Like always, I owe you," I tell him.

Going down to one knee in front of Page, I look up at her face that's filled with sadness. It's only temporary, so that'll be what gets me through it.

"Page Davenport, you know I'm a huge pain in the ass, but you also know that I love you and will do anything for you. So are you crazy enough to agree to marry me?"

"Yes," she says with a smile, and I slide the ring that's a little too big onto her finger.

"You two ready?" the magistrate asks.

"Yes," I tell him getting to my feet again.

"No, wait!" Page exclaims. "Shouldn't we do a prenup?" she turns to ask me, which I have to say pisses me off.

"I don't want your money, but I'll sign whatever you want," I assure her.

"No, silly. I meant for me to sign to protect *your* money," Page replies with a smile. "I barely have a penny to my name."

"Don't be ridiculous," I tell her.

"Are you sure?" she asks.

"You should automatically be awarded half of all his shit just for agreeing to marry the SOB," Jude says.

"I agree," I tell her, then to the magistrate, "Let's do this."

"Right. So do you, Jackson Malone, take Page Davenport to be your wedded wife, to have and to hold, from this day forward, through sickness and in health, for richer or poorer, forsaking all others for all the days of your life?"

"Hell yes," I answer, making Page smile.

"And do you, Page Davenport, take Jackson Malone to be your wedded husband, to have and to hold, from this day forward, through sickness and in health, for richer or poorer, forsaking all others for all the days of your life?"

"I do," she says softly.

"Rings?" he asks, and Jude hands them to the man.

"Jackson, place this ring on Page's hand, and, Page, place your ring on Jackson's as a symbol of your vow made to each other today, and for every day from this day forward."

I take the ring and with handcuffs still on, push it onto her finger. Then she slides the bigger one onto mine with a smile. I try to remember the weight of the metal, and how it looks on my hand, knowing the guards are going to take it away from me in a few minutes. After that, I won't see my wedding band again for six fucking months.

"By the powers vested in me by the state of New Jersey, I now pronounce you husband and wife. You may kiss your bride," he concludes. And just like that, I'm given a wife.

I loop my arms around Page again to pull her to me, kissing her softly at first, but quickly losing myself in her. After a few pats on the back the room empties, leaving us alone.

The moisture on my face tells me Page is crying again.

"Please stop crying," I tell her, resting my forehead on hers. "You're making me feel even worse seeing you so upset."

"I want you to go home with me," she sobs.

"Me, too, princess," I assure her. "I love you. Let me make love to you. Right here, right now because I may not get another chance for six months."

"I love you, too," she says. "Make love to me."

"Okay, but um, you're going to have to do all the prep work since I'm handcuffed."

At that Page starts sobbing again. "I'm sorry. It's all my fault."

"What are you talking about? Did you lie and say I raped you? No. That bitch did, and this is all her fault. Not yours. You did everything you could to help me. If it wasn't for you, I know I'd have gotten a hell of a lot more time for this shit I didn't do."

"Are you sure?"

"Yes. Now take your panties off and pull my cock out, so I can finally get inside my new wife."

That makes her laugh, and she finally goes to work, reaching under her skirt to shimmy out of her panties.

"I don't have any condoms," she says softly, reaching for the zipper on the orange jumpsuit. I've already realized that and knew how this was probably going to go down.

"I don't need one," I tell her. "Are you okay with that? I promise I'll pull out before."

She nods and after freeing my cock she doesn't let go. She goes to her knees instead and covers me with her mouth. Ah, she's going to make me fucking beg.

"God, I love you, woman. But if you don't stop...then your wedding night story...will be sorely lacking."

Getting to her feet she hops up on the small, dingy table, spreading her legs for me.

"Fuck. You deserve so much better than this."

"Jax? Shut up and make love to me. We don't have much time."

"Princess, we've got the rest of our lives," I tell her, moving between her thighs and leaning down her to kiss her lips. Her legs wrap around me, and after she sits up so I can put my restrained hands around her back, her arms snake around my neck, holding me to her. I slip inside of her gently and then our bodies rock together slowly while our tongues explore and tease.

It's heaven being in her without any barriers, but I know I have to be damn careful. I start to pull back, but she stops me, holding me against her.

"Please, Jax...don't leave me."

Reaching up, she pulls my lips back down to hers, and I can't hold back anymore. I claim her mouth desperately with my seeking tongue. It's an incredible feeling, knowing I'm going to fill her with my release. It's like I can't get deep enough inside of her or take her hard enough to show her how much I need her. I want to claim her body, claim all of her as mine, and only mine.

It's over too soon, and then Page is crying again, knowing we're going to have to say goodbye.

"Let Jude take care of you," I tell her while kissing her neck and every inch of her skin I can get to while I still have the chance.

"What?" she asks between sniffles, holding me so tightly they'll have to pry her off of me.

"I don't want you to be alone while I'm in here. Go stay with him and my dad, at least until the media circus calms down. Let them take care of you and comfort you until I can."

The big heavy door comes open, and I let Page go, so she can stand and pull her panties back up, while I zip the jumpsuit.

"All right, time's up," the deputy tells us.

"I love you, and I need you to toughen up and be my attorney now. Figure out if there's anything we can do to make this shorter, okay? Can you do that for me instead of wasting more tears?" I ask her.

"I'll try."

"Good. Don't worry about me, all right? I'm going to be fine. The only thing I'm worried about is you."

"Let's go," the officer says more forcefully.

Page's arms tighten giving me one last hug. I reluctantly, sadly extract myself from her, and head for the door.

"This shit worked out great for me, Page. If I hadn't been incarcerated, I wouldn't be married to you right now. That alone makes it all worth it, princess." After one last long look at her, I follow the guard out of the room. I can still hear her crying even after the thick metal door closes behind me.

CHAPTER SIXTEEN

Page

"Hey, sis, time to wake up."

I hear Jude's voice, and even though I hope yesterday had all been a dream, well most of it, I knew by his nickname that it hadn't. "I don't want to," I tell him, pulling the sheets back over my head. "Wake me up in six months."

"Now that's not the right attitude. I thought you'd be trying to get my brother out sooner than that."

"How Jude? How the hell am I supposed to do that?" I ask through the cotton layers.

"We hire a private investigator or several," my real brother answers, causing me to jerk the covers off.

"Logan? W-what are you doing here?" I ask, finding him sitting on the couch across from the bed, eating a muffin in a ruffled dress shirt and pinstripe suit.

"Trying to help. I put a call into an attorney I know in the area to give me a few PI referrals."

"What's a PI going to do?" I ask.

"Well, it'd be good if we could get the bitch to admit she made it all up, but what we really need right now is to find evidence to force Judge Bray to declare a mistrial."

"A mistrial?"

He nods "We're going to investigate all twelve jurors and hope one fucked up and talked about the case on Facebook or to a friend while it was going on."

"Oh. But why are you helping me?"

"Because you're my sister and you need it. Dad never should've given you this case-"

"I know."

"You did great, Page, don't get me wrong. But this case required a seasoned veteran in criminal defense."

"It's my fault he's in prison, isn't it?" I ask as the tears start again.

"I didn't say that, and I don't think that. All I'm saying is this was too much pressure for a newbie to handle. What's done is done. Maybe another attorney would've had a different outcome...probably not, though, because of those pictures. We've got to find out who put the marks on her. With a good PI, we might luck up and get what we need with that or the jurors."

I launch myself at my brother to hug him. "Thanks, Logie," I tell him, using the name I called him when I first started talking until I was probably thirteen. And then whenever I want to embarrass him.

"You know I hate that name, right?"

"That's why I use it," I joke finally, pulling away.

Glancing down at myself, well, I look like shit. I'm wearing one of Jax's *Havoc* tees that's all wrinkled and a pair of cotton shorts. My hair is such a mess I can actually feel the tangles, and yesterday's makeup is probably streaking down my face. I guess that's to be expected after losing my career and my husband in one night.

My husband.

It's still funny to say that word. But even in the light of day, I don't regret our decision. There was another decision we made last night, and my logical self says even if the chances are slim since my period's due in a few days, it isn't too late for *Plan B* prevention. But my heart, well, it says it'll be okay either way because I'm married to a man I love.

That reminds me of a call I need to make. "Can I borrow your phone?" I ask Logan, sitting down next to him on the sofa. I have no clue where my phone, purse or briefcase are.

"Yeah, sure," he says, handing it over. I pull up the number from his contacts.

"Logan, what's going on?" My dad answers since I'm on his phone.

"Hi, Dad."

"Page? What the hell did you do?"

"For the first time in my life I did what I wanted to - I married a man that I love. I don't care if you approve or not, it's done."

I hear his exhale through the phone. "I hope you know what you're doing."

"I do. I'm happy with Jax, and he's more important to me than my law license."

"At least he's wealthy, so he can take care of you."

Oh. My. God. "I didn't marry him for his money! You just don't get it, do you? Well, I'm tired of trying to explain it." I disconnect the phone before handing the phone back to my brother.

"I give up," I tell him.

"He'll come around," he says.

Yeah well, even if he doesn't I don't care. There's nothing he or anyone else can do about Jax and me now. I feel lighter because of it, and everything would be perfect if he was here with me now and not stuck in a tiny cell. He's probably freaking out, but trying to act all tough like he's fine. It's not fair that he's going through this hell for something he didn't do.

"Page?"

"Huh?" I ask when Logan calls my name.

"Are you hungry?"

My stomach growls, responding for me. "I'm starving...oh no! I bet the food is terrible...and...and they don't give him any dessert," I say, imagining what Jax is going through.

"And here we go again," Jude says when I fell back in bed boohooing.

In bed is where I stay for the next several hours until Jude's phone rings.

"Hello?" he answers from the sofa on the other side of the room.

"Hey, bro! How's life on the inside?" he asks. I make a run for his phone, snatching it from his ear.

"Jax? Is it really you?"

"Hey, my wifie! How are you holding up?" he asks.

"Me? You're the one...that's...locked up."

"You're not still crying are you?"

"No," I say, even though my voice shakes with that one word.

"I'm fine, princess. It's...it's not as bad as before. I called your phone, but it went to voicemail, so I figured you'd be there with Jude. They're getting ready to transport me to the processing facility in Trenton, and then I'll receive a prison designation. So you may not hear from me for a few days. When I get to the assigned prison, I won't be able to call and tell you where I am because the account has to be set up like the one here. God, it's so fucking frustrating. But listen, don't worry. This is going to fly by like you wouldn't believe, and then we're going to make up for lost time, okay?"

After several sniffles, I agree. "I love you and can't help worrying about you. You don't get any dessert do you?"

Jax laughs on the other end of the phone. "Actually, there was some type of pie today at lunch."

"Liar."

"I think it was homemade apple with ice cream on top."

"Really?"

"Sure."

"Liar."

He laughs again. "Sorry, princess, but my time's up so I've got to go. Take care of yourself, okay?"

"Okay." I think about telling him our idea for a private investigator, but I know all inmate conversations are recorded. "I love you."

"Love you, too, wifey. Tell Jude and my dad not to worry."

"I will. Bye."

The crying goes on for a few more hours. Logan fields calls from our parents so I won't have to deal with them. He also talks to three PIs in the area and schedules for them to meet us in the hotel lobby the next day.

...

Jax

Thirteen hours in and I have to say, prison life sucks. If one of my fellow inmates isn't talking or singing loud enough to annoy the fuck out of me, I'm bored out of my mind. Last night I was put in a cell with six badass dudes. I always acted like I was badass, but compared to these guys, I'm a pansy.

There, I admit it.

These men would no doubt stab me in the eye over an orange. No shit.

No one has messed with me, at least, either because of my reputation as a crazy motherfucking fighter or because of my size. Everyone in this place is angry, myself included. They all bitch about their boys snitching on them, their court-appointed lawyers being slack, the judge being racist...the list goes on, blaming everyone but themselves for landing their asses in the slammer.

I feel like I have an actual reason to be pissed since a lying bitch put me in here. But really, after hours of some self-reflection, since there's nothing else to do but count bars, I can admit that my womanizing ways played a part in my downfall. If I hadn't been so quick to fuck anyone that came my way, I wouldn't be here. I should've held out for decent women, or one woman, like my gorgeous wife. I decide starting now that I won't give Jude hell ever again for keeping his dick in his pants.

Speaking of dicks in pants, mine's still thinking about being inside Page last night, how good it had felt, and the bastard is damn eager to get it in again. I haven't had the heart to tell him he'd be going through a dry spell for the next six months.

Six. Fucking. Months. Twenty-four weeks. One hundred-eighty days.

I'm going to lose my fucking mind before I get out.

The only thing that cheers me up is looking at the ring on my finger. The one the guards know about, but thankfully, let me keep for whatever reason. When that day that right now seems so far away finally comes, I get to go home to someone. It'll be a whole new life waiting for me. But fuck if it doesn't blow to know I'll never be able to fight professionally again. Guess it's time to start thinking of a new career. Start coaching instead? Help Jude become the best in the welterweight class? I have no idea, and my choices are fairly limited since fighting is all I've ever known.

And Page, God I hate that she might have to give up practicing because of me. All those years of her hard work in law school, right down the motherfucking drain. Maybe her brother is right, and now that we're married she won't get suspended.

...

Page

I'm standing in the lobby with Jude and Logan, waiting to meet with the second PI when the hotel starts rocking like it's out to sea in rough waters, or we're having an earthquake.

"Whoa!" I exclaim, grabbing onto Jude's shoulder to keep from falling. "Did you feel that?"

"Um, feel what, Page?" Jude asks.

"The floor rolling!" How did they not feel it? I glance around and no one in the whole place seems to be panicking or freaking out.

"Have you been drinking?" Logan asks.

"No. Alcohol is a depressant. I have enough of that, thank you very much."

"Do you need to sit down?" Jude asks.

"When was the last time you ate?" Logan questions me.

Now I feel like I'm on trial.

"I had some toast and a banana at lunch."

"You probably need to eat something else," Logan said.

When the walls start spinning around me like I'm on a tilt-a-whirl, I begin to think there *might* be something seriously wrong with me.

"Um, I'm going to go out on a limb here and guess that the hotel's not really spinning either?" I ask them.

"That's it, you're going to the urgent care," Logan says. "Jude, you take her, and I'll stay to talk to the PI."

"What? No!" I exclaim. "I'm fine. I just need to eat. Maybe sleep. Try not to cry as much."

"Take her," he says to Jude, ignoring me.

"I agree with Logan. You're going to get checked out even if I have to carry you there over my shoulder, and you know I'll do it."

"I don't need to go to the doctor!"

"You are whether you like it or not. Do you need your purse or any other shit?" Jude asks.

"Yes," I huff, and start for the elevator to go hide out in my room, but Jude grabs my arm and stops me.

"I'll go get it, you sit your ass down," Jude says, pointing a finger at me before heading off to the elevator.

Logan stares at me like I'll disappear if his eyes aren't on me.

"What?" I yell at him.

"Just worried about you, sis. You've got a lot on you."

"Yeah, I do. I'm glad you're here to help," I tell him honestly. This whole new helpful Logan is not one I'm used to. I'm used to the criticizing, condescending, and making fun of me Logan. The one I've known all too well for the past twenty-four years. I'm sure that he's now on our dad's shit list for helping me, and marrying me, but he doesn't seem to mind. The old Logan would never think of stepping a toe out of line for fear of our dad's wrath.

"All right, woman, are you going to walk on your own two feet, or am I going to have to drag you?" Jude asks when he comes back with my purse thrown over his shoulder.

Laughter bursts from me at the sight; a big, tough guy with my very feminine white leather purse hanging off of him. It's such a nice feeling to be laughing that I can't stop, even after tears start rolling down my face. "Oh God...it's too funny!"

"Um, Page, I'm glad to see your mood improved and all, but people are starting to look at us, and they might recognize you," Logan warns.

"That's right, everyone, I'm the attorney who fucked her client, an innocent man who's serving time behind bars! But at least he's my husband now!"

"Page!"

"I've got this," Jude says before he hefts me up on his shoulder and walks out the front door.

"Don't worry, he's my brother," I tell the strangers who give us strange looks.

"You okay to walk?" he asks a block later.

"Yes, put me down."

Finally on my feet, I'm a little unsteady, so after Jude gives me my purse, he puts his arm around my shoulders to make sure I stay upright. We walk since the closest urgent care is only three blocks away.

"Should've got a cab," Jude mutters.

"It's not that far. And I'm fine."

"No, you're not."

"Yes, I am. This is such a waste of time."

"What else do you have to do?" he asks.

"Well, there's some more wallowing in self-pity I need to do later, and I should be at the hotel talking to the PIs."

"You can wallow tonight. Logan's got this shit."

The facility luckily isn't crowded since it's the summer. Apparently, not many people get sick at the beach this time of year. I check in, fill out all the pages of medical forms, and sit down to wait. My shoulders hunch over and my eyes water again when the silence leaves me thinking about Jax, remembering the day he brought me in here with the jellyfish stings.

"Am I gonna have to wear your purse again?" Jude asks. "Because I will to keep you from having another crying fit."

I give him a half-smile and shake my head. "I miss him," I mutter.

"I do too," he says with a sigh.

"I'm sorry."

"Don't start that shit again."

"Mrs. Malone," the nurse calls from the door. It takes me a second to remember that I put my unofficial but new name down on my forms.

I jump up out of the chair. "That's me!" I say, and then the floor rolls.

"Easy does it, sis," Jude tells me, helping me find my balance.

"Experiencing dizziness?" the nurse asks with a smile.

"Um, a little."

"Here, have a seat, so I can take your temperature and get your blood pressure," she instructs, nodding to a plastic chair.

"Huh," she says a minute later, looking at the blood pressure gauge. "Your blood pressure's only eighty-two over sixty. That might explain the dizziness."

"What causes low blood pressure?" Jude asks.

"A variety of things, so we'll try to narrow it down. Are you okay with him staying with you?" she inquires of Jude.

"Oh yeah. He's my brother-in-law."

"I'm watching out for her while my brother does hard time in the state pen."

"Jude!" I exclaim.

"I thought you looked familiar. Jackson Malone's attorney?" the nurse asks. "Don't worry, we'd never disclose any of your information or that you were even here today."

"Yep, I'm his attorney. Oh, and his wife now."

"Congratulations. He seems like quite a catch," she replies with a smile.

"He is, and he really is innocent," I tell her. Then the waterworks are turned back on.

"Has she been overly emotional?" the nurse asks Jude.

"Um, considering the circumstances, I'd say about the right level of emotional. Maybe a little...heavy on the tears."

"I'm going to go ahead and draw a little blood from you so we can run some tests, okay?" she asks, handing me a tissue. I nod my agreement.

She's good, and after the swabbing, I barely notice the sting of the needle.

"All right, the doctor will be in as soon as he has the blood work results," she says, leaving us in an exam room.

I hop up on the table and lay down on my side while Jude wanders around the room, fidgeting, and bouncing on his feet.

"When's your next fight?" I ask him, to have something to pass the time.

"Not sure. I had one scheduled in October but...I may postpone it with everything going on."

"Jax wouldn't want you to postpone."

"Yeah, but it also depends on how much time I have to train, and here lately, it's not been much."

"Oh, I guess that's true."

Finally, there's a knock on the door, signaling the doctor.

"Hi, Mrs. Malone. How are you feeling?" a young man about five years older than me asks. He's wearing the standard white coat and gives me a friendly smile. I'm glad it's not the giggling doctor from a few weeks ago.

"I'm a little dizzy, but it's probably just lack of sleep and eating. I've had a lot of stress on me," I explain, pushing myself up into a sitting position on the exam table.

JAX

"I think we've found another cause as well," he says with an even bigger grin. "Congratulations, you're pregnant."

"Um, no I most certainly am not!" I reply automatically, shaking my head. "That's impossible!"

"You are most definitely pregnant," he reiterates, and his smile slips.

"But...but how did that happen?" I ask, and Jude starts laughing.

"Have you had unprotected sex?"

"Only just two nights ago! It doesn't happen that fast, does it?"

"TMI!" Jude exclaims, covering his ears.

"Ah, no," the doctor laughs. "It doesn't happen that fast. When was your last period?"

"Ha! I'm not even late! I'm not supposed to start until Friday!"

"Then you're only a few weeks along."

What the hell is up with this quack?

"No, no, no. You don't understand, we always used condoms! *Always!*"

"Oh," the doctor says, forehead creasing in contemplation. "Let me guess...Magnum Thin condoms?"

"How'd you know?" I gasp in amazement. There had to be at least fifty choices or more of rubbers, but I've seen the boxes and wrappers Jax uses, and they're always Magnum Thins.

"Unfortunately, they've had a recall. A bad batch that was later deemed as *porous* somehow snuck through quality control. They're thought to be a little less than ninety-nine percent effective. More like...fifty."

"Ha!" Jude busts out, having doubled over shaking with a fit of laughter. I'm not as amused.

"This the father-to-be?" the doctor asks.

"Um, no, uncle-to-be," I mutter in shock. Bad condoms. What the fuck!

"Hey!" Jude pauses in the middle of his outburst. "I'm going to be an uncle!"

"Are you sure?" I ask the doctor. "Maybe it's a false positive?"

"Yes. You are very much pregnant. We ran the test on your blood three times to be certain. Based on your last period, I'd estimate your due date to be sometime in April."

"Hey, look on the bright side, Page. At least Jax will be out of prison before the baby's born!"

"Oh God," I groan, covering my face when more tears escape. How am I going to tell Jax he's going to be a father on top of everything else?

"I'd recommend that you start prenatal vitamins immediately, eat every few hours, and take it easy. You should go ahead and find an obstetrician. In early pregnancy, increases in progesterone can cause the widening of your blood vessels, and that sometimes can reduce your blood pressure. Try sitting up and standing up slowly to let your body adjust."

"Come on, hot mama. Let's get you back to the hotel so you can rest," Jude says, jumping up out of his seat, acting way too excited and happy about our predicament caused by ineffective prophylactics. As if I didn't have enough to worry about, now add to that a baby on the way.

"Oh God. I'm going to have a freaking baby," I mutter.

"Um, doc, does pregnancy cause brain damage?" Jude asks. I swat at him.

After checking out and paying the bill, we start walking back to the hotel.

"Do we need to get a cab?" Jude asks.

"Really? I can see the lobby of the hotel from here," I tell him, and instead of laughing and joking he seems oddly serious as he stares straight ahead. "What...what do you think Jax will say?"

Jude finally smiles. "He'll be surprised I'm sure, but also ecstatic. He'll worry about you, both of you. He'll be pissed that I was with you when you found out, and he wasn't."

I choke on the air in my lungs, knowing he's right. Jax should've been the first one to find out. He should've been with me.

"I'm sorry, Page," Jude says softly, putting his arms around me.

"That stupid bitch," I mutter against his chest.

"Hey, if it weren't for that bitch, you and Jax wouldn't be together," he reminds with a smile.

That's true. "I guess this also explains how Jax's DNA was found in the bitch."

"Damn." Jude laughs. "I guess you're right. Oh shit, I hope there aren't any more little Jaxes on the way."

That thought sends me into a panic, and then later that night I had horrible dreams about diaper wearing babies cage fighting.

CHAPTER SEVENTEEN

Jax

I've been in the prison in bum fuck for two goddamn days, after a three-day stay at the intake facility. I haven't been able to talk to Page, Jude, or my dad since the day I was moved. Each second that goes by makes me angrier. I can't call them except collect, and apparently that doesn't work on cell phones. Despite having millions of dollars in the bank, I don't have any money on my account here, so I can't even buy a damn stamp for a letter to tell them where I am. The lack of control, loss of freedom, and shitty conditions are wearing me down, quicker than I thought possible.

"Yo, Malone. I got a magazine you might want to see," my cellmate says. He's a scrawny blond kid, several years younger than me, and according to him, he's in for selling drugs.

"No, thanks," I tell him. I have no interest in looking at his jerk off material.

"You sure? It says this is your wife or some shit, Page Davenport? She is fucking hot."

I'm out of the bed and jerking the magazine out of his hand a second later. I stare at the picture of my wife, relieved to see her after what's felt like forever, even if it's only been just a week. But seeing her in my brother's arms feels like my heart is being cut out of my chest.

Okay, I'm sure it's completely innocent, just a comforting hug because she's upset. But that doesn't really seem to fit since she doesn't look upset. She's smiling up at him, and his smile is even wider.

I flip to the front to find the date of the sleazy tabloid and see that it's three days old. I go back to the picture and read the caption.

"*Court documents show that the infamous MMA fighter, Jackson Malone, and his attorney, Page Davenport, were married in the early morning hours of July sixteenth, shortly after he was convicted on an assault charge by a jury, and received an active prison sentence of six months. Two days later, Jackson's new bride looked awfully cozy with her new brother-in-law, Jude Malone in Atlantic City. Maybe she got a two for one deal on the Malone brothers.*"

I throw the damn magazine so hard it hits the opposite wall with a thud. Guess that explains why they haven't bothered finding out where I am.

How did I not see it before? They were always flirting and teasing each other. Has my own brother fucked the one woman I've ever loved? And if so how long has it been going on?

Page wouldn't have married me if she'd been with him before, right? But actually, she only married me to try and keep her law license, not because she wanted to spend the rest of her life with me.

And my brother...he was the one person in the world I trusted more than anyone except our dad. He's never messed around with any women, so has he fucked me over to screw Page? Out of all the women in the whole goddamn world, why did he have to go after her?

The next three days I spend working out, trying to sweat off my rage, but it seems to be growing rather than easing up. I'm at combustion level when the weekend rolls around. The only reason I know it's Saturday is by the excitement of the other inmates, looking forward to visits with their families. I'm shocked as shit when the guards call my name.

JAX

Walking into the family room and seeing Jude and Page, all I can think about is that fucking picture. That's all I've *seen* since that day. I can't sleep because of that fucking photo.

"Hey," Page says with a hesitant smile. She stands up as if to hug me and the guard stops her.

"No contact!" he barks, and she sits back down with tears forming. My eyes cut to Jude's, and based on how his gaze keeps flickering back and forth between my face to my clenched fists, I know he recognizes my about-to-explode look. He should since he knows me better than anyone.

"You won't believe the hoops they've made us jump through to find you and then get here," he says when I sit down at the table across from them.

"We put money into your account just now, so you can finally call out. They wouldn't let us do it over the phone, and no one would tell us where you were until yesterday," Page explains. "They kept saying you were in transit and that they couldn't disclose the details. And then yesterday they said we couldn't visit you until today."

I lean back and cross my arms over my chest, taking deep breaths, in through the nose, out through the mouth, trying to calm the rage.

"How...how've you been? We've been worried to death," Page says. God, she's a really great actress and I almost actually believe that she's concerned.

"I've been a helluva lot better."

Page looks at Jude as if asking him a silent question and that's when what little restraint I have left starts to snap. "There's something I need to tell you," she starts.

"Goddamn right, you do. What the *fuck* was that picture about?" I snarl, making Page jump.

"What picture, and what is your problem?" Jude asks.

"What's my problem? Really? You want to know what my problem is? I'm sitting in fucking prison for shit I didn't do, wondering what my own *brother* is doing behind my back with *my wife!*"

"Watch it, Malone, or you'll be removed," the guard warns as he walks by.

"I don't know what the fuck you're talking about, and I'd *never* do that to you!" Jude replies. I can't even look at Page when I hear her start crying.

"Pictures don't lie! You were all over each other! And it's not like it's the first time!" I can't help but remember all the times the two of them flirted with each other, like the day on the elevator, and how they'd danced together. How could I have been so blind?

"Jax, I don't know what picture you're upset about...but *you know* how the media can make an innocent picture...look like something else," Page says between sobs.

"She doesn't need this shit from you right now!" Jude yells at me.

"Don't," Page says quickly to Jude before jumping up and walking out the room.

"You are fucking up in epic proportions right now," he tells me after she's gone. "And if you don't calm the hell down you're going to screw things up with her to the point they can never be fixed. Page needs you, and you just destroyed her! She's-"

"I'm sure you'll take care of her after you two leave here."

He closes his eyes and takes a deep breath. "Jax, I get that you're angry about being in here because you're innocent. Page and her brother are working their asses off trying to get you out. They've got three PIs working for them. But whatever you're upset about, you can't take your anger out on her. Take it out on me, or anyone else, but she doesn't deserve that shit. You don't know what she's been through or how hard this is on her. She's...she's been sick, okay? I had to take her to the urgent care the day after they moved you when she almost passed out because her blood pressure was so low. I can hardly get her to eat, and she barely sleeps, crying and tossing and turning all night-"

"How would you know?" I ask.

"Because I see her every damn day."

JAX

"No, how do you know she doesn't sleep?" I ask, clenching my jaw so hard my teeth might break.

"I..." he opens his mouth and then shuts it, avoiding my eyes.

"Straight up, Jude, are you fucking sleeping with her?"

"I...yes, but I swear, Jax, *all* that we do is sleep. She cries nonstop..."

"Fuck you both!" I yell, and then get the hell out of that room before I choke him out. I even refuse to see my dad because I'm so fucking pissed.

I don't know why I'm surprised. My own mother loved Jude but couldn't care less about me, so why did I expect Page to be any different?

...

Page

I'm still in shock and feeling ... numb. After days of not knowing anything, we finally found Jax. I couldn't wait to see him and unburden the news that he's going to be a father. Instead, he accuses the two of us of ridiculous shit and flips out on us.

"We've got to get him out," Jude says after the three of us get back in his dad's SUV to leave the prison. Jax wouldn't even come back to talk to his father. "He's losing his grip on reality and shit. I'm sorry, Page."

"Maybe I should've just told him..."

"No, not when he's like that. He was empty, like right before a fight. There was nothing but anger left in him."

"I'll ask Logan to get the PIs to work overtime on their digging. Maybe when he gets out..." I start, but I can't help but worry that the Jax I know and love might be completely lost.

...

On Monday morning we finally get some good news.

"So, my IT person is *really* great at her job. The only problem is she doesn't always ... follow proper procedures."

LANE HART

"You mean what she does is illegal?" Logan asks Dan Jones, one of our three PIs.

"Right. But we've got to find a way to get evidence of it legally and then I can guarantee you, Malone is a free man."

"What is it?" I ask, trying not to get too excited yet, but praying he's right.

"Juror number seven, the foreman Steve Yates, the thirty-four-year-old accountant? Well, he received a wire transfer the day before the verdict. A very large sum of money, half a million dollars."

"What?" I exclaim.

"Like I said, my IT person is damn good. She traced it back to a bank in New York, then to another bank in Maryland, and finally to the account of a certain politician."

"Elliot!" I yell.

"That's the one."

"That son of a bitch!" I exclaim.

"That is great and all, but, Page, you know we need hard core proof, not the results of fraudulently accessed, federally protected, bank records," Logan points out.

"What if I can show the prosecutor in Atlantic City that Elliot had a personal vendetta against Jax? One that Elliot developed after Jax kicked his ass in a hotel room. Elliot almost choked me to death when he thought I'd been with Jax. Oh, and Jude was also a firsthand witness since he had to pull Jax off of Elliot."

"You're kidding, right?" Logan asks. "Did that really happen?"

"Yes!"

"When?"

"Um, it was in June," I say as I think back through the weeks. "It was Monday, June second, the day Jax went to court!"

"No one's going to believe Jax or you now that they know you're sleeping with him. And relatives are always shitty witnesses that side with their own people."

"Good thing we've got it on video," I tell him with a smile.

"No fucking way!" Logan exclaims.

"It's on Jax's phone. Shit, where the hell is his phone? Did it get transported with him from prison to prison? We've got to find it!"

"You'll need him to sign something releasing it to your custody, then it should be handed right over," the PI tells us.

"I'll go see him," Logan says right away. "As his attorney, I can stop in for a visit anytime, and after last weekend ..."

We'd told Logan about Jax being upset with us over a stupid picture, but only Jude knows I'm pregnant. I couldn't bring myself to tell anyone else until Jax knows. Although when that will be, I'm not sure. He doesn't want to see us. He hasn't called anyone but his dad once since Saturday, and there's no way for us to call him. But maybe he'll actually be getting out sooner than six months.

...

Jax

"Let's go, Malone," the guard says, interrupting my weightlifting routine. "Your attorney's here to see you."

Page.

Just the thought of her tightens my chest. Despite how hard I try to hang on to the anger, at times I can't help but miss her so much it hurts. But the pain of her and Jude's betrayal hurts even more.

When I walk in the small attorney conference room, I don't know which is worse, my relief that it isn't her, or my disappointment.

"You again?" I ask Logan, taking a seat across from him.

"Yeah, I'm officially your attorney, even though you're my brother-in-law now."

I bark out a non-humorous laugh. "Page hasn't filed for an annulment yet?"

"No, of course not."

"Right, because then she'd get disbarred."

"That's not why I'm here. You won't believe what we've uncovered, and if all goes well, you might be out of here a helluva lot sooner than six months."

"Only one hundred and sixty-eight days to go."

"If you'll sign this paper turning your cell phone over to me, and if the dumbass security guards haven't lost it, then my guess is, you won't be doing even a quarter of that time."

"Okay. So why's my phone so important?" I ask while signing the form, trying and failing not to get my hopes up.

"Do you still have the video from the day Elliot attacked Page?"

My fists automatically clench at the memory. "Oh yeah. I backed that shit up on my computer too, and it's on the cloud."

"Thank fuck!" he exclaims.

"But how does him hurting her, help me?" I ask.

"It doesn't. But the part where you beat the shit out of him, and he gets angry that you've been with Page does help you. Elliot was so pissed off at you that he paid half a million dollars to one of the jurors to make sure you got convicted."

"No fucking way," I mutter in complete and total shock. "How do you know all that?"

"One of our PI's has a damn good hacker on staff. Now we just need a reason to give to the District Attorney to go through his bank account records. I'd say revenge is a pretty good one. I'd take a guess and say Elliot's juror couldn't sway the whole jury to convict you on the rape charge, but he strong armed them on the assault, and they caved. Page and our PIs are talking to them all right now."

"Good."

"Look, I don't know which picture you got upset with Page and Jude over, but believe me, I've been with them almost twenty-four seven since you got locked up, except for when he took her to the doctor and then they came to visit you. There is *nothing* going on between them. Page is a complete mess over you, and she's seemed to fall even further off the deep end after her visit Saturday."

"Do you sleep in the same room with them?" I ask sarcastically.

"Some nights, yes, back when we were all staying at the hotel. None of us really slept the first few days, but Jude and I took turns trying to comfort Page during her more...extreme crying fits. Yes, he was in the bed with her, just like I was some, but they were both fully clothed, and there was nothing sexual about it. Your brother is your biggest supporter, and even after whatever happened last Saturday when they came to visit, after days of getting the runaround about where you were, all Jude said when I saw him was, 'We've got to hurry up and get him out because he's losing it.'"

"Um-huh," I grumble.

"Oh and the only way they found you on Friday was by Page calling every prison in the state asking them to check their roster to see if you were listed. This place, Northern State, was listed seventh on a list of ten."

"So you really think there's nothing going on?" I ask, more of that ridiculous feeling of hope filling me up.

"I'm certain there's not anything going on. She loves you, and treats him just like me like he's her brother," he says before he chuckles. "Actually, I'm a little jealous because I think she wishes Jude would've been her funny, easygoing brother growing up instead of having to put up with me being an ass to her."

"Maybe...maybe I overreacted after seeing the picture. I mean, I know they did the same thing to one of the pictures of Page and me when she first started working on the case."

"You probably did overreact, but I know they'll forgive you given the circumstances."

"Will you ask them to come back and see me this weekend? Tell them I've cooled down and I'm sorry."

"I'll do it," he agrees.

CHAPTER EIGHTEEN

Page

"Adam, I know I screwed up this case, but there's more to the story," I tell the District Attorney.

He leans back in his chair, steepling his fingers in front of him. "I'll give you five minutes."

"Great. Okay, I'll talk fast. I was engaged to Elliot Winters, the Maryland state senator. He came here to Atlantic City after Jax's, I mean after Jackson Malone's court day on June second. I was...I was with Jax...in my room...when Elliot knocked on the hotel room door. Even though Jax made up a story about me switching rooms, later when Elliot found me, he attacked me. He accused me of sleeping with Jax and then grabbed me by the throat asking if that's what I liked now. He was...he held me down on the bed, and I couldn't get his hands off of me. I yelled for Jax, who was thankfully in the room next door. He and Jude came in and got Elliot off of me, and then Jax started hitting Elliot, beating the crap out of him. Elliot said he was going to blame the whole thing on Jax, and no one would believe us."

"I do have a hard time believing that."

"Then I guess it's a good thing I have a video recording," I tell him. "Here," I say offering him the thumb drive. He takes it curiously, plugs it into his computer and then we listen to the conversation we had without Elliot knowing.

"Okay, so now I believe you. But why do you think this is reason enough for the judge to declare a mistrial for Jackson Malone?"

"Well, as you heard, Elliot told us it wasn't over, and he figured out a way to get back at Jax. He paid juror seven, Steve Yates, half a million dollars to sway the jury to convict Jax."

"How the hell do you know that?" he asks, sitting up straighter in his chair.

"I can't give you sources or the proof I have, but if you could just get a warrant for his bank records after you charge him with attempted murder against me, you'll find it."

"I don't know, Page. That's a stretch, to ask for bank records for an assault case."

"Then what about getting the feds involved. Tell them he's a dirty politician. They can investigate to see if he's accepted bribes or misused campaign funds."

"That might be possible. I could make a call to the local bureau."

"Could you get a search warrant for all the jurors' bank records to investigate juror fraud? I'm begging you, Adam. Jax didn't do anything to that woman but have sex with her, and he doesn't deserve to be locked up. Help me convince Judge Bray to declare a mistrial."

He sighs and taps a pen on his desk. "There is something I debated telling you before the trial, but I didn't. The victim, or alleged victim, asked me about money. She wanted to know how much she could get from Jax for what he did after he gets convicted. I told her this is a criminal court, not civil."

"So this whole time, she wanted his money."

"Yeah, that and revenge that he didn't want anything to do with her most likely. I probably should've told you that she asked about restitution."

"Don't worry about it. Just...all I'm asking is for you to do what you can now to help Jax."

"All right, let's go to the judge's chambers and see what we can get him to approve. If nothing else he'll probably agree to bring the jurors back in for questioning."

"Thank you so much!" I exclaim.

Now we're finally getting somewhere! With any luck, we'll convince the judge to give Jax a new trial, one with a better attorney.

...

Jax

I'm pissed that they're moving me and not telling me where the hell I'm going. But then I start to see the signs for Atlantic City outside the prison bus windows. Why are we going back there? It has to be something to do with the case since there's only a jail there and no state prison facility.

After sitting alone in a holding cell for at least an hour, I'm finally taken into the courtroom. The same judge from the trial is on the bench. Logan is sitting at the defense table instead of Page. I look around the room and...my heart stops when I find her in the front row, sitting beside my dad and Jude. They're all smiling, so I take that to be a good sign about why I'm here, even though it looks like Page is about to cry.

"Mr. Malone," Judge Bray starts. "You've been summoned to court because we've reopened your case after an investigation of juror fraud. There is evidence to suggest that one of the jurors was bribed during your trial. Therefore I've declared a mistrial and ordered that you be granted a new one. Until such time you will be released on the same bond conditions as before, a fifty thousand dollar secured bond, no travel without prior approval is permitted, and you are to have no contact with the alleged victim."

They're fucking letting me out. After only two and a half weeks I'm getting released from prison. Jesus!

"Thank you, your Honor," I finally manage to say.

"We'll go ahead and calendar the case for retrial the week of September third. Any objections?"

"No, your Honor," Logan responds.

"No objection," the District Attorney says.

"Then let's adjourn court for the day. Bailiff?"

"All rise. This honorable court now stands in recess until tomorrow morning at nine a.m."

With that, my handcuffs are removed, and I'm once again a free fucking man.

Logan is wearing a cocky grin that he definitely deserves.

"Thank you so much. I don't know how to ever repay you," I tell him.

"Oh, you already have in a big fat fee." He laughs. "Now go see your wife," he says with a slap on my shoulder. "She missed you."

I turn around and look for Page. She hadn't moved, so I go to her.

"Hey," I say, unable to help my smile.

"Hey," she replies hesitantly.

"Hey, bro, glad to see you out of handcuffs," Jude tells me.

"Good to have you home, son," my dad says, giving me a hug.

"It's damn good to be free. I'm sorry about how I acted last weekend," I apologize to them all. "That place...it does something horrible to a man."

"You were being held in a shitty prison for something you didn't do. That would make anyone go a little crazy," Jude replies with a shrug.

"Yeah, it was pretty shitty, but it's no excuse for how I acted. Now let's go home," I say, talking to Page. "Forgive me?"

"Yes. Even on your worst day, you're better than Elliot on his best. Oh and he's sitting in a cell right now, getting drilled by federal agents," Page replies with a smile.

"Welcome back to the free world," Page's dad, who had gone unnoticed, says from beside me. I turn toward him and shake his offered hand. "And welcome to the family."

"Thank you, Mr. Davenport," I say in surprise. I'm glad he doesn't seem pissed at Page for marrying a jackass like me. Turning my attention to Page, I ask, "Come home with me?"

"Of course," she agrees.

"They're ready to release your belongings back to you, and as soon as that's done you can go," Logan tells us.

After I get rid of the orange jumpsuit, I change into the jeans and tee Page brought me, then slip my wedding ring back on. All that was left was for us to make our way through the maze of reporters to my dad's SUV.

I reach across the backseat to hold Page's hand, but that's not enough contact. I grab her and pull her on top of me so that she's straddling my lap, and bring her lips down to mine. Our kiss is hesitant at first but quickly escalates until we're clinging to each other like we can't get close enough. I feel the wetness of Page's tears on my cheeks, and at least now I know they're happy ones.

We kiss like that for the entire three hours home. After saying goodbye to my dad and Jude, I carry her up to my apartment and start undressing her before the door shuts. I need her, need to feel her warm skin against mine to truly feel alive and free again.

Page is gorgeous laid out underneath me, her blonde hair down and fanned out on the bed, her blue eyes lit up with happiness.

"I missed you so damn much," I tell her.

"I missed you, too," she says with a smile. "Now make love to me."

"Do you want me to get a condom?"

She bites her bottom lip and smiles wider. "No, and you don't have to stop either."

"You don't have to tell me twice," I say as I ease inside of her. She's definitely ready after three hours of foreplay. "I love having you like this, with nothing between us. Whatever happens...well happens, if that's okay with you."

"Um, well, you don't have to worry about getting me pregnant," she says, making me go still.

"Oh?"

She's gone on birth control. I shouldn't be surprised. She's several years younger than me, right out of law school. We just got married two weeks ago, and I've been a jackass the entire time. I guess it shouldn't come as a shock that she doesn't want to get knocked up so soon.

Even understanding all that, it's still hard not to take it personally. That she just doesn't want *me* to get her pregnant.

"If you want to wait that's fine...I just thought, after that night..."

"Jax?"

"Yeah?" I ask, pulling back to see her face.

"You don't have to worry about getting me pregnant because, well, I already am," she says, practically flinching away from me while her eyes stay locked on mine.

"You're already..." I rewind her words to make sure I understand them. "You're...pregnant? Like right now?" I ask, and she nods.

"We're gonna have a baby?"

"Yes," she confirms. "Are you freaking out? Because...I'm sorry, Jax. I knew you'd be upset..."

I lean down and kiss her lips to stop her rambling. But then...has it even been long enough for her to know? "Oh princess, I swear I'm not upset. I'm just surprised. I mean, are you sure? How do you know, because it's only been what, just two, maybe three weeks?" I ask.

She exhales likes she's been holding her breath the whole time. "I'm sure, and I'm, um, about six or seven weeks along."

"Okay, you lost me." I'm not all that great at math, so maybe I'm missing something.

"There was a condom recall."

"You're shitting me." I laugh, and she shakes her head with a smile. "I'll be damned. So the night we got married, you were already..."

"Yeah. I found out the day after they moved you from Atlantic City. I was dizzy so Jude went with me to the doctor's office and they told me."

"God, and I acted like such an asshole to you!" I exclaim, now understanding what Jude was trying to tell me. What Page had been trying to tell me when I went ape-shit on them at the prison.

"Don't worry about that. It was a stressful time. I can't imagine how hard it was on you. Being in there, all alone."

"I missed you so damn much," I tell her. "So when? When are you due?" I ask, rubbing my palm over her lower belly, that doesn't feel any different yet.

"April fourth."

"April? Wow. Do you think we'll have a girl or a boy?" I ask with a smile.

"If it's a girl, you're not going to make her fight are you?" she asks.

"I guess we'll just have to wait and see if she comes out swinging," I joke. "All I know is that we're going to let him or her do whatever the hell they want."

Then I make love to my pregnant wife. I've never been so damn happy and have no idea how I could be this lucky. I have everything I could ever want, and I owe it all to a lying bitch. Who would've thought that in the end, I'd be thanking her? Instead of making my life hell, she helped me find my way into heaven.

EPILOGUE

Page

The sold-out crowd of ten thousand at the Patriot Center in Fairfax is a force to be reckoned with. Kind of scary actually.

"These people are nuts," I have to yell to Sadie, so she will hear me over the noise.

"Yeah, they are. Especially the women," she giggles.

"Jax is clearly the fan favorite," I notice, from all the signs and the *Havoc* griffon logos in the stands.

"Uh-huh. Jax is the best, and I'm betting Jude will be, too, soon," she says wistfully.

I know Jax is incredible, but seeing it is a whole different thing.

The lights in the arena dim and the theme song from the *Halloween* movies pump into the stadium after the announcer finishes the intro for Jax's opponent, Michael Evans. A few fans chant the first name of the man with a shaved head and solemn expression as he makes his way down the aisle to the raised octagon. Both of his arms are covered with black tattoos of screaming skulls and fire, which up his badassness.

Jax will never have any ink work done on his magnificent body. He's afraid of needles. Needles and small spaces are what freak out my big, incredible husband. But he doesn't need the ink to be tougher. He manages that just fine on his own.

Once the ref cleared the psycho looking dude to enter the cage, the announcer goes through Jax's many wins. The world championship belt is on the line with this fight. Jax is fighting to keep the title that was taken away after the criminal charges. If he wins, this will make it six consecutive years as the reigning champion.

The first guitar riffs of Sick Puppies' rock song *"You're Going Down"* comes blasting from the stadium speakers, making the crowd go even wilder.

The colored spotlights swirls, searching the arena for him until he finally steps out of the tunnel. He's wearing tight black shorts, with almost every inch covered by sponsors, and a red *Havoc* hoodie pulled up over his head but unzipped to show his cut upper body. Incredible is the only way to describe him.

Watching one of the big screens in the stadium, the camera goes in for a close-up of him walking to the cage. He's the raging volcano again, scary and beautiful at the same time. I can only stare and drool as he approaches the ref and strips down to his shorts. I don't care much for the roar of approval from the thousands of women cheering for him. That's my husband, damn it!

Finally, he's cleared to enter the octagon, just six months after his case was dismissed by the district attorney.

We found a witness to testify that the bitch had confided in her that she'd lied and given herself the marks on her neck. And somehow, mostly because of my brother, I'd managed to keep my law license. I've finally figured out what type of law I want to practice. I decided to specialize in sports contracts, and I already have a few MMA fighters as clients. Now that we're married, I can even represent Jax. I also plan to spend some time volunteering at the local animal shelter after the baby's born. We're currently looking for a house with a backyard to move into, and once that happens, Jax has promised me all the puppies and kittens I could ever want. I know that if it were up to him, he'd give me the world.

I'm doing great with my nerves seeing Jax in his very first fight, or at least I was until the bell rings and the two men collide.

"Oh shit!" I exclaim when fists start flying. I hold my breath as I watch the two angry men face off.

The psycho fighter dodges one of Jax's jabs and starts laughing like a cocky bastard, motioning to himself with both hands, telling Jax to bring it on. The leer stays on his face right up until Jax lands a cross on his jaw. The other man falls back so stiff and fast there isn't even time to yell, "Timber!"

"Oh my God! Jax won?" I ask Sadie, jumping, well easing to my feet as fast as an eight-month pregnant woman can. "But it just started like ten seconds ago."

"Oh yeah. That dude won't wake up until next week!" Sadie replies before we both shout and cheer for my man.

We yell louder when Jax's arm is officially raised by the ref. Once again he's the undisputed, middleweight champion of the world. To celebrate he climbs to the top of the cage, straddling it with both hands in the air while waving the black and white *Havoc Fight Club* banner proudly.

Jude and Sadie's dads head into the cage to congratulate him with hugs when he jumps down, and cameras begin circling. One of the TV announcers shoves the microphone in Jax's face that shows up on all the big screens around the stadium. My husband didn't even work up a sweat.

"How does it feel to get back in the cage and come out with a win in the first thirty seconds of the first round after all you've been through this past year?"

"It feels great. It's been a helluva year, and I've faced a lot of challenges, but it's the best feeling in the world to get back to fighting," Jax says, finding me in the front row and winking.

"For a while, it seemed like we might not see any more from *The*

Mauler because of the criminal charges. How did you deal with the stress of your court case?"

"I've got to say that if it weren't for my beautiful wife, I probably wouldn't be standing here today. She fought for me through it all, so I credit this win to her. I'll have to spend the rest of my life trying to repay her for saving me."

"Um, Page? You're leaking," Sadie says.

"Oh, I know. He's too freaking sweet," I reply, wiping the tears from my cheeks. I wasn't a crier until I got pregnant.

"Ah, not from your eyes, Page," she says, pointing down at my toes.

"Oh my God. Did I just get so excited I actually pissed myself?" I ask, glancing down my long maxi dress, finally noticing my wet legs. Then I feel a sharp pain in my lower back when my belly tightens like a fist. Again. "Oh shit!"

"I'm guessing your water just broke?" Sadie asks. I nod, sitting gingerly back down in the seat until I figure out what I should do. We're in Virginia, hours away from my OBGYN and hospital. I'm not even due for four more weeks!

I notice movement in the cage. Jax is climbing up and over the top, heading for me the quickest way since it's filled with people.

"What's wrong?" he asks going down to his knees in front of me.

"Congratulations, Jax, you were awesome!" I tell him with a hug. "Oh, and the baby's coming."

"Shit, you mean like right now?" he asks several octaves higher than normal, his eyes wide. I worry he might be freaking out when his tan skin pales.

"Yep. My water just broke, and there's this pain in my back I've had since this morning. I thought it was just the shitty hotel bed, but-"

"You're in labor?" He finishes for me.

"I believe so, yeah. I think your son's decided to bump up his birthday by a month."

"Holy shit!" he says before getting to his feet and scooping my fat ass up into his arms with a smile. "Then let's find you a hospital, princess."

"Good idea. You want to let your brother and dad know it's go time?"

"Dad! Jude!" Jax yells to them across the huge arena. "Let's go! It's time to meet Xavier!"

The End

READ MORE COCKY CAGE FIGHTERS!

Thank you so much for reading Jax!
Jude and the other Cocky Cage Fighter books are currently available in my store individually and in exclusive bundles that are 50% off!

Visit now and get 20% off when you use the discount code: **CCFSAVE20**
https://www.authorlanehart.com/

ABOUT THE AUTHOR

New York Times bestselling author Lane Hart was born and raised in North Carolina. She continues to live in the south with her husband, author D.B. West, and their two children.

When Lane's not writing or reading sexy novels, she can be found in the summer on the beaches of the east coast, and in the fall watching football, cheering on the Carolina Panthers.

Connect with Lane:
Twitter: https://twitter.com/WritingfromHart
Facebook: http://www.facebook.com/lanehartbooks
Website: http://www.lanehartbooks.com
Email: lane.hart@hotmail.com

Made in United States
North Haven, CT
08 November 2025